Garibaldi

and Rio Grande do Sul's War of Independence from Brazil.

The Memoirs of Luigi Rossetti, John Griggs, and Anita Garibaldi

By

William Rosenfeld

Dante University Press, Boston

D1376793

Library of Congress Cataloging-in-Publication Data

Rosenfeld, William.
 Garibaldi and Rio Grande do Sul's war of independence from Brazil : the memoirs of Luigi Rossetti, John Griggs, and Anita Garibaldi / by William Rosenfeld.
  pages cm
 Includes bibliographical references.
 ISBN 978-0-937832-53-0 (paperback : alkaline paper) -- ISBN (invalid) 978-0-937832-54-7 (e-book)
1. Garibaldi, Giuseppe, 1807-1882--Fiction.
  2. Garibaldi, Giuseppe, 1807-1882--Friends and associates—Fiction
  3. Revolutionaries--Brazil--Rio Grande do Sul (State)--Fiction.
  4. Rio Grande do Sul (Brazil : State)--History--Revolution of the Farrapos, 1835-1845--Fiction.
  I. Title.
 PS3618.O836G37 2013
 813'.6--dc23

                              2012046730

 Dante University Press
 PO Box 812158
 Wellesley MA 02482

 www.danteuniversity.org

To Irma

Giuseppe Garibaldi

Preface

Anita Doarte, Luigi Rossetti, and John Griggs were Garibaldi's closest comrades during Rio Grande do Sul's war for independence from Brazil (1836-42), Garibaldi's formative years as a military leader. None of the three left a memoir, so I have written them. My purpose is to present a balanced portrayal of Garibaldi by relating the reactions of those closest to him.

Designing Anita's voice was easy because she was relentlessly honest and forthright. Rossetti's was more complicated because he presented two separate personae: one as propagandist for the revolutionaries and the second as devoted, admiring and at times critical comrade to Garibaldi. My design of Griggs's voice had to wait until I had identified the real person from among the several inaccurate, earlier representations. When, after three years of research, I identified him as mate on a New England merchant ship, who threw in his lot with the revolutionaries—one of my most satisfying pieces of scholarship, by the way—Griggs's voice followed readily. To help set the three memoirs in their historical context, I invented one additional voice, that of a scholar-editor, who furnishes the contexts and analyses that the companions could not. I also include chronologically relevant excerpts from Garibaldi's memoirs. Finally, I base the fictional memoirs on the legitimate sources I cite in my bibliography.

Coincidentally, my interest in the Revolution in Rio Grande do Sul derives from my year as Fulbright Professor of American Literature at the Federal University in Rio de Janeiro, during which I lectured in Porto Alegre. That interest piqued when I discovered an enticing footnote naming John Griggs, a United States Citizen, as one of Garibaldi's comrades in the revolution. (1)

William Rosenfeld
Marjorie and Robert W. McEwen Professor of English
Emeritus

Contents

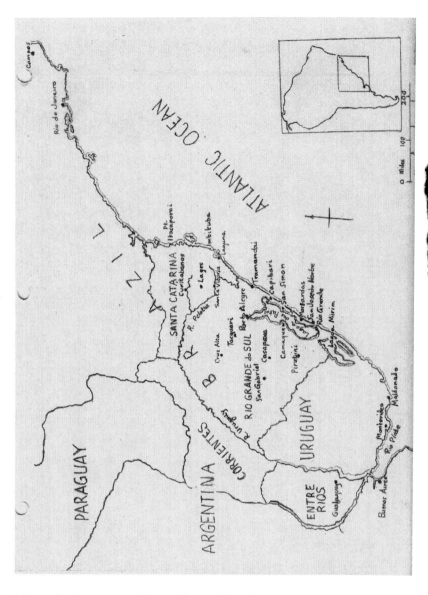

Map of relevant portions of Brazil and Uruguay.

Editor's Foreword

With apologies, I must begin by dragging you, my readers, through a tangle of locales, circumstances, and dates that form the background to Garibaldi's and his companions' entry into the revolution in Rio Grande do Sul. I place them here to disclose the political morass that engulfed the four comrades as well as the motives that drew them into the larger conflict in southern Brazil, Argentina, and Uruguay. (2)

At the time, the borders between those countries and territories were ambiguous. Both Argentina and Brazil wished to incorporate Uruguay, hence the constant skirmishes and political realignments. Throughout this embroilment, the Emperor of Brazil repeatedly offered the rebels in Rio Grande do Sul amnesty plus a generous measure of self-rule, which their leaders consistently rejected. Even after the Imperial General Caxias, the best military leader on either side, entered the war, the imperial government offered to end the revolution amicably. This particular war for independence, as the reader is aware, is one of several throughout Latin America at about the same time.

Now to the persons whose motives and actions are most immediate to this study. I was already familiar with Garibaldi's part in the nineteenth century campaign for reunification of Italy. However, I knew little about his involvement in the Rio Grande do Sul's war for independence. So, to indulge my curiosity, I read several books about Brazil during the period, four biographies—for a start—of Garibaldi, and as many versions of his memoirs. In all that reading, the names of the three companions appear repeatedly.

In November, 1835, Garibaldi met Rossetti almost at the moment he stepped ashore in Rio de Janeiro. The two immediately became close friends.

Four months later, on March 9, 1836, far to the south in the port city of Rio Grande, John Griggs, mate of the American merchantman Toucan, jumped ship, carrying little more than a load of counterfeit coins and galloped north to the rebel capital in Piratini.

In May of 1837, back north in Rio de Janeiro, a small group of imprisoned rebel leaders issued a letter of marquee commissioning Garibaldi and Rossetti to sail as privateers for the Free and Independent Republic of Piratini. Soon afterward, Garibaldi and Rossetti sailed south to Montevideo, from where they hope to join the rebels.

Near the end of May, Rossetti went ashore near Montevideo.

On June 27, during a naval engagement with Uruguayan and Brazilian naval ships, Garibaldi was captured, imprisoned, and tortured by Uruguayans antagonistic to the Brazilian rebels.

After learning of Garibaldi's capture by unsympathetic forces, Rossetti, helpless to do anything else, rode north to the rebel capital in Rio Grande do Sul, where he met Griggs.

Garibaldi was released in April, 1838.Shortly after Rossetti learned of Garibaldi's release, he returned to Montevideo, and escorted his comrade up to Piratini, where he introduced him to Griggs.

As for Anita's place in the chronology, she left her family to join Garibaldi some time between July and October, 1839, after the rebels moved north into Santa Catarina. Ample information about Anita Garibaldi was already in print when I began my research. Less existed about Rossetti, and, as for Griggs, aside from a few brief allusions in Garibaldi's memoirs, nothing either consistent or verifiable existed in any of my sources.

What, I wondered, did these closest comrades—by Garibaldi's own designation—think about him? That enticing question prompted my search for these memoirs.

Following are a few items about the text. For the sake of convenience, I have indicated the memoirists' names and all dates relevant to their activities. My own comments follow the title Editor. At relevant points, I include passages from Garibaldi's memoirs, as they appear in the Theodore Dwight translation of 1859.

CHAPTER 1
Rossetti Meets Garibaldi

The Memoirs of Luigi Rossetti
Written at the times when his Duty allowed.

These I offer as a Record of my Experience in the New and Independent Republic of Piratini, formerly the Province of Rio Grande do Sul in Brazil.

With my Love and Admiration for my Compatriots in Young Italy and Brothers in Freemasonry, Heroes of Oppressed People Everywhere.

Villa Settembrina, Capital City, near to Porto Alegre, June, 1840.

Rossetti, November 1835: The vessel I watched at anchor in Guanabaro Bay on that November morning was a modest French packet, the *Nautonnier*. Did its passengers see Rio de Janeiro as I first did, the great sweep of its beaches, each crescent a golden strand lined with monumental royal palms, the white buildings like marble cliffs facing the bay. Sugar Loaf Mountain rising abruptly from the shoreline, like a breaching whale. Lofty Mount Corcovado, a Cathedral of Nature thrust upward from the inland range? Even now I marvel at its beauty, especially after sunset when torches line the streets like tears of joy above a sparkling necklace.

But I also know that when those passengers in the *Nautonnier* penetrate the delicate aroma of spices mixed with banana, papaya, mango, and other flora that ride the offshore breezes down from the tropical forest, then they will smell the sewerage lying in the streets, and soon they will see the beggars everywhere, cast-off human beings with twisted limbs and running sores, and the tigres, those poor black wretches who carry the barrels of viscous filth from the houses above the beaches down to the outgoing tides.

But these poor tigres carry another stench, one that putrefies the hearts of all who love freedom—slavery. In physical beauty, Rio is equal to Napoli. The difference is in the detested custom of one human being claiming ownership of another. I cannot say that my own countrymen in Italy are free, bowing and dancing as they must to their French and Austrian masters. But these poor Blacks along the waterfront and in the streets of Rio de Janeiro. How much more wretched are they than I! Many times I think to show one of them a kindness, a pitiful child—a master's bastard, no doubt—clinging limply to its mother's arms, or some ancient slave, no longer useful, left to perish along the walls of a dim alley. Even if I managed a kindness to one, what of the thousands in even sharper misery?

Under those shifting moods I lived, the cerulean skies overcast by the mists of inhumanity, cut off here thousands of kilometers from Italy. So on that morning in November, I looked at the *Nautonnier* and dreamt about crossing the Great Ocean to my beloved Ligurian Sea.

Later in the day when her crew came ashore, I stood again in the waterfront praça, when one of the seamen stopped me. In stature he was not nearly as tall as I but broader of chest and shoulder. In attitude, he was vivacious, self-confident, as if he alone could set the terms by which others might share his world. Penetration was the message of his eyes, a glow of expectation that something important was imminent. I can say now that the difficulties that came with our association have been many but the rewards are immensely greater.

From Garibaldi's Memoirs: While walking one day in a public place in Rio, I met a man whose appearance struck me in a very uncommon and very agreeable manner. He fixed his eyes on me at the same moment, smiled, stopped, and spoke. Although we found that we had never met before, our acquaintance immediately commenced and we became unreserved and cordial friends for life. (3)

Rossetti: "I must know your name!" Those were his first words to me. The accent was my own Piedmontese. The clear ring of his voice was so bold that I confused his meaning. When I gave him my name, he responded, "And I am Giuseppe Pane."

I pointed at his seaman's garb, "Bread and salt."

He laughed and put his hands on my shoulders. It was a gesture possibly too abrupt, too familiar, but genuine, nonetheless. "Yes, Luigi Rossetti, salt from the tears of gratitude for having found a compatriot, and bread for the sustenance of our fellowship."

I could not know then that our embrace would fasten our careers like links in a chain of iron, for not two months earlier, the very same month in which the *Nautonnier* left Marseilles, the Revolution in Rio Grande do Sul had broken out.

As we walked along I asked if he was a regular officer on the *Nautonnier*.

"Of no ship," he told me.

"How is that? Are you not in the crew of the brig from Marseilles?"

"No more. The captain is a thief, like all Frenchmen who have authority over Italians. I used her only for passage here. Why else would I take fifty francs less pay than I deserve?"

"Why indeed?"

He studied me for a moment, then leaned close and whispered, "Maybe the captain supposes that I did not protest because the police are interested in me." He saw that my reaction was exceptionally cautious." I really came because I understand that all poor Italians who stop here become rich and satisfied." Then he stepped back and laughed uproariously at the clouds above, his muscular neck bared. I felt myself carried upward in the genuine joy of his emotion. I have recalled that image many times since, wishing, as I did then that we could remain floating, suspended above the rot and corruption, the injustice that infested the city.

"But come," he urged me, "show me where we can break bread together."

I was pried from my reveries and led my new friend up a side street to a clean café, which I and my friends frequented.

Editor: Clearly Rossetti was wary of the stranger, attractive though he might be, speaking out with such bold confidence. When they met the next evening Garibaldi had removed his sea chest from the *Nautonnier* and told Rossetti that he must find himself a place to stay.

On the same night that Rossetti met Garibaldi, he had told Dalecazi, leader of The Young Italians in Rio, about his new acquaintance. The organization of Risorgimento met regularly at the home of the Veronese engineer. Rossetti told Dalecazi that he was suspicious of the newcomer. When asked why, he said that Pane, the only name by which he knew Garibaldi, seemed too eager to meet with the Young Italians, a little too forthcoming.

The fact is that Rossetti was overly cautious. The Young Italians, although anti-imperialists were in no danger from the remarkably tolerant Brazilian authorities, even though the French Charge d'Affaires kept trying to harass the Giovine Italia, and the Sardinian ambassador complained about them constantly. "Still," Rossetti pointed out, "we have to take care not to alienate the Brazilians" because, after all, they knew the Young Italians were already in touch with Tito Zambeccari, one of their number in Rio Grande do Sul, and thereby implicated in the revolution down there. If the Imperial Brazilian authorities should become incensed by that connection, he pointed out, the Italians could face imprisonment, and Brazilians jails are far from pleasant. Rossetti told Dalecazi that he still felt Pane seemed too anxious to join their ranks, a bit too zealous, he thought. So Dalecazi suggested that, if Rossetti thought it necessary, he should learn more about the newcomer before he brought him to a meeting. To that purpose, Rossetti took time to escort Giuseppe around Rio in order to observe him for a while.

In late November, the days were not as hot as they would be in January and February. Rossetti lounged about with Garibaldi, strolling the beaches, each one as inviting as the next, Flamingo, Botafogo, Vermelha, Leme. They also took the ferry across the bay to the Island of Niterói. When back on the mainland, they trekked westward along Copacabana, then over the ridge behind Sugar Loaf, called Arpoador, or Harpoon, and then waded in the pristine beach of Ipanema. Rossetti studied Garibaldi's responses to everything they saw. As his journal entries show, he gradually appreciated that Garibaldi reacted with the innocent, childlike responses of a keen but uncomplicated observer.

Rossetti, November-December, '35: One evening, the newcomer, Pane, went off by himself. I followed at a distance. When he had finished two days of his solo wandering, he rejoined me near our first meeting place. "I could not stop myself," Garibaldi exclaimed. "I walked the entire length of Copacabana, and stood on a shelf of rocks at the very southern end. The spray from the breakers striking the rocks cleansed the bitterness from my heart." He told me he had slept on the beach among the boulders, and in the morning continued along the length of Ipanema--"A beach whose beauty is unmatched in all my visions." It is indeed a glorious sweep of golden sand, with the double peak at the farthest end—he meant The Two Brothers. "Such a paradise! Ah, Luigi," he rhapsodized, "I could build a tiny hut and settle there. Let the affairs of ambitious men pass me by." Although I sympathized with his impulse, it was hard for me to believe, even then, that this man could settle into such a tranquil life. Picture him as a beachcomber, scraping the raw insides of mussels among the tidal pools to satisfy his hunger. Not likely!

When I reported to Dalecazi and the others, they laughed at me, in good nature, of course. "Ah, Rossetti," our leader told me, "you joined us not much before Pane arrived. You are more suspicious of the newcomer than we were of you. You will learn to relax." But they approved of my caution. On that basis, I could not desist in watching closely Garibaldi's movements for some time afterward. I admit that, as unlikely as it seems, I foolishly continued to expect that something about Garibaldi might surface to vindicate my caution, especially after I learned that Dalecazi had written to Mazzini to inquire about him and learned that Mazzini identified him as "Borel." So I stopped asking myself, Pane or Borel, how trustworthy is this newcomer really?

Editor: Mazzini's reply relaxed the Young Italians' anxieties sufficiently for them to accept Garibaldi as one of their number.

We will return to that period in Rio de Janeiro, but to maintain the chronology into which all the memoirs fit, I now introduce John Griggs's personal log. From this point on, his and Rossetti's memoirs alternate according to the dates and relevance of their entries (see the Chronological Outline).

CHAPTER 2

Griggs Joins the Revolution/Meets Ruthie

Griggs's memoirs, as we shall see, reveal fully as hearty a personality as Garibaldi's, obviously as adventurous, even though their enthusiasms follow from markedly different motives. Especially noteworthy is Griggs's eye for practical details about the management of his responsibilities as a ship's mate, ship-builder and -fitter for the rebel navy, and for the natural settings and the people he encounters after his flight from the *Toucan*. Readers may be as amused as I am by his sprinkling of this New England seaman's colloquialisms, which color his otherwise standard usage.

In his heading, Griggs refers to his memoirs as a personal log, which calls for a special explanation. Keeping personal logs, as such, was forbidden on board ships in the U.S. Navy, although midshipmen were encouraged—at times required—to keep one. In such circumstances, however, their logs were part of their training toward the time when, as commissioned officers, they would be required to make entries in their actual ships' log. (4) As in the navy, merchant ships were, by maritime law, required to keep a log as the official record of anything of significance that occurred on board at any time. Usually the entries noted routine matters such as the time and personnel involved in a change of watch, including the ship's course and position on the charts, scheduled drills as well as unscheduled occurrences, cargoes taken on board or discharged, and the like. In short, they were filled mostly with routine data, which would thereby be made accessible for any official examination or inquiry into a ship's business.

Griggs's own log, then, is more properly a memoir, for he kept it outside the strictures of maritime law after he had left The *Toucan*. Therefore, much of what he enters pertains solely to his observations about his personal involvement in the rebellion of the Rio Grandenses.

JOHN GRIGGS
Formerly Mate of the *S.S. Toucan*, of Boston
(Nathaniel Hamlin, Master).

Now a Volunteer in the War to Liberate
The Free Republic of Piratini
from the Empire in Brazil.

His Personal Log
The likes as other seafaring men have written before him.

This record is intended for the eyes of whosoever
will take time and trouble to read it
but in the main for my own progeny,
—as God may grant me by His favor—
once my seafaring days are done.

Griggs, March 29, 1836: Twenty days ago, I found myself in a tight spot. I had no choice but to jump ship and flee. I was sorry to leave the *Toucan*. She was a good berth and a likely step in my advancement to a ship of my own. So leaving her meant shearing off into unknown waters and tricky currents. But the Imperial Brazilian constabulary were just at that moment on their way to arrest me as a smuggler of contraband for the rebels in Rio Grande do Sul, so I daren't have waited to dicker with them. I was guilty, no use fudging the truth. I used the personal cargo space granted me as mate to hide false Brazilian coins. That was the agreement I entered into with Captain Hamlin. Except for that sack of coins, I fled without so much as a ditty bag. Ending up in a Brazilian brig is not for me. Once I skipped ashore, the rest went Boston style. The rebel agents had horses ready and we galloped steadily from the Port of Rio Grande due west until we crossed the narrows below the Lagoa dos Patos and entered rebel territory.

From there we made our way Northwest by North over a vast and fertile country. Grass so tall our horses' chests brushed it aside. The vista was as endless as the horizon. I'd never seen anything to match it. That vast, open country of wild grain was like the reports I've heard about our own Western Prairie. I would have been lost within an hour without our guides leading us from one settlement to another. We had the benefit of few marked tracks because the tall and hearty grass blades close over them soon after anyone passes through. Our native guides—gauchos, as they are called—set their courses by the sun and stars, same as we sailors do when we're far off soundings. Except they use neither compass, sextant nor Bowditch tables, nothing but a glance aloft from time to time.

We made stops at clusters of huts widely scattered along the way. The people in that inland stretch are mainly herders, (5) not much for setting their hands to farming more nor they have to. They would have a hard time turning that sod, anyway, even after they cut the grasses back. And what they managed to grow would have to be a plentiful cash crop, seeing as they had no need to plant fodder for their cattle. These people realize ready cash, some from the flesh but mostly from the hides of their wild longhorns--hides on the hoof, as you may say, before they're slaughtered. Once they reach the ports, the tanned hides are stacked in our cargo holds bound for profitable markets in the north end of our trade routes where the shoe factories in Massachusetts await them. Some of my own kin, in fact, are engaged in that part, so I know the wherefore of it. (6) I calculate a long future of such payloads going north and manufactured goods carried back down here, especially if Rio Grande do Sul gains its freedom from The Imperials. We Americans should be able to claim a favored place in their mercantile traffic. Maybe then we will cut the Brits clean out of the exchange.

For those that want to know, my main reason for tolerating this hard ride toward the Rebels' headquarters on up into the hills of this Province, my main reason, as I say, is no different from any of the early explorers, including the great Henry Hudson and those even earlier than him—trade and raw materials thereof. Otherwise I could as easily a-ridden down to Montevideo and taken a berth back to Boston on one ship or another. But the time I've already put in sailing into these Southern Latitudes gives me a leg up for trading with these Rebels later, so long as I avoid getting caught helping them out.

That is why I chose to hide the contraband coins in my own cargo space. If I was caught, I'd take the blame and the Captain and Owners of our company remain untarnished. Anyway, I'm the one who now gets to have a look at the inland stretches of this country and observing the habits of these gauchos. I've put down some details of their ways while my recollecting is fresh. Now that I'm settled in Piratini, I'll lengthen it into proper sentences and such.

They live practically their whole lives on horseback, which is the way I begin to feel after these several days in a saddle. Nor would I have seen the shanty huts they make from mud and whatever sticks of wood they can find in this grassland. Near to their huts they put up arbors for shade, caramanchaồs, as they call them, pronouncing it with their noses into the last syllable. Between chores, they take their meals and lounge beneath them arbors. They lash the boards with rawhide rope or chord twisted from the long grass that grows plentiful all around. It makes good stout rope for the short lengths they need to hold the thatch together. I've given that twisted grass some hard yanks and snaps, and it stands up well enough for the purpose the gauchos put them to. They also braid leather thongs into lariats, quirts, bull-whips and such to aid their herding. I didn't poke my nose around too much, but these folks saw I was curious and explained things to me.

Looked at from whatever angle you like, their houses are naught but muck hovels, efficient for their needs but pretty much sham built to serve for shelter from weather and safety at night. I wouldn't down-mouth them outright to these gauchos, for they gave me the best of their hospitality all along the length of this jolting journey.

The women tend the outdoor hearths for cooking, but they are fully as able as the men for hard riding, altogether a hard-bitten lot, dark as Indians from the sun and steady winds. I doubt not that plenty of them, men and women alike, trace mixed blood through their veins.

As for the Revolution wherever our group stopped along the way, the locals talked with us about the war and seemed more animated by the prospects of fighting than about the idea of a New Government. I liken these gauchos to our own hearty countrymen who carry their families and all their goods into the Western Reserve and beyond. Hardy folk top and bottom, with little energy for political concerns. From the scars I see on most of these sinewy fellows, cheek and arm alike; any one who brings them together as an army will have a brutal company of fighters who won't take readily to defeat. Aside from rifles and pistols, every one of them carries a pointed, two-edged dagger in his belt. Most are fashioned from silver, which seems to be the favorite decorating metal. They use the knives for herding chores and for eating. I doubt not they use them for settling personal fallouts as well.

There's farming tools, spades and the like, mostly fashioned at their own forges. Machetes, too, a flat blade some four inches broad and of a length from elbow to fingertip, fashioned with a handle long enough to fit a full-grown fist. But as there seems precious little farming, most of what they eat is beef fresh off the bone and charred over an open fire. They also keep a store of jerked beef, charque, as they call it. Nearly tough as rawhide, a testy exercise for tooth and jaw alike.

To see them use their daggers for eating is a treat. They take a-hold of a strip of flesh between their teeth and draw their dagger a swift stoke across it right near to their nose-tips. If I'd had tried it, I fear I'd end up with a shorter beak by half. So I made them laugh as I laid a slab of meat along my thigh and drew my sheaf knife across it to just before it got to my own flesh, then picked up the meat and finished the cut from the bottom. Well, they clapped my shoulder and admired the way I could just miss cutting into my thigh and allowed that their way or mine took skillful handling and slaked our hunger equally well, no matter whose gullet it went down.

It's not all swank and sweat among these gauchos. They add whatever bits of bright coloring they can to their garments—bandanas, sashes, buckles, wristlets, link belts, a fair amount of gaudy jangling stuff. But most all whatever they wear has some useful purpose for making their way through this rough country and herding their wild cattle. Dark and calloused as they are, they make a proud picture in their low-crowned, narrow-brimmed hats and bright kerchiefs, sitting their saddles and sipping maté, a kind of herbal tea, which recalls to my mind Labrador tea or livery tea as was brewed back home from evergreen shrubs. Down here they steep their maté leaves in dried out gourds and draw the brew through filtered silver straws made special for the purpose of straining out the bitter sediment.

At least one among them in each of these settlements has a guitar, and the music they tease out of those stringed boxes is a wonder. But they show their best energy when they are on their mounts, willful, fiery ponies, few of them more nor 14 hands and full of weasel juice. (7) Some of them stand on long legs beneath big chests, which seems to echo Arabian stallions a few generations back, but most are stubby bodied and close to the ground. All of them look as ready to throw as carry a rider.

These gauchos are are good match for them. They rein them steady and heel over in their saddles—left or right—almost to the ground and wheel about in tight turns. That's when every bit of gear—rope, stirrups, reins, short, leather aprons—serves its purpose.

It's all of special interest to a seaman like myself. A sailor has a purpose for every bit of tag and tackle on board his ship, even though a lubber may pass them by without a thought. I told these gauchos so, and that fixed a kind of camaraderie among us.

One thing I couldn't tell them is my disapproval of the cruel bits and spurs they use to keep their mounts under control. I suppose with so many wild ponies around for the taking, these riders think nothing of bloodying a few flanks with spur and stirrup and raking their mouths with spiked bits until they're either subdued or discarded. But that's my way of looking at it. Back home, horses are bred and trained for dependable compliance and valued accordingly. They are dear enough in trading, and the old saying holds among livery folk, "If you can't ride 'em, don't buy 'em."

Editor: As is obvious by now, Griggs leaves no doubt about his quick-eye for detail and appreciation for the gauchos' functional fittings. By the end of March, 1836, he had not yet reached Piratini, headquarters for the rebels. But his escort left him off at the fazenda of one of General Gonçalves' sisters, Donna Anna. Her land stood along the banks of a small river that fed into the southernmost banks of the Lagoa dos Patos. It was Griggs's first real rest since he climbed into a saddle for the hard ride north of the Uruguayan frontier. The orderly, well-settled ranch furnished a far different scene from the humble shacks he had seen back in the open pampas.

Donna Anna lived in a well-appointed house with tidy gardens and orange groves almost all the way down to the river bank. These were real plantations with broad stretches of land seeded in wheat, cotton, and kitchen gardens. All the buildings, domestic and others, were low, single-storied structures. A veranda ran the length of the main house. The ladies and young men were well dressed in tailored outfits with buttons and fine stitched seams, obviously imported patterns or even made abroad. Even their servants wore decent, if humbler, clothes.

Griggs felt self-conscious in his rough, sea-going togs, bedraggled as he was from the hard ride up from Rio Grande, but the Gonçalves family seemed to take no notice of it. They intended to usher him into the main house but he declined until he could tidy himself up, so the ladies ordered hot towels brought out for him on the veranda. In his journal entries he makes abundantly clear his appreciation of the comely young servant woman's attention.

Griggs: She went ahead and swiped my face and neck without asking. It felt fine, no denying, both for cleaning away the grime and her gentle touch, too. Then I'll be bowed if she didn't pull my boots off and make as if to peel off my socks and wash my feet, but I hauled my leg back and did it myself while she stood by blushing. I thought maybe I'd insulted her because the way she went about it seemed to be her job, but soon as I pulled my feet from the bucket, she knelt right down and patted them dry before she carried off the towels and all.

Putting aside the comfort I felt at that good girl's hands for swiping and patting, the routine of being waited upon in that way went counter to my custom. And here I was being fondled, in a way. Although it was only my feet, extremities, you could say. Still I knew that just round the corner the Gonçalves family would be going about their business as if they didn't know any of this was going on, even given that my feet needed the grime washed away. I can see the likelihood of some married couples, depending on their personal inclinations, standing still for that sort of patting. But I'm not married to this girl and not likely to be by a long way round.

After the girl left, I cleaned up the rest of me as best I could before I was called in to sit at the family table, trying hard to put that good girl's attention far away. The Gonçalves folk considered my status special, seeing as I was a ship's officer. I gave up trying to make them understand that my rank carries no special privileges how-so-ever. Though I can't say I didn't enjoy the special attention--every bit of it.

We dined on charred beef—excellent cuts grilled over charcoal, more tender than what the Gauchos served— sweet potatoes and manioc meal, the latter covered in a sauce of minced greens, tomatoes, onions, wine vinegar and a little oil, followed by oranges picked fresh from their own trees. And as excellent a wine as I have ever swished beneath my palate, being more accustomed to cider and beer, I might observe.

Editor: Griggs's initial caution about exposing certain of what he considered racy passages in his personal memoirs clearly dates him in one way. Fortunately for us, Griggs maintained his frankness in style and substance, even though he apparently intended to eradicate at a later date those he parenthesized above, especially such passages about Ruthie. Fortunately for us, he changed his mind later, thereby leaving an honest and dynamic self-portrait, as we shall see.

He was clearly uneasy with the attentions of the Gonçalves family and protested his impatience to get to General Gonçalves' headquarters in the new capital. So, at the end of March 1836, he went off with an escort in the morning for a whole day's ride to Piratini in the high country west of the Lagoa dos Patos. During the early hours he made his way through the grassland, which sloped gradually upward along the Rio Piratini into hillocks and coppices until the forested hills came into view. At the forest edge, the trail described a fairly steep series of cross-backs up through pine, deciduous, and dense shrub. On the last day of March the riders reached Piratini.

Griggs, end of March 1836: Arrived in Piratini, Headquarters of the Revolutionary Government. The town is hard to reach. My crotch can answer for that after all those unaccustomed days in the saddle. Piratini has a fair status as a metropolis in this remote area. Most of the buildings, eight or so, are built of mud bricks, stuccoed over and covered with roofs of brown tiles. Not more nor a few of which are two stories high; and those are the only official ones. All of them are connected in a line and abut the street, such as it is, with its hard-packed dirt continuing right on into the buildings. Not prettied up but they stand the hard use of these frontier types, who are all business. The Ministry of War is one of the best structures. Like the few other official edifices, it has some fancy outside terracotta work, scrolls and such along the tops of windows and at the gable ends. Handsomely paneled doors and broad plank flooring set it off from the others. Dusty and unkempt as the town is, I'm relieved to be here after my flight from the Port of Rio Grande.

April in these latitudes brings cooler days and downright chilled nights. I have to remind myself that back home the winter snows have begun to run off along with maple syrup, for our seasons are the reversed of what they get down here.

I met with General Gonçalves and a few of his staff. He stands out among the others. He's a good fathom tall and stately. He looks to have a quiet, dependable strength and much patience, the sort who fore-thinks his decisions before he acts. Most others around him are rugged looking, except for another foreigner, an Italian, name of Zimbockackra, or howsoever it's spoken. I can't make out his stake in this brouhaha. He mostly stayed out of conversations but jotted away in his notebook while the general and I talked. Without so much as a thank you, Zimbockackra took the counterfeit coins I'd smuggled in. That followed the General's generous show of gratitude.

The General asked after Captain Hamlin. (8) He knows that the Brazilian authorities detained the *Toucan* last August on suspicion of carrying contraband. That was a half year after he and his comrades broke off from the Imperial Government in Rio de Janeiro. What with the coins I brought with me, he told me, "You are already an agent of this revolution." And he said it with congratulations and true appreciation, as I calculate it. That pleased me a good bit. It's near enough to the whole truth, leaving out my and Captain Hamlin's intention to gain a favorable foothold in trade with this new Nation of Rio Grande do Sul, should it come to reality.

But I'd better allow the General to form that conclusion in his own time and manner. He knows that the *Brown* was stopped early in '34 in San José do Norte. That was when the Brazilians found boxes of false coin on board and put Captain Pierson in prison. They freed him after he paid for his own release. Gonçalves also knows about the *Trafalgar*, the *Arabian*, the *Emma*, the *Duan*, and the *Oriental*, all American merchantmen held in port on suspicion. The searchers found nothing on those other ships, but the warning was clear: no contraband for the rebels unless agents were willing to face imprisonment or worse.

Still end of March 36: As I already observed, the General is a true aristocrat, the sort who furnishes dependable leadership. At the same time, if what I saw in this center of the new government gives a proper measure, he will need help to keep it organized enough to fight a war against the Imperials. Everybody here is ready to grab their muskets and jump into a saddle quick enough. But I see nothing like an orderly army. I see no barracks, nor drilling, nor stores of weapons and no regular uniforms, which is why, as I come to understand it, the Imperials call the rebels Faroupilhas, or rag-tags. As to their taking to being organized into a fighting army, I'll keep my doubts to myself.

Gonçalves asked what he could do to make my stay more comfortable until they could get me back among my countrymen. That's when I told him I decided to put myself at his disposal. I am in a tight spot here, for my government can do nothing to protect me. I have not actually taken up arms for this nation, but it may come to that. By law it is the same thing. And that is compounded by my joining in a rebellion against Brazil, a nation that is still a bona-fide partner in trade with the U.S.

If the rebels succeed, then our company is in a good place to set up as a favored business partner with them. Captain Hamlin, who is part owner of the *Toucan*, has assured me of a vessel of my own when he stands ashore as a broker for our shipping company. I may even have the *Toucan* herself. She is a good sailer, hardly a year since she slid down the skids at Sampsons' shipyards in Duxbury where I signed on as Mate.

Today I rode back to the Ministry. A good number of gaucho types were milling about. Aside from them, some true Black Africans gathered in their own groups. None looks fiercer. They are Freedmen for volunteering into the militia, mostly as cavalry, which comes from their being expert at handling horses. Watching them sit their saddles and grip their long lances, as if their threatening looks were part of their standing rigging, you'd never guess they were ever anything else.

Editor: Griggs was a phenomenon to the Riograndenses, an American putting himself directly at their service. Understandably, the U.S. War for Independence was fresh in their minds, an inspiration, just as it was for others in South America who fought to separate themselves from European monarchies, but the Riograndenses kept at him to explain why he decided to join their cause. So, without revealing his fundamental intentions, he obliged them with an account of his forebears, which credentials he hoped would quench their curiosity.

To begin with, he told them about Thomas Griggs who sailed as purser with Hakluyt and put into various ports in Brazil, including the Isle of Santa Catarina, which he pointed out occurred two hundred years before America's own war for independence. (9) They sang out bravo to that. But closer to current time, he told them about the Colonial John Griggs, who was bodyguard to General Washington himself. And later a Captain Alex Griggs sailed the *Harpy* out of New York in the War of 1812 and fought off several British ships. He took 17 prize vessels in all, and in 1814, one day before July 4, took the British brig-of-war *Princess Elizabeth* in as fierce a battle as any Griggs was ever in. That was enough to mark a place for Griggs among the Rio Grandeses.

He wasn't surprised when his listeners called his forebears heroes, but he was uneasy about their identifying him so readily for his selfless devotion, as they saw it, to their cause for freedom. All of which, as we shall see later, set him to cogitating over the traits that characterize heroes.

Griggs: These Gonçalveses are fine people. I have already written down as how, being a ship's officer, I rank pretty high in their eyes, but that's the way these aristocrats cipher it, no matter how Bay Staters feel about it. I intend to cast no word against them, but these Gonçalveses would be more at home among Virginia landholders than Massachusetts trader-types like my own people. That aside, I enjoy their gracious treatment and their enthusiasm for the cause of Political Independence, just as I feel toward Independent Enterprise. So, I'll stand by them; for, it will likely help both them and myself in the end.

Still, I can't help thinking on how people measure others as relates to their own sight and setting. What I mean is they fit me in to their own view of things, whereas I know how I came up through the ranks, as we say, from my original berth as a forecastle seaman with the stain of tar still fixed in my knuckles. I have yet to see a show of dirt beneath the finger nails of the Gonçalves family, nor a bit of tarnish on the braid of the General's shoulders and cuffs. Yet, they call me into their drawing room as an equal for courteous attention.

Maybe could they have seen me sharing my practical skills as a sailor with the Gauchos, or find me at home at a forge or pitching in with the shipyard workers. If they understood my outlook in carrying contraband to their capital for the purpose of gaining a trade advantage down the road, maybe they'd measure my risks and adventures in another way. I don't know for sure, but for the moment I'd best let them believe what they wish. Seems to me that's not really misleading them.

I had heard some shipmasters and mates charge that these new breakaway governments are not trustworthy toward merchantmen from the US and others. To be sure, some of the old practices still stand. For one example, a shipmaster must still slip some cash so the port-masters assign him a favorable anchorage or a handier docking spot. And most foremen hold their paws out for a bribe to guarantee swift and damage-free long-shoring. Other than that, I've seen nothing but steady cooperation at these ports along South American coasts. Of course, now that I have become a marked man, all other U.S. vessels will have to stand special scrutiny for a while, especially the *Toucan*, if they accept more of her business at all. (10) That will go on until the Imperials satisfy themselves that our contraband traffic has stopped. Captain Hamlin has a good name among them, so he may be able to convince the Imperials that I was a renegade acting on my own.

Enough of such gamming.

It's nearly mid-April [1836] and I am getting edgy with nothing to do. As we say, a hard day's work makes a bed soft at night, and I have not been sleeping soundly.

After a bit of poking around I came across a likely project and suggested that the General permit me to move to a clearing I happened across down near the mouth of the Rio Camaquã. It stands a few miles east of Doña Antonia's estançia, where I found a kind of warehouse, or work-shed—a galpoa, as they call it. And there scattered along the shore lay several hulks, including two sizeable sloops that appear to be in fair condition for repair. Nearby the galpoa is a scattering of other out-buildings, altogether a sham-built bunch of sheds but serviceable enough. With the general's go-ahead, I spent a fortnight at the estançia to arrange for putting in stocks of food and equipment enough for a few men to settle in there to the purpose of working on the hulks. Enough men are already hanging around down there for me to pick a trainable crew of workers.

A special word about these hang-about types: Some down there were black slaves turned to such chores as gathering and drying yerba leaves and smoking strips of beef into jerky. Others are whites who either tried fitting out the vessels on their own or just served to guard what there is.

Since the war started, this whole Province has attracted a lot of runaways, fugitives of one kind or another, thieves and cut-throats amongst them, for all I know, or maybe just some restless souls, but more of the former, I wager, by the way they sulk and look over their shoulders, except when they're slopping down dregs of rum and carousing with unlovely ladies.

In my own experience, I've shipped a few of their sort as crew when none better were about. They're one-trippers, usually, good for one leg of a journey until they get enough tin in their pockets for a few drinks and a whore. Then you've seen the last of them. Of course, I've seen some fine seamen rise from out of unlikely looking stock. But most of them are worth less than thinking about. I've got to admit, that sort are the exception on most American vessels these days, for our ships are manned mostly with native born seamen who have naught but honest bones in their bodies and some with high ambitions. (11)

After taking the measure of the lot drifting in at the galpoa, I have picked three former slaves for the hard and steady work around the boats. They seem likely fellows, sturdy and alert. If the others can't stand me putting the Blacks over them, then they can up stakes and leave. I've got to make proper use of the best of them. It's not like I claim a place among the abolitionists. I have read through one of John Woolman's tracts that my grandfather on my mother's side kept round the house, he being a Quaker off and on.

Anyway, slavery is due to end after Gonçalves and his compatriots succeed with this Revolution. Then they'll all be freedmen alike, so whatever the light skins don't like, they will have to get used to it. Of course, Brazil outlawed the slave trade some ten years ago. Not slavery as such, but even the outlawed trade has all sorts of loopholes, which means that trade goes on, especially in ports such as Recife. We put in there on an occasional trip when cargo demands, so I've seen the slavers there. Fact is that I've been offered berths on slavers, where the pay is equal to the risk. I'm ashamed to say that some U.S ships with New England seamen are in the trade. Howsoever they are registered it's a filthy business making money on others' misery, packing the blacks in below decks, knees to butts, with little relief for an entire journey. I couldn't do it. I've whipped a man or two for neglect of duty, but I couldn't lay that sort of suffering on a fellow creature.

On another tack, one special person came down from the Gonçalves' estancia to join me. I did not send for her. She is the same girl I made note of, the one who started to wash my feet after my long horseback flight from the *Toucan*, a fine looking maid of mixed-blood, mostly Indian, as I reckon but who's to say for certain? She's of somewhat shorter height than most, although she seems to me full grown. Oh, yes, I'd say so by the inviting proportions of her. But that's not a concern I ought to get involved with.

Doña Antonia or some one in her household must have assigned her to me. I don't know her status. Could be a slave but I've never asked. All I can say is that she has a favored place in the Gonçalves' household. Ruth—that is her given name, although it took me a few tries to figure it out. The accent down here makes it sounds more like Rootchie. Or sometimes the way they flutter their r's it comes out Hootchie. She'll have to answer to Ruthie for my purposes, how-so-ever they hail her. When I first tried saying her name, she turned her head aside and covered her mouth, embarrassed but ladylike with concern for my feelings, it seemed to me. It's one of the habits that makes her more attractive than not. Anyway, she tried my way of pronouncing it. May take her time to get the *th* right in Ruthie, but watching her body shake gently with laughter took no getting used to. Back at the estancia she is always nearby, gathering up my soiled garments and bringing them back clean, tidying my quarters in apple pie order, first thing in the morning and answering my needs all day without a word from me, right up to the time I turn in for the night.

(After a while, I might as well say here, she stayed on for the night. That was after I asked Domingo, the plantation foreman, about her. He's the one told me that Ruthie asked to serve me and Doña Antonia gave her permission--"A clean girl," as he put it. "No sickness," he assured me, and cautioned me, "Don't let her know you asked. An insult, you understand?"

I've always stayed away from the girls who hang around the devil's half acre in our ports-of-call, unlike some seamen whose careers end early and nasty with the pox. But as for Ruthie, as long as she rode down here to stay with me—by the way, she sits her horse better than I do mine, it's no doubt true—I will let her stay on until we sail out of here. Then it's back to the estancia for her. I want no ties with the shore. Putting it all in all, she's bright and orderly and, I'll be frank, cozy to the touch.

And I have made another thing clear, while she's here. If any of my men gives her so much as a glance, I'll put my quirt to their hides, one side and the other. I steer clear of saying anything about them hauling wenches in from where-so-ever they find them. Such women seem to generate like maggots and no doubt spread them, too. That's their lookout, do what they will as long as they know Ruthie is off limits to them.)

CHAPTER 3

Griggs Begins Work on the New Navy

Editor: Immediately above stand three or more of the parenthesized paragraphs Griggs intended to strike out whenever he got
around to reading over his private log.

In mid-April, 36, in one of his treks down near the shore of the
Lagoa, Griggs spotted the scattered hulks lying high and dry at the
mouth of the Camaquã. The Brazilians, by the way, designated all
such vessels barcas, which doesn't mean anything as large as a
barque-rigged vessel but is just a general reference to sailing vessels of average size. Each of these vessels displaced approximately
30 tons, which describes them as far smaller than American merchantmen such as the *Toucan*, for instance, which registered at 207
36/95 tons gross. (12)

Griggs saw that their hulls and decks were reparable, a few
new planks and fresh caulking would do it. They had been rigged
originally as schooners but Griggs decided to limit each to one
mast until they proved seaworthy. He could step a second mast
when he needed to.

Griggs's ship-fitting compound was on low, sloping ground
under good cover, and far enough upstream from the Lagoa dos
Patos to remain hidden from Imperial patrol boats. (13) It had a
sort of general storage and repair shed in addition to the galpoa,
with a decent forge and generous piles of scrap metal lying about.
He set about transforming it into a shipyard to fit out his random
collection of vessels for running supplies to depots up and down
the shore lines and up the rivers as far as soundings allowed. Aside
from the two small sloops, he didn't have much to work with until
he found the bigger hulls. But he proceeded to fashion proper fittings and riggings. He even armed one of them for possible raids
on the merchant vessels in the lagoa. It would be a jury rig navy at
best, but seaworthy.

Griggs: I set about taking an inventory of the usable supplies
we have on hand at this Shipyard of the Republic, as it's been ti-
tled. The best I can say for it so far is that it is safely located. The
shallow shore along the lagoon will prevent any close-in raids by
Imperial patrol boats. If any of them should try to come up river,

we would know it soon enough and fight them off easily from the foliage along the banks. I have drilled a likely troop of musketeers for the task. Several of the freebooters who were foisted on me made too meager a show of working, so I ran them off. It's mostly the former slaves that have wind enough for the tasks ahead. They're bright and grateful and know how to stay at their chores. I can train them to do what I need in the way of repairs and even fitting out some of these hulks we've inherited.

Some few of the idlers have stayed on, anyway, picking up enough work-habits to be useful. I'd had to take a cane to a parcel of them who were holed up with some whores in the storage shed, where they were interfering with work. After that they became reliable enough for some of the simpler tasks of stacking planks, laying out tackle, caulking and such. Filthy louts with no self-control. I'd run the lot of them off into the bush if this was my show. But the General is against it. Says they're not the sort to work hard but they'll fight when they have to. Well, it's his call, and I'm not one to reform conditions down here. The rules a Bay Stater holds to mean nothing to this lot of drifters. I could make a more reliable crew out of the common fishermen hereabouts, for they have the habits to stick to their purpose. I just hope the scoundrels I do have won't forget what I've taught them about handling lines, once we launch these vessels. Likely they will be ready for action when they know some booty's to be had, but I won't take the worst on board any vessel with me for any reason. The scum! I'll make bos'ns from among the freed slaves. For quickness and dependability, they'll do handsomely. Perhaps I'd better take it up ahead of time with the General.

May '36: It is cold nights, but the work on the schooners goes on, although slowly through this month. I have plentiful planking but little else for ready use in the way of fittings. Four of Doña Antonia's slaves turn out to be good joiners. Working iron is a bigger problem. I've learned since that one particular Freedman here name of Procopio has skills at the forge. He's a black of great stature and a fast learner. I'll show him how to fashion some of the fittings we need—cleats, mast-rings and footings, and chocks. I had to long-splice various spare lengths of hemp for the rigging. They will do until we get some proper cordage. I used that chore to train some of the other Freedmen—that and fashioning sails, which will be none too fine, I fear. We have some serviceable canvas, but for spare sails we'll have to make do with sacking for now. Patching and double hemming all around.

Procopio has a will to learn, a real boon hereabouts. He's admirable to view, sculpted like an Ajax and the fiercest of his band. Two of the Maltese sailors unsheathed their knives on him when he stumbled across them rutting a slut in one of the sheds, but they saw he was not one to back off so they did instead. He is a true Branco.

That needs a bit of explaining. So I'll pick up on what I wrote a few pages back. The Brazilians have all range of designations according to skin color—mulattos, mestisos, moranhos, mamelucos, caboclos, cafuzos, cambos, cabujos and others reflecting unions of whites, Africans. (14) Branco stands for white, but that's not all of it. White also stands for anybody they mark as a leader among them, as you might say. So here comes the strange part of it. A few of the darkest skinned are called Brancos because their skills and dependability put them in positions where the others look up to them. So that's how rank and respect come about.

To me it works out more fairly than other ways of seeing it. Some of the best seamen I've known were blacks. Some few of them have been promoted to bos'n on U.S. vessels—rare as that is—but not a grumble heard among their white shipmates. That happens mostly in the whaling fleet, where I've heard blacks often get the smallest lay and even some times little or nothing at all, except those who can throw a harpoon.

It's true, blacks on board merchantmen, of whom I've known more than a few, are taken on mostly as cooks. But there's been many a black topside seaman as well. I've never heard those that make bos'n referred to as White or Branco, as they'd have it here among the Brazilians. When I sailed before the mast, I had a few blacks as shipmates. I've heard many a debate about how much blacks can learn, that they are limited to imitating whites but only up to a certain level of skill. I say there are other measures, too. Take the whalers again, where blacks serve as harpooniers and even mates on some ships. I've heard some speculate that one day a black will serve as master of a whaler, where the worth of a captain is measured in barrels of oil he delivers to his home port.

In my own experience of seamanship, I've seen blacks make a long splice as handy as any able seaman afloat. I myself learned to tie a masthead knot, rolling hitch, and fashion the Napoleon bend, all from a stumpy old black seaman named Samson Tyre, out of

Marblehead. He also taught me the difference between a standard bowline and a tow bowline, and best of all, when to use a becket bend and a barrel hitch. Samson didn't stand as tall as my shoulder, nor was he near as handsome as my man Procopio here, but for skill he could hold his own against any seaman I ever saw.

Of course, sailors in general tend to be a more alert and a brighter lot than most men ashore. What sets a limit on learning, as I see it, is a man's attitude more than any natural limitation. Not being a philosopher, I daren't carry these speculations any further than I have. But I do offer them up to this last piece of reckoning to show that I am not altogether dim—the slave-blacks I've come across in and around Boston are careful to limit their skills to satisfy their owners' sense of superiority, whereas the freedmen-blacks don't need to fence in their abilities for any rules other than this: a man's work is a man's worth.

September '36 marks six months since I arrived, and the weather grows fairer with longer days. By now we've made decent headway with our navy. We have a proper shipyard, jury-rigged though it be, two sloops and two smaller craft that are broad beamed and lateen-rigged. Not quite Hampton boats but serviceable. With General Gonçalves' permission, I finally gave Procopio the title of Foreman, and he has taken the task of training other Freedmen. The worst among the white mariners—if you can call them mariners—grumbled some, but none of them is his equal for skill or industry. Once we form crews, I will make Procopio bos'n. I kept an extra peak-cap to give him as a mark of rank. Perhaps later I'll give him his own sloop to sail.

Editor, October 15, 1836: In the middle of this productive stretch, disaster struck the rebels In late September, one of the large land owners, Bento Manoel Ribeiro, with Imperialist sympathies, formed an army and attacked Gonçalves' forces up near Porto Alegre at the head of the Lagoa dos Patos. The General led a brigade to engage them at Pelotas, north of the Imperial capital, where Ribeiro defeated him and took Gonçalves prisoner, along with Zambeccari and other leaders of the revolution. Gonçalves and the others were imprisoned far to the North near Rio de Janeiro. The Imperials continued to control Porto Alegre. General Lima, next in rank to Gonçalves, was left in charge of the rebels. He withdrew the main body of remaining troops into the highlands west of the lagoa but ordered Griggs to maintain his position at the shipyard. All refitting work, however, came to a standstill.

By the end of November 1836, Zambeccari managed to get a message from prison to the rebel headquarters, which subsequently reached Griggs, that two ship owners—Young Italians in Rio—had made plans to sail down and join the revolutionaries. He referred to Luigi Rossetti and a man less familiar to him, Giuseppe Garibaldi.

Griggs: We have received word that more Italian volunteers are making their way here. That is extra good news. The Italians are mainly an energetic and dependable lot, but I don't see how they can sail directly to this locale. They can't enter directly into the Lagoa dos Patos. It may be they plan to slip past the Imperial forts on either side of the entrance channel. That's not likely for they are already identified in Rio de Janeiro as Young Italian supporters of the revolution, so the Imperials will be laying for them. I don't know their ship's draft, either, for passing over the bars in the entrance channel is tricky even at high tide. I wish them success, for we could use another good ship and a few more seasoned sailors, especially if they have experience in battle. Someone has warned them, I hope, against the obstacles they face down here.

CHAPTER 4

Rossetti and Garibaldi: More Adventures in Rio de Janeiro

Editor: Of course Griggs was right. With no chance to enter the Lagoa dos Patos, Garibaldi had to sail on down to the Platte Estuary, collect some other Italians there, and somehow join the rebels overland in Rio Grande do Sul, the same way Griggs had. But no one anticipated the trouble they ran into after they'd sailed into the Platte.

Before we proceed to that point, however, we need to go all the way back to their ventures in Rio de Janeiro. The account is full of twists and turns but reveals much about Garibaldi and Rossetti both.

On November, '36, after resolving his suspicions, Rossetti took Garibaldi to meet the Young Italians. On entering Dalecazi's apartment, Donna Dalecazi ushered him and Rossetti into the parlor, where all stood to greet them. Rossetti made introductions, following which Garibaldi told Dalecazi right off that, in Marseilles he had heard his name. Dalecazi asked whether Garibaldi had known other Young Italians. At that Garibaldi laughed and told them that his real name was not Pane, which he had used with the French ship captain as a convenience to slip away from Marseilles. Then he referred to his earlier alias: Borel.

At that point, Delacazi broke in to indicate that he was already aware of Borel's role in an incident that had occurred two years earlier. "You planned a mutiny on board the French ship *Euridice* at Genoa, did you not?" Garibaldi acknowledged as much and told of how, when the plot was uncovered, he had to run for his life, literally by foot, all the way to Marseilles, and of how, once there, he took berths on various merchant ships, mainly to ports in North Africa until he was able to sign up on the *Nautonnier* bound for Brazil.

Rossetti: Of all the names of fellow mutineers Garibaldi mentioned, Cuneo's was the only one I recognized. I told him, "He is here, you know." Giuseppe was clearly excited and asked immediately why Cuneo was not present. But Dalecazi informed him that "here" meant Brazil. To meet Cuneo, he said, Garibaldi would have to go far to the South in Uruguay. "He is there with other Young Italians," and added, "but your reputation is already known to us."

Dalecazi then cautioned Garibaldi that he was already under sentence of death by both the French and the Sardinians, to which we raised our glasses and saluted him. Tears spilled from his eyes, and I remember his exact response. "Understand me, Compadri, I weep not in pride. What I have done is nothing measured against what must yet be done for our homeland. I would gladly give my life ten times and ten times again to see our beloved Italy free and united, to regain her past glory as the greatest Republic the world has ever known, and crowned by her future power and benevolence for all mankind!" He fairly sang those elaborate phrases in his ringing, tenor voice. We could not help being moved by his rhapsodic enthusiasm.

Certainly now as I look back through those years at the risks he has taken, his numerous encounters with death, his recklessness, and yes at times his foolhardiness, I know that he understood himself very well as a person motivated by a simple, childlike commitment to freedom and the dignity of those he encountered, enemies and friends alike, I might add. And most striking of all was his absolute rejection of personal gain, even, at times, of personal comfort. The thought came to me suddenly that if those are the characteristics of heroes, then Garibaldi surely qualifies.

When he asked about traveling down to join Cuneo, Dalecazi told him that, for the present, he must be satisfied with an exchange of letters. "The distance is vast," Dalecazi explained. "A few days sailing from Rio and you are only part way to Montevideo. Do you understand how large this continent is?" He instructed Garibaldi that it would take weeks to reach Cuneo.

When, in November, 1835, I followed Dalecazi's instructions and wrote to Mazzini about Garibaldi, I did not know, that Garibaldi had already written to tell Mazzini where he was and about his flamboyant plans to find a ship and sail as a privateer against the enemies of Italy in this region. By the time Mazzini answered [January, 1836] with a letter for us to share, verifying Giuseppe's career as "Borel," Garibaldi had already posted provocative broadsides around Rio against the Sardinian Ambassador. He did this at first on his own, and Dalecazi had to chide him. Nonetheless, he soon became a regular member of our meetings in Dalecazi's home where we knew him by his real name.

As we learned, even Mazzini knew Giuseppe only by his pseudonym. I include the substance of his letter as a point of interest and as a touchstone for my own observations. Mazzini wrote that "Borel" had earned a voice by his actions at Genoa. He called him a rank-and-file revolutionary, but naive, impetuous, ideologically uncultivated. Still he called him a valuable force for action, at times the only sort we would be able to count on. He ended his letter with a three-word directive to Dalecazi: "Useful if controlled." With Mazzini's over-all assessment I now agree, but at the time, my own evaluation of Giuseppe's traits was still forming. I have had occasion to test Mazzini's assessment, and have concluded that Giuseppe is indeed naive—not at all intellectually disciplined. His claim to be a disciple of Saint-Simon, for example, is merely an enthusiast's passing familiarity. Some of his favorite references— derived from Saint-Simon—were that the Roman Catholic Church was most heretical to true Christianity that all men should be motivated by a sense of brotherhood, and his one quotation was that the Pope was at the head of a "hateful system of mysticism and trickery." His own strong arm, he avowed, will are guided by pure intentions.

Editor: Garibaldi's irrepressible need for action both amazed and alarmed his companions, but he showed different moods as well. They sensed his withdrawal, and once, when they asked him why his mood had turned so, he told them that he was often overcome by a vision that his life would contain few respites between moments of fierce struggle. Rossetti includes yet another consideration about Garibaldi: his impetuosity and the resultant gaps in judgment, his apparent inability to foresee the consequences of his actions. That factor began to play a more frequent concern in Rossetti's assessment. We shall see that it was shared by Griggs and Anita

Rossetti: In the streets of Rio, excitement was always waiting, especially in the late afternoon when the heat lost its intensity and celebrations broke out spontaneously among the Cariocas, as the residents of Rio de Janeiro are called. Carnaval, Saints' days, Indian Festivals, Macumba rites, national and provincial celebrations, all ran together. In that daunting confusion, Giuseppe constantly surprised me by the intense penetration with which he saw each object, each action. Although our friends Zambeccari, Dalecazi, even I, all of us are more deliberate about measuring peoples' worth, Garibaldi became the spontaneous judge among us. How does one explain such a characteristic? He sometimes exasperated me because his forceful commitment was so unswerving that he would make what he did, what he said, what he thought seem more important, more perceptive, in short more necessary than anything the rest of us did or thought. I knew and still know that at times he is wrongheaded, that he makes foolish decisions, that he can be impolitic to the point of endangering himself and his friends. But when the need for action comes, he is in the forefront, whatever the likely outcome.

Where are we left with all this conjecture? Do not we all make mistakes? What have our own hesitations to act cost others? Nevertheless, for Garibaldi each moment is still the center of immediate necessity, and each person, while he speaks to him, is the center of his concern. And such respect touches even the lowest person! I give an example.

One evening we stood watching a procession of Flaggellentes hobble along half naked. Crowns of thorns pierced their scalps and necks. Blood trickled from their wounds and joined the rivulets from the spiked whips with which they slashed through the hairshirts on their backs. The people along the streets stared, some knelt and prayed. But Garibaldi was forthright in his disdain, insisting aloud for all to hear that he would turn those whips on the priests who inspire such inanity! "The body of a man is a beautiful thing," I recall his words exactly, "given by God to care for, to love and be loved, not for such senseless brutality as this."

I ushered him into a small praça in a side street, and we sat on the edge of the fountain. I dipped my kerchief into the water and handed it to him. While he wiped his brow, he told me the reason for his passionate outburst. On the previous day he had passed by the Praça de Sant'Anna, where a statuesque Black had been fastened to the center-post. His wrists were pulled high by the thongs. Other strands were pulled tight around his waist, his knees and ankles. His pants were pulled down to bare his buttocks. "Think of the humiliation!" he gasped. I will never forget his words nor the fierceness of his empathy. "The leather cords were drawn so tight that they nearly cut into his flesh, puffing his skin with the pressure. Then the whip came down on his bare flesh. Infuriatingly, even the police, the so-called minions of justice, joined the crowd in urging the whipper to strike his hardest. I felt the lash myself--

each searing stroke." He hissed through clenched teeth that the man who swung the whip was also a black slave, as huge and muscular as his victim. "He himself wore an iron band around his waist, linked by a chain to his ankle ring. Two more slaves were stretched face down on the flagstones awaiting their turns at the whipping post. Their heads were so close that the blood drawn by the lash splattered them. Other slaves were forced to watch the torment that could as easily fall to them.

"And the whites in the crowd," he told me, "some strolling by, stopped to watch the spectacle, to chatter or laugh like magpies, without pity, without the slightest sympathy. To them it was an entertainment. Among them stood a man dressed in an elaborate uniform and wearing a cocked hat with huge ostrich feathers trailing. By his side stood a little boy, dressed in imitation, thread for thread, feather for feather. Their frilled frocks and wide tails swung as they bowed their heads together and smirked at the half naked wretch at the post. I tell you, Luigi, I could hardly keep myself from taking the whip from the man and turning it on the spectators."

When I think of how outspoken Giuseppe was, what danger he put both of us in, it only tells me what a benevolent destiny he lives under. For all his daring, the risks he takes—often thoughtless, unnecessary risks—he has survived, although not without scars to himself and at times to others supposedly close to him, as if they were of no consequence separate from his own.

I must not seem to suggest here that he was not himself destined to suffer, both physically and emotionally, as a result of the unrestrained expression of his principles. But whether that suffering should have guided his discretion, his proper concern for the well-being, even at times the immediate safety, of others, remains an openly ambivalent judgment of his character. Well, perhaps I should ask myself, who am I, after all, to assign blame for such lapses?

Editor: In Uruguay Garibaldi was indeed to feel punishment similar to that suffered by the slaves he'd seen in Rio. His careless, arrogant gestures toward the police whenever he met them, his jokes about the Brazilian officers, their postures, their equipment, their pretentious uniforms, the high cockades, their glistening boots had often shocked Rossetti and the others, as we have seen. As Rossetti pointed out, Garibaldi did not disguise his disdain, and his companions constantly had to remind him of the danger his indiscretion put all of them in. Still, no matter how reckless he might seem at times, his input gave his fellows much to admire, and Rossetti, to be fair, still called him "a giant of selflessness among us."

Here is another instance of that trait.

One day he dove into the filthy water at the waterfront to rescue an elderly slave who had fallen from the pier. A crowd had formed on the edge watching the poor soul gasp and struggle to stay afloat. He was close to sinking to his death. "One slave more or less," Rossetti observed, "what could it matter to those heartless beasts watching him? Some of them actually laughed at his plight." But Garibaldi threw off his hat and jacket and dove in. He pulled the poor Black around to where Rossetti could help them both out, and they sat gasping, the slave with his head between his knees, unable to gather enough breath to utter his thanks before his master approached and cuffed him for his carelessness. Without pausing to thank Giuseppe, the brute jerked the slave to his feet and shoved him along the street, not even allowing the poor fellow to cast a glance of gratitude toward his rescuer. How could anyone fault Giuseppe for that act of heroism?

CHAPTER 5

Partners in Business and Revolution/ Griggs on the Scene in Rio Grande do Sul

From Garibaldi's Memoirs: I spent several months in Rio, unoccupied and ease [sic], and then engaged in commerce, in company with Rosetti [this is Garibaldi's spelling of his companion's surname]: but a short experience convinced me that neither of us was born for a merchant." (15)

Editor: By January 1836, Garibaldi had objected to his dependence on his friends so forcefully that Rossetti finally suggested a business partnership to keep him occupied. He might better have paused to consider whether Garibaldi's sense of management might be any better than his own. The subsequent history of their venture soon enough exposed their incompetence as businessmen. They spent too much energy agonizing about the selfishness and dissemblance in others, including some of their fellow Italians. The partners quarreled about everything except their trust in one another. Rossetti's account of their venture is as colorful as it is perceptive.

Rossetti: I was optimistic at the beginning. So I told Giuseppe about my scheme for delivering macaroni, spices, and hardware to the several Italian resorts along the coast north of Rio de Janeiro. I argued that the chance for success was good. I had my savings and he had what remained of his pay from the *Nautonnier*. He would deliver the goods and I would manage our business in Rio. That settled, the next day we began to look for a suitable vessel and a small crew to help sail it.

Our kind compatriots took a collection for us to purchase a sloop of adequate size (Ironically, so much for our independent enterprise!).Giuseppe estimated it at about seventy tons. Most of our customers were the restaurateurs in Cabo Frio, a beautiful resort city somewhat less than a day's sail north of Rio. We carried pasta, spices, and cooking wares. Our customers welcomed the idea but when Garibaldi delivered the goods, they almost always tried to pay him less than they had agreed, and he had to let the goods go at the narrowest of profits—even sometimes at a loss. It was not altogether his fault, for he could not bring the cargo back and thereby waste an entire journey. When he lost patience and argued with our clients, they threatened to cut us off from future business.

If it was trying for me, it was twice so for Garibaldi--almost a full day's sail to go one way and then to deal with such connivers. He hated it. But I had my troubles in Rio, too. Part of the delivery might get "lost" before it reached our storehouse; sometimes the goods were not loaded in time to depart on a favorable tide. And then the graft that port officials demanded: storage fees, duty fees, dock-clearance fees, fees for the slave drivers to get the goods loaded. I finally resigned myself to these bribes as a necessity. I tried to explain the system but Garibaldi could not accept it. By now all of us knew his ideals well enough. But I must tell you that they made an inappropriate attitude for business.

At times he was impossible, absolutely. To him, our business was little more than a reason to place a ship under his feet. He was more interested in treating her as a vessel of war. He renamed her the *Mazzini*, purposely to convey a belligerent association. Whenever he saw French or Sardinian ships in the bay, he flew the tricolors of Young Italy, and he sailed close to them and shouted oaths and insults. It was a dangerous game that gratified his own bellicosity, but soon we received word that the Sardinian Ambassador had complained to the Brazilian authorities. Of course, I hated them too, traitors to Italy and tyrants all, but I was afraid that they might conspire with the Brazileiros to revoke our license or worse. My attempts to restrain Garibaldi were ineffective. If anything they made him angrier. I told him I was as committed to the cause of liberty as he was, but now we had a substantial investment and were indebted to our friends for it.

By December of the same year, the income from our business grew. Finally we had made a good name everywhere, even established new customers at Macãe and Campos. In February, 1837, one year after we started the business, we entered our first profit. But almost at the same moment our business was ended. We had joined the Rebellion in the South!

Editor: Late in October of 1836, new developments brought them closer to the sort of involvement Garibaldi craved and changed the direction of their careers forever. Rossetti heard from Zambeccari, who, after the Battle of Pelotas was imprisoned in Guanabaro Bay along with General Gonçalves and other leaders of the Revolution. After several applications, Rossetti and Garibaldi gained permission to visit him at the Fortress Prison in Santa Cruz. They told the police that they wished to bring Zambeccari and the others some food, linens and soap.

From Garibaldi's Memoirs: Zambeccari arrived at Rio, having been sent as a prisoner from Rio Grande, when I became acquainted with the sentiments and situation of the people of that province. (16)

Rossetti: We put ourselves at Zambeccari's disposal. Garibaldi wasted no time telling him of his plan to use our merchant vessel as a Privateer in the service of the Revolutionaries in Rio Grande do Sul, to make raids on cargo ships, especially those flying the Sardinian flag, and to give the prizes to the Revolutionary Treasury. At that meeting, Zambeccari told us that sailing as a privateer was unnecessary. The Republic in Rio Grande do Sul had, after all, declared itself independent and would furnish its own official documents and a flag for our ship to sail under, so that Garibaldi would be a Commissioned Captain in the Navy and legally at war with Brazil. Garibaldi's enthusiasm was boundless, and his expression of gratitude elaborate enough for both of us, as it needed to be, for I had serious apprehensions about my suitability as a naval battler. But what sacrifice, I convinced myself, could be more profound?

On our next visit to Zambeccari's cell, he told us that he had gained Gonçalves' permission to grant us Documents of Commission and wrote immediately to General Netto for Letters of Marqué. What we did not consider at the time is that the Brazilian Government would refuse to acknowledge our credentials. To them we would be treated as pirates. Just as well that I did not learn that until later. Thanks nevertheless to the amazing tolerance of the Brazilian Police, we did not fail utterly.

Editor: Progress toward their new career in Rio Grande do Sul was quite slow because even the promptest communications with their compatriots in the revolutionary province took weeks each way. But the prospects of joining other Young Italians in a just struggle sustained them through the remaining weeks of their commercial tedium. The best and the worst came after the letters of marqué finally arrived (May 37) from General Netto, who was then in command of the revolutionary forces.

From Garibaldi's Memoirs: Having obtained the necessary papers, we engaged a small vessel for a cruiser, which I named "The

Mazzini." I soon after embarked . . . with twenty companions, to aid a people in the South, oppressed by a proud and powerful enemy. I was at the head of a resolute band, but it was a mere handful, and my enemy was the empire [sic] of Brazil. (17)

Rossetti: Right under the noses of the Imperial Police, we had been preparing our sloop, the *Mazzini*, for her new career as a Man-of-War. To get our official documents we played a game of secrecy and intrigue. Although Lima's letters were signed on November 14, 1836, we waited until May 1837 for them to arrive. During that time we continued to make our trade runs to Cabo Frio, Macãe and Campos. Our satisfaction at showing a profit at last was mixed, for we would never be able to earn enough to repay our friends for all their help.

To arm our Mazzini, we needed additional, large amounts of money from our fellow Italians, almost £10,000 in all. When our documents arrived in early May, we sped up our preparations and recruited the last of our crew. Among them were the Giovine Italia Mutru, Luigi Carniglia, and as fate would have it, another man named Garibaldi, this one Maurizio, who bore no relation to Giuseppe. With two Maltese sailors, three other adventurers, who made their homes wherever they laid their heads, and several others, we had a crew of eighteen. To disguise our true intentions, I signed on as owner-passenger under my own name. Finally, on May 7, 1837, we set sail from Rio de Janeiro.

Editor: During almost six months of the time Rossetti and Garibaldi spent to arrive at that momentous development, Griggs and his workers in Camaquá had been following an orderly routine. Then in March 1837, he learned that General Lima, had succeeded in arranging a coup by which one of the rebels' prominent enemies, General Manoel Ribeiro, who had defeated Gonçalves in September, switched his loyalties to the rebels—which typifies the abrupt shifts among the Riograndense land barons. By this arrangement, in mid-April, Ribeiro attached his army to General Netto's in the hills north of Porto Alegre. In just three days their newly combined armies drove the Imperials back into the Capital. Had they coordinated their conquest to include the ports at the mouth of the Lagoa dos Patos, the rebels would have gained control of the entire inland waterway south of Porto Alegre.

In the middle of May, 1837 the welcome news came that Gonçalves had escaped from his prison in Rio de Janeiro. Unfortunately for Zambeccari, he did not escape with him. Then by the end of May they had to check their elation; the news was incorrect. Gonçalves, instead of making it out of prison after all, had been merely transferred to a different compound in Bahia, nearly 20 degrees north of the rebel capital in Piratini. They couldn't be sure they would ever see him again.

Griggs: Winter weather has set in. It is not so bad as winter in New England. The days here are still warm. The evenings are chilled. The weather doesn't force us inside so we still do what we can to fit out our little navy here at Camaquã and await happier developments. By now, along with all the clutter and clutch, we've collected a decent store of iron bands and bars for repairs on our bigger vessels. If things don't liven up soon, I'll take leave of this location to see if I can do some good elsewhere, although just where that might be I cannot say. Procopio has turned into a true yoke-fellow, but aside from him, a few of his fellow Freedmen and the Italians, the workers under my charge don't know a granny from a reef knot. They lounge around all day. It's too long a time of idleness for them and for me, too. Truth is, we don't have much to do aside from guarding our area.

Mid-June, 37: Things may brighten up after all. After two more weeks of doldrums, the Italian Rossetti is here and told his story of what happened in Uruguay. When he and his shipmates on board the *Mazzini* found their passage through the mouth of the Lagoa blocked, they sailed the long way round into the Rio Platte, just as I foretold. Rossetti went ashore alone at Maldonado and trekked to Montevideo where he linked up with Young Italians there and arranged to sell the cargo he and Garibaldi captured south of Rio de Janeiro, mostly a large consignment of coffee.

Sounds like I'll have to go on waiting for more real shipmates, for Captain Garibaldi, I'm sorry to learn, is not with them.

After talking some with Rossetti, one thing was clear, between the two of them, Garibaldi is the sailor. Rossetti is a bit too lacy around the cuffs for a deck seaman—a book-keeper, maybe, but no sailor. Not that there's anything wrong with his type, but it sounds like I'll have to go on waiting for more real shipmates. Here's the rest of what Rossetti told us about his delay. While Rossetti was ashore arranging the sale of their coffee, Garibaldi got caught in an off-shore battle with hostile warships and had to make a run for it, leaving Rossetti behind. Bad luck for him and bad luck for us, too. Now I daren't go into action, even though this jury-rig navy is pretty well pasted together. I might as well give Garibaldi a week or so longer to join us. So with that in mind, I will send word to Captain Hamlin in Porto Alegre. Tell him about my whereabouts and my plans to stay on for a while longer, at least until Captain Garibaldi joins us.

CHAPTER 6

Rossetti and Garibaldi Sail South
to Join the Revolutionaries

Editor: I must back up a bit to give Rossetti's complete account of
the comrades' ventures when they first sailed south out of Rio de
Janeiro. Back in May of 1837, with the eyes of the Imperial police
on them, Garibaldi, Rossetti and their crew sailed out of Guanabara
Bay. On that day, Rossetti clutched the table from the cabin and
wondered how he'd ever survive the journey to Rio Grande do Sul,
whereas Garibaldi took charge of his new cockleshell as if she
were a forty-gun man-of-war. The little *Mazzini* was after all his
first true command, and treating her like a proper naval vessel, he
raised the colors of The Free and Independent Republic of Piratini.

Rossetti: On May 7, 1837 only three days after the Letters of
Marqué came, which is when we officially joined Gonçalves' Revolution, we sailed out of Guanabara Bay disguised as a coastal
trader. We kept most of the crew behind bulwarks until we cleared
the harbor. I was excited by the prospect ahead but just as much by
fear, I must admit it, to say nothing of my sea-sickness, and I
placed my faith completely in the skilled hands of Giuseppe.

Only then could I appreciate how easy life had been in Rio,
where our friends were always near us with good food, decent
wine, and especially solid land under our feet. Now uncertainty lay
ahead. We wondered about the fate of Zambeccari, Gonçalves and
the others. On the other side, we enjoyed the prospect of finally
being active in the Revolution. For us, the words of Barrault,
which Garibaldi quoted so frequently, would become reality: "The
man who offers his sword and his blood to all peoples who struggle against tyranny, he is more than a soldier; he is a hero." Obviously my comrade took those phrases seriously. Giuseppe was in
his glory. After we reached the open sea, he had the crew pull back
the tarpaulins, shift the casks of dried meat, fruit, and manioc below, and clear the decks for action. He fairly sang his orders. Soon
enough the others responded to his enthusiasm.

The weather was still fine, even though we were in the autumn
of that latitude. The daylight was warm and we had a strong wind

pushing us along. I sat huddled against the cabin table until Garibaldi shouted for me to get up on deck. "You will feel better, Luigi, if you lend a hand. Work! Start to sweat. Be a sailor now!" He was right, of course. I staggered onto the main deck to help adjust the sails. In a short time I was indeed warm from the exercise and stayed that way until we drew near to the south shore of Grande Island, where a large merchant ship came round its eastern end.

From Garibaldi's Memoirs: We sailed until we reached the latitude of Grand Island, off which we met a sumaca, or large coasting boat, named the Luisa, loaded with coffee. We captured her without opposition, and then resolved to take her instead of my own vessel... I...transferred every thing from the Mazzini on board the sumaca, and then sunk [sic] the former (18).

Rossetti: Immediately Giuseppe commanded everyone to take up muskets, stay out of sight and remain silent. He fairly hummed. "Stay low, calm, calm. Do not show a sign of action until I say so."

Someone put a rifle into my hands. I could not breathe, nor could I clear my mind of the notion that I was about to face death and, perhaps worse, deal death to others! It was all too soon for me. Nothing had prepared me for this, not the heated discussions in Dalecazzi's home, not the inspiring essays from Mazzini, my own declamations in our broadsides. On board that little boat, my spirits were tangled until I felt Giuseppe's hand on my shoulder: "Well, Luigi, soon now you will see why we have come this far." When he saw the uncertainty in my face, he pressed my shoulder and said, "You will do your duty." He moved along the deck saying something of the sort to each of his crew. Then to all of us at once, "Look up slowly. Lift your heads, but do not show much of yourselves. See the fruits of our first victory!" I did so, easing my head up. Alongside the dock in Rio, our *Mazzini* seemed small. Now as I squatted on her deck she seemed infinitesimal. The merchant ship looked huge, twice our size at least, and under full sail. How, I wondered, were we to conquer such an imposing vessel? But Giuseppe moved casually to our helm. When we were within hailing distance, he called out: "On board the *Luiza*. Heave-to in the name of the Republic of Piratini.

We could see them stirring on board the *Luiza's* quarterdeck, and soon from the cabin an officer came on deck and directed his glass at us. Giuseppe called for the helm to be brought over and shouted for our sails to be shifted for an interception.

Garibaldi ordered all of us to rise. "Up, men, show yourselves. Hold your guns high!" We did so and followed his example with a series of savage shouts. On our leader's command, three of our crew fired musket shots in front of the *Luiza*, following which she lowered her sails and sat waiting for us. Garibaldi directed Maurizano to steer alongside, and we lowered our sails. Our brave captain was moving and shouting rapidly: "On the alert! Carniglia and Maurizano and you, Rossetti, stay on board the *Mazzini*. Everyone else, ready, your arms, and on my word board her and take positions at all points on her main deck. Watch the hatches and companionways for surprises. Don't touch anyone or anything unless they resist. Now, at once, go!" The *Luiza* was secured in minutes. Garibaldi saluted and presented his papers. The *Luiza's* captain, still showing his shock, returned the salute. If only all of our campaigns from then on could be so easy.

One tense incident followed immediately, however, which taught me anew that Giuseppe's respect for humanity was to rule almost all his actions. At the moment when the captain saluted Giuseppe, a struggle broke out on the foredeck. One of the *Luiza's* young officers made a show of defiance and two of our crew pressed him against the forecastle bulkhead and pointed their carbines at him, while another drew his dirk. Garibaldi flew toward them, and with a bellow that cut the air like thunder, he drew his sword. "This blade," he shouted to his mariners, "is my authority!" No one could have withstood his will. "I gave orders to harm no one." Alert as always, he called to the rest of our crew, "Watch the others!" He faced the young mate. "What moves you to resist us, my young hero?"

The youth snarled at Garibaldi, "You are pirates, scum of the seas!" Giuseppe took the insult calmly. "Not so. If we saw pirates in these waters, we would protect you from them. Believe me; I know what it is to face marauders. Besides, if we were sea bandits, the blood would be spurting from your throat by now. We sail in the name of the Liberated Republic of Piratinim, with papers properly drawn. So you have fallen to honorable foes who will do you no harm, as long as you do not provoke those who are as honorable as yourself."

He barked at his two crewmen, who backed off, still scowling at the young mate, and Garibaldi turned to the *Luiza's* captain.

"Sir, show us your log and your cargo papers. Mutru," he snapped, "take two men and search the ship. Be alert!" He then turned back to the captain. "Sir, assure your crew and passengers that they are safe in our hands, and escort me to your cabin, please." The captain, now with regained composure, bowed. When they came back on deck, Garibaldi told the *Luisa's* crew that we would re-commission her into the Navy of the Republic of Piratinim. At that point he set six of our crew to transfer our possessions to the *Luisa*. While that went on, he had me write up a new document of commission with the name *Mazzini* and the details of her dimensions and cargo drawn from her current papers. She was a 100-ton merchant schooner. In addition to her few passengers she carried furniture and sacks of coffee, all of which became ours. Among the black slaves in her crew, five indicated their desire to join our cause and thereby to gain their freedom immediately.

From Garibaldi's Memoirs: A Brazilian, a passenger in the sumaca, took the first opportunity . . . to offer me a casket containing three valuable diamonds, in a supplicating manner, as if afraid for his life; but I refused to receive it, and gave peremptory orders that none of the effects of the crew or passengers should be taken from them. . . . And this course I pursued on all subsequent occasions, whenever I took any prizes from the enemy. . . . (19)

Rossetti: Mutru returned from his search with another passenger, obviously a merchant--either the owner or commission agent for the cargo. He stepped forward and bowing repeatedly to Garibaldi, motioned to a small strongbox cradled in his arm. He spoke in a hushed voice. Garibaldi stepped back from the man and spoke so that all on deck could hear. "I have designs on neither your life nor your valuables. Both are safe as long as you obey our orders with the rest of the passengers." Giuseppe motioned him toward the other prisoners near the foredeck. All alike showed their surprise at his speech. Even I wondered at the wisdom of such a promise. The man's small treasure would surely fetch hard money, which we needed badly, but Giuseppe's will was firm on the matter.

As for our prisoners, I saw nothing but skepticism in their expressions. I could see that the *Luisa's* captain in particular was still despondent, but he had to feel assured by Garibaldi's conduct and bearing. I certainly was relieved to hear Giuseppe speak with such firmness, for nothing could have disturbed me more than to associate with the spilling of innocent blood. I would have been surprised if Garibaldi had allowed it, but then, I knew little about the conduct of military encounters.

I would soon enough learn what Garibaldi already knew: to kill a foe, no matter how respected or how despised he might be, is no dishonor in war. Likewise, to be killed in a battle is not what I would choose, but no one controls all the conditions of war. So from that point on I was ready to accept death if destiny dictated. Certainly I had worked the prospect over and over in my mind. For Giuseppe, on the other hand, I heard him say in more ways than one, "War is the way of mankind," which I found to be a sobering portion of his credo.

Editor: As Rossetti noted: When the papers were in order and all the battle gear was transferred on board the new *Mazzini*, Garibaldi sent Carniglia below to open the scuttle valve on the little sloop in which they had conducted their trade and in which they had sailed so boldly from Rio de Janeiro. When Carniglia and Maurizio jumped on board the new ship, they let go the mooring lines and stood off to watch the first ship of the Revolution slip beneath the waves. They could not know, of course, that in Rio Grande, John Griggs had already fit out other vessels for the purpose. Rossetti's personal reaction to the scuttling is poignant enough to include here.

Rossetti: A huge hiss was the only echo of her brief but victorious career. Long after we had hoisted the sails on our new and far more substantial ship, I looked over the taffrail, trying to keep my eyes on the spot where our little sloop had sunk beneath the ocean swells. What a terrifying sight it was to me, to see a ship on whose deck I had huddled with my comrades, a small set of boards to which our souls had clung for survival and for glory, to see her go down with nothing to mark her departure from our lives, no mound, no monument, nothing but an unlikely recollection of her phantom reality. I felt how vast the ocean that gulped her and how grateful that none of our compatriots had sunk with her.

From Garibaldi's Memoirs: The passengers and crew were landed north of Itaparica, the launches of the *Luisa* being given to them, with all their movables, and as much brandy as they chose to take with them." (20)

Editor: 17 May 1837: After about five days sailing, Garibaldi found a place along the coast to put the prisoners ashore. On the chart it looked like Itapacaroi Point in the Republic of Santa Catarina. Garibaldi piloted the Mazzini in to where the calm surf allowed the captives a safe landing. There he had sails lowered and ordered the ship's boat over the side. He assembled the prisoners on the main deck and had them place all their portable belongings in the boat, to which he added a cask of brandy from the ship's stores. Then he told the passengers, the captain, and the remaining crew members to climb into the boat and row ashore. Carniglia asked about sending along two of the crew to return the boat to the ship, but Garibaldi was concerned that the castaways not be stranded in that desolate place. Carniglia's objection proved to be well founded when the rebels themselves fell into bad fortune.

28 May 1837: After the new *Mazzini* sailed past Rio Grande do Sul, Garibaldi put Rossetti ashore at Maldonado in Uruguay, a small port city just outside the entrance to the Rio de la Plata. In the eleven days it took them to reach there, they had run short of food, and the crew grumbled about Garibaldi's misguided kindness in sharing their supplies with the prisoners they had put ashore earlier.

CHAPTER 7

The Partners Arrive in Uruguay/Rossetti Rides North and Meets Griggs

Rossetti: At Punte del Este, I left my shipmates for Maldonado. I hope to stay on firm land from now until this Republic is secured and I return with Garibaldi to Italy. If I could have looked ahead and prevented the terrible ordeal that my friend faced before I was to meet him again, I would have gladly faced a lifetime on a ship with all its discomforts and dangers.

At the moment, however, I looked forward to meeting Giovanni Cuneo and other Giovine Italia in Montevideo and to gain their sorely needed help with our expedition. So when the *Mazzini* put into port, I rode on to Montevideo to arrange the sale of the coffee we had taken in the *Luisa*.

In Montevideo I made my way to Cuneo's house. The meeting would have been happier if I had not been so worried about our situation. When I left the *Mazzini* Giuseppe and the others were in good spirits, but I was uneasy about our reception in Uruguay. Our compatriots in Young Italy were as secure as those in Rio, but President Oribe was a bellicose Blanco, the party aligned with Uruguayans antagonistic to our cause. So we had to make all of our negotiations for selling our cargo with the Colorados faction, who considered the Gonçalves Family their allies and were more sympathetic to our Republican ideology.

From Garibaldi's Memoirs: I received unexpected notice, quite different from what I had been led to expect, that the flag of Rio Grande was not recognized, and that an order had arrived for our immediate arrest. (21)

Editor: Rossetti's journey from Maldonado to Montevideo, his meetings and arrangements to sell the coffee, and the return took him about two weeks. When he arrived in the port, eager to rejoin Giuseppe and the others, the *Mazzini* was no longer there. His friends told him that, with the collusion of Oribe, a Brazilian warship had been sent to recover the former *Luiza*, now renamed the *Mazzini*. Giuseppe had left a message that he would pick Rossetti up at the Point of Jesus Maria further up the estuary. When he arrived there, no Mazzini was in sight. Rossetti waited for as long as he could, almost two days. During his wait, his Young Italy compadri urged him to ride all the way up into Rio Grande do Sul to contact the revolutionaries there. So after they assured him they would remain alert for news of Garibaldi and his shipmates, Rossetti departed northward.

Rossetti, End of May: My guides and I traveled by horse, a long and hard ride with few rests, which gave me time to notice various fascinating details about the hardy inhabitants of that vast country. Most of the horses are small, not more than fourteen hands, but energetic and sure footed. We rode Gaucho style in deep, Spanish saddles, laid over thick woolen blankets and sheepskin, which the Gauchos also use for bedding. The stirrups are broad and strapped long for the rider to stretch forth his legs, not the sort I was accustomed to in Genovese Riding Academies, but they are remarkably stable. Also, the extended stirrups allow the rider to dismount and remount swiftly and even dip far to either side and ride along the horse's flank to manipulate their ropes and lariats from all angles.

We rode at a quick and steady pace. These little horses are nearly wild and very erratic. I did not like to use the Gauchos' cruel bits but I could see that absolute control was necessary, for if a rider is thrown off and his comrades do not see him, he must watch not only his horse but the others run out of sight and leave him helpless on these endless grasslands. That could be the end, for various beasts of prey roam the pampas, let alone the untamed cattle with their long, sharp horns.

Mid-June, 1837: Even with the cold winds and rain sweeping down from the higher terrain to the North, we were warm, for we wore thick, broad ponchos over all our other clothing. So I could appreciate in comfort the beauty of this natural paradise.

It took us more than two weeks to reach Piratini and that distance was just a tiny part of this continent. Think of its size! We went through spectacular, wild country, an unsullied natural splendor. For all that time traveling, we saw nothing but rich grasslands, sometimes the blades reached above our horses' chests. A few small, forested hillocks, like islands, relieved the oceanic swells. Near dusk each day, we stopped at a gaucho settlement, many only small clusters of families, staged at a full day's ride between them. Wild cattle and herds of horses roam in great numbers.

As soon as we crossed the Rio Santana we were in Rio Grande do Sul. The terrain became hillier with more frequent forest covering. We stopped in various places for rest and refreshments: Jaguarão, Osorio, Pinheiro, but none more gracious than Arroio Grande, the estancia of Doña Ana, sister to Colonel Bento Gonçalves. There I could have enjoyed a much longer stay, such cultivation, grace, and generosity, an oasis of civilization in this remote region. But I was on a mission that disallowed selfish comfort. I should note that at each stopping place, the inhabitants told me about the tall *oficial da marinha norte americana* who had passed through bound for the same destination. Of course, that made me even more eager to reach Pratini.

I soon met him, the other foreigner who had joined the Revolution. John Griggs has been here for some time fixing boats to form a Navy for the New Republic. On my way down to his compound in Camaquá, I had many factors to consider about this mysterious Griggs. When we finally met, I found a taciturn fellow, who, as I could see, was willing to let others make of him whatever they chose. He is tall and of a powerful physique, enough so to intimidate anyone who dares stand against him. I soon learned of his reputation as a brawler among those who challenged his authority. But he also shows a contemplative demeanor with more than a hint of gentility--a high forehead above full but well shaped brows, a small, straight nose, and trimmed mustache and beard. He studies the world from under heavy lidded eyes that seem calm, perhaps at times with a hint of disdain for the incompetents in whose company he finds himself. Happily, he values us Italians among his associates as dependable colleagues. Altogether, he is a striking presence. He is the only citizen of the admirable, new nation, The United States of America, among our comrades. I can see that, as an experienced mariner, he will make a valuable associate and, I must say, a handsome one.

Editor: Rossetti soon got news from the Young Italians in Montevideo that Garibaldi had run into trouble down in the River Platte and had sailed the *Mazzini* abruptly out of Maldonado.

As was always a threat, the Argentinian collaborators in Uruguay went back on their assurances of neutrality and, as Rossetti had heard, allowed the Imperial Brazilian Navy to send some ships down to intercept Garibaldi. The blame fell not to them alone because Garibaldi skirmished with a Uruguayan gunboat and put himself in bad graces with that navy. So he was forced to run up the Rio Paraná to Carameio and then north into the Gualeguay River, whose waters, as the map shows, are narrow and thereby leave little room to maneuver. To make things worse, although that course follows the Uruguayan border, it put Garibaldi 200 miles deeper into unfriendly territory. He and his crew, it therefore seemed, would be out of touch with their allies for months at least.

About mid-June, 1837, in response to that unwelcome news, Rossetti returned to Montevideo to see how he could help his comrades from there. At about the same time, Gonçalves' Republican Government in Piratini had accepted Rossetti's offer to begin publishing a newspaper to support morale among the revolutionaries. The equipment necessary for printing a newspaper was back in Uruguay, so he had to transport a small printing press and secondary supplies along the same route he had first taken to join the rebels.

On reaching Montevideo, Rossetti met with Cuneo, and to his surprise almost the entire crew of the *Mazzini*. But his joy was not complete because Garibaldi was not among them. Carniglia, who had recently returned separately from Gualeguay, told Rossetti that Garibaldi remained a prisoner. In mid-June, during their battle with the Brazilian and Uruguayan gunboats, one of their comrades, Fiorentino, was killed—shot in the head. Garibaldi took the helm from him and was himself shot in the neck but, despite his great pain and grave danger, he managed to navigate the ship beyond the range of the Imperialists' guns. When he could handle the helm no more, Carniglia steered the ship up the Rio Paraná and into the Gualeguay. Along the way, they received help from other shipmasters and citizens ashore who remained sympathetic to the Unitarians.

At the end of June, nearly two weeks later, they arrived in Gualeguay City. The authorities there, although antagonistic to Garibaldi, got medical help for his wound and let the rest of the crew return to Montevideo—only Carniglia was allowed to stay and help Garibaldi recover sufficiently to get around on his own. Carniglia assured Rossetti, that Garibaldi was at last recovered from his most serious wounds and that the local leaders were civil to him. Rossetti wanted to stay in the region and make plans to rescue Garibaldi but his companions dissuaded him.

Garibaldi, it seems, had been caught in a political crossfire. (22) The revolution in Rio Grande do Sul had its turns and twists but it was simple compared to what had been going on between

Uruguay and Argentina. A General Rosas in Argentina kept trouble brewing in the region between the countries known as the Banda Oriental, which was tossed back and forth between the contending factions. Standing against Rosas was a group called the Unitarians, or the United Party. General Rivera, leader of the Unitarians, was a fugitive from Argentina and a good friend to the Gonçalves revolutionaries. He had held the Presidency of Uruguay as far back as 1830. But after about three years, a General Lavallejo, with Rosas' backing, formed an army to depose Rivera. A few years after that, Rivera got up a force strong enough to drive Lavallejo off, then resumed the Presidency some time in 1836.

Obviously, the boundaries between Uruguay and Rio Grande do Sul were not delineated with precision or formal agreement between the inhabitants of the contiguous provinces. With the next turn of events Rivera was beaten again by Lavallejo and General Oribe, a sympathizer to the Argentinians. As a consequence, Rivera and his Unitarians fled north into Rio Grande do Sul, where they enjoyed the hospitality of the Gonçalves family. But soon enough, they returned to Uruguay and tried to regain control of their lost territory. Very confusing.

Coincidentally, that was about the time John Griggs left the *Toucan* Griggs, as an interested observer, had been working out his own analysis and evaluation of the tangle of intentions among the various factions contending for power in the region.

CHAPTER 8

Hamlin Runs The *Toucan* Aground

Griggs: All of these groups—The Gonçalveses and his followers in Rio Grande do Sul, the Riveras and Lavallejos in Uruguay, also Oribe and his cohorts in Argentina—they all claim rights to sections either side of the southern frontier of Brazil. On top of that, almost every large landholder wants to be a leader. Maybe that's what their patriotism comes to, having their own power without any of the authorities far up in Rio de Janeiro or south in Buenos Aires telling them how to manage their affairs.

I heard that, most of the time during this squabble, the Imperials headquartered in Rio de Janeiro have offered Gonçalves and his comrades several chances to leave off his fighting, with promises not to punish them. From the practical angle, I can't really see why Gonçalves wants independence as long as the Imperials make good on their negotiations to let him run things the way he wants to. It is true enough that people like him, big land grantees, settled this land and worked to make it pay. So, in a sense, they've owned it right along. Maybe it all comes down to honor, maybe not paying taxes for what's already theirs. Honor of that sort carries a heavy price, as my own countrymen would agree. But a lot of people have already paid dearly for honor on both sides of this struggle.

Anyway, Gonçalves seems to be the only one who can hold this particular revolution together. His followers, in the main, are pretty wild people with a good many of them shy of dependable. Their spirits can flare at any time. But most are come-and-go soldiers who fight when their own homes are threatened. Likely as not they break off fighting when they get too far from home. I wonder how different that is from most wars.

Editor: Despite his skepticism, Griggs's commitment to the revolution was strengthened when he was drawn in deeper by an unforeseen development. It came in the form of a reply to his earlier note to Captain Hamlin, Master of the *Toucan*. Hamlin was angered out of patience with having to keep his ship tied up in Rio Grande after Griggs had fled. He had been promised that the *Toucan* would be released in short order, after which Griggs hoped to be back in his former berth and sailing for home. But, driven by his frustration, Captain Hamlin's new and unexpected action pulled that strategy from under him.

Griggs: Captain Hamlin's arrangements for the *Toucan* are not what I expected. He got word to us at the last possible moment. That was right after word reached him that the imperials planned more interference to his unloading schedule up in Porto Alegre. So he made contrary plans. He chose an isolated spot on the eastern shore about one-third of the way up the Lagoa, and, on July 31, 1837, rammed the *Toucan's* prow aground near Bojuru. I know the place. It's just across the Lagoa from our Port of São Lourenço do Sul, both are in Rebel territory. From there he sent word that whatever we could salvage from her—planks, rigging, and cargo—was at our disposal. So I sailed across with our largest vessel and met with Hamlin on the beach where the *Toucan* lay a tilt, starboard side up, her keel showing.

When we met, Captain Hamlin brought me up to date on what happened after I jumped ship. The Imperials boarded the *Toucan* and arrested Warren Hathaway, who had taken my berth as mate. I am sorry for Hathaway, but he's a hardy soul, and they freed him as soon as they saw they'd taken the wrong man. I feel sorrier for The American Consul Hayes. The Imperials will be sure to blame him, so he will have to tip-toe through a diplomatic mess, now especially.

Putting the *Toucan* so close in to the shore was convenient for us. We had no trouble collecting nearly all of her cargo. Afterward we transported Captain Hamlin and the crew down near Pelotas and let them escape in one of the *Toucan's* boats across to Rio Grande.

Of the *Toucan's* cargo, the food stores were still usable. I managed to float off most of the hatches, the sky-lights, tackle and fittings onto jury-rig barges, even the windlass and a good stock of planking. Most of the ship's spare rigging, ropes, and sails, along with such bos'n tools as fids, marlinspikes, belaying pins, and mallets. Tar buckets, too. Nothing wasted. They will serve our vessels well, for I was shy of well-wrought fittings for both standing and running rigging. We turned the cargo of silks and sundry fancy items over to the Gonçalves ladies. (Later on, I noticed that some pieces showed up in Ruthie's wardrobe. Maybe the ladies reckoned it was a proper use for them, seeing as I was the one who brought them from the *Toucan*. Much appreciated, especially seeing how handsomely those strips of fine cloth draped along Ruthie's flanks.

So all in all, the old *Toucan* has served this revolution well in utility and beauty. Ruthie, for her part, was prouder than any bird-of-paradise I ever saw, and at least twice more huggable. I ought to allow that the male carries the fancier show of plumage. Well, for my purposes, we'll let that pass.)

CHAPTER 9

Garibaldi's Failed Escape
and Sudden Release

Editor: Captain Hamlin's was a daring move, especially because his motives doubtless were transparent to the Imperials. Just about one month after Hamlin granted his former mate, Griggs, the benefit of the *Toucan's* grounding, Rossetti announced his equally bold intention to help Garibaldi escape. His compatriots in Montevideo, however, convinced him to leave Garibaldi's rescue to those more suited to the task. So he shifted his energies to become the revolution's chief propagandist by writing, printing, and disseminating his new journal, *O 'Povo*.

Rossetti, Montevideo, September 1837: I arranged for the *Mazzini's* crew and other Young Italians who wished to join us to ride overland to Rio Grande. Our most burdensome cargo was the printing machinery, which I packed on mules with as much paper and ink as I could purchase. By the end of the long journey, more arduous than my first, we were welcomed by the citizens of Piratini. And after they helped me put our printing press in working order, the mariners who accompanied me—Carniglia, Lodoba, Lamberti, Mutru, and Maurizio Garibaldi— went down to the Lagoa dos Patos to help the American Griggs with the boats. That was a suitable occupation for them and Griggs, too, for they would be dependable co-workers.

Editor: Griggs, who knew about Rossetti's return, welcomed the experienced Italian sailors, but he was disappointed with the small number. On meeting Maurizio Garibaldi, he was also disappointed to learn that the Garibaldi, about whom he had heard so much, was not among the new comrades. But he accepted them all with his usual equanimity.

Griggs: I wondered why so few came up from Uruguay, but Carniglia explained that other Italian crew members decided against leaving Montevideo. At least these few Italians who came are an orderly looking lot and welcome. After a day of trying to take the measure of Garibaldi, I learned that this one was not Captain Garibaldi but a deck seaman. The questions I put to those who had escaped yielded more complete information about the Italian refugees' ventures in Uruguayan waters. Their captain, his ship taken from him, was still held captive up the Rio Paraná and into the Gualeguay. Carniglia was the last of the Italians to see him. He told me that the whole crew sailed up river and put in at Gualeguay, where they were taken into custody by Rosas' people. Then all of them except Garibaldi were released to return to Montevideo. By his own request, only Carniglia was allowed to stay behind to help take care of his captain, who was badly wounded during the fighting off Maldonado.

Editor: Garibaldi was well recovered when Carniglia finally left him, which was about one month after they had arrived in Gualeguay. He came away with assurances that Garibaldi would continue to be treated respectfully. The Argentinians announced that they would hold him for ransom or some sort of political trade-off.

In his conversation with Griggs, Rossetti gave more details about the troubles in the Rio de la Plata. He told of how Garibaldi had put him ashore at Maldonado and sent him to Montevideo to collect supplies and horses for the journey to Rio Grande. During the two weeks it took to complete those tasks, Garibaldi and his crew enjoyed their leisure in Maldonado, but they had to scramble back aboard the Mazzini when they learned that the Uruguayans and Brazilians had plotted to arrest all of them. They left word behind for Rossetti to meet them back at Point Jesus Maria, where they had first dropped him off.

Meanwhile, back north in Rio Grande do Sul, in mid-October, '37, good news arrived that General Gonçalves had escaped—this time for real—from his prison in Bahia. By the end of the month, he was back in Piratini, arriving shortly after Rossetti and his fellow Italians came up from Montevideo. The General was in good spirits and called a meeting of all officers and advisors. He asked his fellow donarios to furnish an orderly list of their men and equipment. He also wanted to begin military drills for some of the new cavalry, which included the freed-slave volunteers. He promised that large armies would clash in the next campaign. At the same time, he ordered Griggs to make haste to have his vessels ready to transport men and equipment from point to point along the shore of the Lagoa dos Patos. With spring weather setting in, Griggs's men would be in a good season to complete their work.

Shortly afterward, Rossetti, although he had been dissuaded earlier, returned once more to Montevideo to see how he might help Garibaldi escape from Gualeguay.

Rossetti: October '37: I heard from Giuseppe. Although he was still a prisoner, the officers of Oribé's government treated him with full courtesy. Apparently they understand that he is a valuable hostage, someone for whom they might arrange favorable negotiations with our side in the Revolution. Why else they kept him captive I could not guess.

From Garibaldi's Memoirs: My wound being healed, I was allowed to take rides on horseback, even to a distance of twelve miles, and was supplied with a dollar a day for my subsistence, which was a large sum for that country, where there is but little opportunity to spend money. (23)

Rossetti: So Giuseppe has freedom to roam the countryside within a limited range. He writes that he has a horse at his disposal and rides more every day as his health improves. Even acknowledging his harsh situation, I must admit that I am amused to picture Giuseppe on a horse. As awkward as I was as a sailor, he must be equally inept in a saddle without the benefit of the schooling I had enjoyed. I am sure, for example, that Giuseppe has never heard of, let alone read, Federico Gorsone's historic manual *Giardini di Cavalcare*, which all academic students are required to read. Well, I put that aside. I am sure that he will benefit from his experience and in time become a decent horseman, and possibly a better man for it. The sound of horses' hooves, as well as the odor of the noble beasts will make the universe more pleasant for him. I am sure Colonel Gonçalves, a fine horseman who was schooled in the ring from childhood, feels that way. Even John Griggs sits easy in his saddle, although he admitted to me that the long ride across the rough country to Piratini left him with aching legs and back. He was not trained to sitting in academy saddles but he tells me that he spent his boyhood on a farm, where he rode all sorts of mounts, including, without saddles, broad-backed truck horses.

Most fascinating to me is the picture of Giuseppe pressing his hind parts into a deep Spanish saddle, while he holds his reins in one hand, as these Gauchos do. I have watched his forearm muscles ripple when he holds a tiller or a carbine or saber aloft, so supple and yet so powerful. He should have no problem managing a horse, even an unruly one, for sheer power and will, aided by the sensitive balance in his sturdy thighs.

I can hardly wait to return to Montevideo to discuss plans for his escape with Cuneo and the others. I cannot tell whether his letters carry a secret intention, although, restless as he is, he feels honor bound to remain a prisoner.

But I have learned just in time of Rosas' plan to turn Giuseppe over to the Imperialists in Brazil. I sent a message to our sympathizers to urge Giuseppe to make a run for freedom. Certainly if he could slip away from his captors and reach some Coloradans, they would not refuse to help him. Through friends in Gualeguay he could procure a guide. From there he could make a run for the Eastern Frontier on the New Year. I had hopes that my dearest comrade would follow our suggestion and be back among us soon.

From Garibaldi's Memoirs: Having after a time formed my plan, I began to make preparations. One evening, while the weather was tempestuous, I left home and went in the direction of a good old man, whom I was accustomed to visit at his residence, three miles from Gualeguay. On arriving, I got him to describe with precision the way which I intended to take and engaged him to find me a guide, with horses, to conduct me to Hueng, where I hoped to find vessels in which I might go incognito, to Buenos Ayres and Montevideo (24).

Editor: As we learn later, in Rossetti's entry for January 1838, this plan went awry and resulted in terrible consequences for Garibaldi. During the period between Garibaldi's ill-fated attempt to escape and his actual release by Oribe, Griggs, although ignorant of the Italians' strategy, went about his business of fitting out the rebels' little navy for active duty.

CHAPTER 10

Griggs's Navy Is Ready/His Thoughts about Ruthie/Garibaldi Joins the Rebels

Griggs: On November 1, 1837, Gonçalves rode north to the vicinity of Porto Alegre to confer with Lima, Netto, and Manoel. He ordered me to test some of our vessels on the Lagoa. I have sloop-rigged our two larger smacks and already taken them for excursions along the shoreline southward from the Camaquã. With some few adjustments in the rigging, they handled well and will be able to run the shallows better than our schooners. I have trained our crews to jump over the side in the shallows and push the launches over the sandbars and into the cover of the undergrowth out of sight of Imperial patrol vessels. It is a trustworthy maneuver, although when these vessels carry heavier cargoes, we will have to stand farther offshore and depend on darting quickly up the rivers or into the cover of the deeper shoreline to shake off the Imperial patrollers. I trust these vessels to sail anywhere on the Lagoa, even in heavy weather when the swells run high and the troughs are short and choppy.

December 1837: Summer has set in with fair and dependable weather. Our work on the larger vessels goes well. I have rigged one of them with fore-and-aft gaff sails for better cruising. I've left the other with a Marconi for swifter maneuvers so it can come about even, in contrary winds. The ships' stores taken from the *Toucan* helped greatly with fitting out our vessels. I have worked gun-ports into the bulwarks, a tricky business. But with the helpers I have trained so far and the more experienced seamen who have joined us, I am encouraged enough to see ahead to some snug battens. After all, I am simply following the good example set by the first U.S. Navy, when merchant ships were purposely built for easy refitting as warships. (25)

Editor: At the end of December 1837, General Gonçalves received word that the Imperials were preparing a full offensive to break the revolution, bringing together troops from other provinces for transportation south. All the while, offers of clemency continued, urging Gonçalves to accept a peaceful settlement of his grievances.

By mid-January, 1838, sad news arrived about Garibaldi. He had tried to escape but was recaptured not far from Gualeguay. Argentinian soldiers awaited him at his first resting place, and his comrades despaired because they knew that Garibaldi had gone back on his word not to attempt escape. His captors would be merciless.

As expected, they treated him brutally. Their local leader, a Colonel Millan, ordered Garibaldi put to the strapado. They tied his wrists behind his back and hoisted him to a bar high overhead so his toes barely touched the ground. The weight put a terrible strain on his neck and displaced shoulders. Breathing was a torment, and to increase the punishment they lashed him with canes.

Then in April, 1838 his comrades suddenly received news that Garibaldi had been released. No reason was given on either side but all his friends gasped their joy.

From Garibaldi's Memoirs: I was then informed, by Governor Echague, that I should be allowed to leave the province. . . . Good fortune and misfortune thus often succeeded each other. (26)

Rossetti: In Montevideo, we waited impatiently to see Giuseppe after we heard of the happy turn of events. Each day of waiting was like an eternity. But when we saw him, we could only shed more tears. Some for happiness at his release, some for the sadness of his condition, but most from guilt, for we had encouraged him to try to escape. He seemed years older, weak and thin, dark hollows beneath his eyes, his mouth drawn down from the constant pain in his shoulders. Will he ever use his arms freely again? Will I ever see the muscles in his magnificent forearms ripple, I asked myself? But a man of his indomitable will is also resilient in body. We will help him heal. Our happiness was restrained only because the local Blancos in Montevideo might still try to harm him. So when he arrived, we moved him around among our friends. We could not let him stay with Cuneo. Too many people knew about their friendship and might direct the police to arrest him anew. Instead we took him first to the house of Angelo Pesante, who coincidentally had been Giuseppe's ship captain many years earlier.

Editor: Meanwhile, in Rio Grande do Sul, Gonçalves' preparations to meet and resist the Imperial campaign continued with nothing to interrupt them. Near the end of February, confirmation came that, in the face of Gonçalves' stubborn refusal to capitulate, the Imperials would soon start a large-scale campaign from the North. In response, Gonçalves ordered weapons placed at the ready and supplies distributed among the far-flung fortifications.

Griggs's two schooners were already in service, transporting several cargoes of ammunition and weapons to secured depots at points along the western shore of the Lagoa, from Pelotas, São Lourenço, Camaquã, and as far north as Tapes. They did not dare sail farther north than that for fear of encountering the heavier armed Imperials.

In a short time a large army of Imperial regulars from Rio de Janeiro reached Porto Alegre, where they organized local militias. Clearly, the main action was to take place at the north end of the Lagoa dos Patos.

In mid-April, after more than a month, word came that a large force of Imperial cavalry was riding south from Porto Alegre, and that several imperial ships had transported infantry via the Atlantic sea-lanes south from Rio de Janeiro. With news of the latter development, Griggs stepped up his preparations, among them sending his personal companion, Ruthie, back to a safer locale. We can note with special interest, evidence of his changing regard for the young woman, quite surprising even to himself.

Griggs: With fighting soon to commence, I have sent Ruthie back up river to Donna Antonia's estancia--a sad parting. I have developed strong feeling for this girl, more than I can account for by any casual satisfaction. It's a new sort of attachment for me, especially—I put it frankly—with her being of mixed breed, a mestisa, most likely, not the sort who would settle in among Backstaters at home. But I must admit to thoughts in that line creeping in. For now I'll have to release her sweet presence to a safer spot, for the long and short of it is, now especially, I must part all ties with the shore.

I couldn't let her go off without some show of my feelings, so I braided a wrist band for her out of fine linen whipping cord and gave her my best linen shirt to fashion a garment for herself. You'd a-thought I gave her an engagement token and something for her trousseau. She shed tears a-plenty at that but left me without too great a splatter and splurge. She's a fine and handsome girl. I did nothing to earn her devotion. If the true measure of worth be taken, she holds the balance of credit: Lonely nights ahead.

I have to turn my attention back to making things ready for the ruckus that soon may come, Distracting work, especially because my vessels can do little in the way of fighting for now. After using them to supply our battle stations up and down the shoreline, Gonçalves has ordered me to place them in safe hiding. We have run them up the Camaquã nearer to our work-sheds. I un-stepped their masts and hid them as best I could in the brush that overhangs the river. I cannot see that much real fighting will take place near here, but I have posted sentries and we are ready to serve as militia ashore if the enemy comes this far. Every one is jumpy but I expect that most of our men will stand fast. I am pleased to see how alert and committed they have become with the prospect of fighting close ahead. I've taken time to drill them over and over. Can do nothing more for now.

Editor: Within two weeks, that is about April 30, 1838, battles commenced on a large scale near Porto Alegre. Leaving those engagements to his capable confederate General Netto, Gonçalves proceeded from Piratini to engage the enemy forces advancing around Pelotas to the South. All stations were on the alert and the rebel forces defended their posts stubbornly.

Far to the South, in the beginning of May 1838, Garibaldi decided he was strong enough to leave for Rio Grande. So, with a small troop of adventurers, he began his journey north to Rio Grande do Sul. The trip, it seems, hastened Garibaldi's recovery. By then, and much to Rossetti's admiration, he had become a competent horseman, the one benefit of his captivity. The journey to Piratini, long days in the saddle, his quickly returning energy; the beautiful autumn weather, all helped Garibaldi become stronger in body. His spirit had recovered already.

Indeed, his many sufferings at the hands of Rosas' cohorts had done nothing to diminish his will. Neither man was aware of the outbreak of hostilities, but soon after they reached Gonçalves' family, they learned of the widespread fighting between the revolutionaries and Imperial forces, and they hastened to join in the fray.

Rossetti: Safe in the company of those he knew to be his Friends and Equals, and most of all in the Fresh Air of Freedom, our valued compatriot regained his spirit of usefulness to our Just Cause.

We had now joined our compatriots in a land where the cause of Human Dignity was foremost, an alliance refreshing to us all. On our journey northward, we saw the evidence of that comraderie in a most joyous way when we stopped again at the estancia of Doña Anna in Arroyo Grande. Her entire family and their servants treated us with the utmost grace. To tell the truth, I was somewhat embarrassed by Giuseppe's elaborate obeisance towards them. It reminded me of his first meeting with Seniora Dalecazi in Rio de Janeiro. But Giuseppe cast such an air of self-confidence that they were quickly won over. Perhaps it was the positive reputation others and I had cast before them prior to his actual appearance that disposed them to a favorable response. Anyway, in the face of his self-confidence and his natural, gracious presentation, who could resist? He is the very model of a Natual Aristocrat, even though possibly an amply stated one.

As if by magic, Giuseppe became fully rejuvenated. I think it was these beautiful people, so refined in dress and manner, whose attention cured him. His response was like one born to that life, instead of the life and manners of a sailor's family. And why was he not? The generations of hard and honest work by his father and grandfather in Nice and Genoa and their fathers before them preserved and strengthened the Noble History of our Homeland, once the most powerful civilization in the world and destined, God willing, to become so again.

Some may be interested to consider that, in our families Giuseppe and I were both the youngest sons. As such, our parents' expectations for us were a career in the Church. Think what might have happened if our parents had succeeded in their encouragements. We would not have been here among these gracious people to be acknowledged by them as allies in the Worthy Labors for the Liberty and Equality of All Mankind. Destiny! May it bring victory to the righteous among us all!

But as much as we felt at home among our sympathetic hosts in Arroio Grande—the good wine and food and the constant attention of our hosts and their servants—we had not traveled all that way to settle softly into a tranquil life. So we left our friends, the family of Doña Anna, with warm gratitude and promises to return when duty allowed. A great temptation, whenever we had time to think about it.

From Garibaldi's Memoirs: Being unoccupied in Pirati[ni], I requested permission to join the column of operations under S. Gonzalez, near the President, and it was granted. I was introduced to Bento Gonzalez, and well received; spent some time in his company, and thought him a man highly favored by nature with some desirable gifts. But fortune has been almost always favorable to the Brazilian Empire (27).

Editor: On May 7, 1838, the comrades arrived in the Capital City of Piratini, Garibaldi met Almeida and his staff and, after a necessarily hurried welcome, made it known that he was eager to meet the General and enter active duty. So after a brief pause for rest, he joined Gonçalves at Pelotas. Gonçalves met very briefly with Garibaldi before he returned his attention to forcing the Imperials' withdrawal from the battle zone. Then, on May 10, 1838, the good news came that the battles were over, both north and south. Gonçalves and his confederates pushed the Imperials into swift retreat from Pelotas--hundreds of the enemy killed on the way. At about the same time, General Netto sent the northern Imperials running back into Porto Alegre. That done, General Gonçalves was free to give Garibaldi a warm welcome.

Soon thereafter, he moved his capital from Piratini to Caçapava, which is situated in the high country about 100 kilometers north. Now, the territory of the Republic was even more secure. Only Porto Alegre and the ports at the mouth of the Lagoa dos Patos remained in Imperial hands. The latter were more essential to the progress and wellbeing of the revolution and therefore became the object of a subsequent campaign, which had some nasty incidents, to the discredit of the rebels and which Rossetti neglected to note.

CHAPTER 11

Rossetti Initiates *O 'Povo*/His Thoughts about Griggs/Griggs's Thoughts about Garibaldi

Rossetti: Once settled in Caçapava, I busied myself with my printing operation. Although transported with great difficulty, the small press was a simple mechanism with paper and ink of adequate quality. So I chose two Freed Slaves, Neiton and Paolo, as my apprentices, and in an amazingly short time they learned to operate and maintain the equipment like experts, much to my gratification. I compared my progress to Griggs's in his work on the navy boats. Griggs' band of sailor-warriors was soon expert at refurbishing their ships for efficient service on the Lagoa dos Patos. He seemed fully satisfied with his new assistants but was unwilling to say more about them. That may be because the sort of work he trained his Freedmen for is simpler manual tasks than running the sophisticated machinery and stages of preparation for my printing press. Also, I think he may not be inclined to praise ex-slaves because of the enormous numbers of Blacks still used by his countrymen, a prejudice which, I am happy to observe, my own countrymen reject.

For some time I have seen such traits in Americans, their assumptions that African Blacks lack the ability to learn more than rudimentary skills. I do not force Griggs into such discussions. Also, he himself is exercised in the simple life of a sailor—much like Giuseppe, I think—and less inclined to such topics as politics and philosophy. For the moment, we should concentrate on working together to bring about Freedom for all citizens in Rio Grande do Sul.

Let me put down this thought in the interest of justice. Griggs seems by nature a taciturn man, so he may hesitate to express his feelings or beliefs about slaves or blacks in general. Or he may be conditioned to keep his feelings to himself. Abolitionists are not treated with respect in his young country. He does not hesitate to use the blacks as his crew where they show talent and energy, obviously despite what the whites say.

Also there is the young woman he keeps nearby when, in the consideration of her safety, he can do so. She is a peasant house servant, obviously a mestiso. Griggs is her protector for all that he uses her for his own purposes. I have heard that he has warned others away from her, but that may be as much from jealousy as respect—just some ideas to think about, as I say, in fairness to him as to all men. Hold them in good faith, in trust, unless they prove themselves unworthy.

Editor: Rossetti's analysis is as revealing about himself as about Griggs, who welcomed Giuseppe and the other Young Italians to his ship-fitting operation in Camaquá. He quickly took a systematically detailed measure of the man. Like the seasoned ship's officer that he was, Griggs omitted nothing from his evaluation, as we see in his strikingly balanced portrait of Garibaldi. Consider the similarities between his own and Rossetti's.

Griggs: The real Captain Garibaldi has arrived. He seems to have rebounded from the torture he suffered at the hands of the Argentinians. He is the sort you take to right off: Stout-chested, light-haired and clear, wide-set eyes beneath a broad brow. I have become accustomed to cockiness among my Italian comrades, but I could see right off that this man has as full a measure as you could find in anyone. He has a mite of roughness about him--every hair a rope-yarn, as you might say, yet he carries himself with more than a shading of dignity—the stamp of a leader, as I observe. There's no denying the appearance, for I've seen the like among fellows who're just as forth-putting as he is. We'll see if it bears out.

May 17, 1838: Garibaldi has had a look at my work on the vessels and has allowed that I know what I am about. We see eye to eye on that, I'd say. He rides frequently between here and Piratini, but when he is here, he makes himself good company. A man to show interest in everything around him, even though he listens fitfully and is ready most of all to talk about his own ventures in the service of a just cause, as he puts it. I must admit that, by my soundings, he went through some harsh weather all the way. He is lucky to be here in one piece. Most would have crumbled under the strain. That much can be said for him, surely.

As for his ship handling, I know well enough how unforeseen winds and currents can put a ship on a course for disaster, but there's also skill of foresight learned by hard experience that can help one head off the worst of problems. Caution and precaution both have brought many a ship's crew through contrary conditions.

But as for Garibaldi's judgment, I began to hear some evidence to the contrary. I'd best get down to that. Putting it in my personal log is not the same as tattling to others, as I see it. Anyway, I'll not make accusations without giving my reasons.

For one, there's his caper with the *Luisa's* boat. He captured the merchantman along his course down from Rio de Janeiro. As Rossetti tells me, the hard-bitten among his crew wanted to cast the captives ashore, or worse, and keep their goods for themselves. Garibaldi held them off until he'd sailed further down the coast, where he found a safe stretch for landing and put the cranky members of the *Luisa's* crew and their passengers ashore along with some of their personals and enough provisions to see them safely through two or three days. That was a decent act. So far so good. But Garibaldi let the cast-offs keep the only boat on board the *Luiza*. A poor decision, worse than poor, as it turns out, for there he was sailing in strange waters without a longboat on board for his own emergency use.

A landlubber might think I'm fussing about nothing. But any sailor worth his salt would see that that is exactly what brought him to trouble after he sailed into the Platte Estuary, where soon enough he got word that ships of the Imperial Brazilian Navy were coming for him.

So he had to weigh anchor and sail the *Mazzini* out of Maldonado before he resupplied her. It wasn't that he did not have time to do so earlier. He and his crew had spent precious days carousing in port, which should have come second to replenishing his stores and—here's where it all comes a cropper—to getting another boat on board. He soon found himself cruising off an unfamiliar coast with short supplies and no emergency boat handy.

From Garibaldi's Memoirs: Rossetti set off for Montevideo, to arrange things connected with the expedition. . . ; and during eight days we enjoyed one uninterrupted festival among the hospitable inhabitants (28).

Griggs: Sure enough his crew soon ran out of food altogether, so he anchored at night off an uninhabited stretch of beach up river from Maldonado, and despite a strong blow, took a cabin table and lowered it overboard as a jerry-rig raft for him and one of his sailors to hand-paddle through the surf. That sounds like a resourceful answer to a tight situation. OK as far as it goes, but the whole caper came about as a result of him leaving the ship's boat with the cast-off crew of the *Luisa* back up the Atlantic coast, and thereby putting himself and his own crew in peril. In the middle of it all, he and his shipmate had to keep re-righting that makeshift raft each time it flipped over. When he finally made the beach, he found his way inland, where a herder who happened to be nearby gave him a whole bullock carcass. A piece of good luck, that. Well, he and his man got the beef on the table and somehow paddled it back out to his ship, during which they almost lost the beef a number of times and barely saved themselves.

Cheers for them making it back to their ship all right, but it was a damned fool risk that never should have been taken. And that's my point about it.

Here's another thing. Some might say that going after food was a worthwhile risk under the circumstances, but I can't see why a ship's captain took it on himself to paddle ashore to forage for food. Why didn't he set some dependable crew members to the task? Suppose his ship was forced to sail off while he, its captain, was riding the surf and foraging ashore?

Here's yet another part of it. Suppose him and his crew had to go a day more or less without food. Plenty of crews have done that, as long as they had water in their casks. Water can be more precious than food. You can go without food for days until you have a clear chance to gather it.

His next caper gives me even worse shakes by a long shot. It's about his ship's compass. It may sound like nitpicking to a land-locked reader, but it is one of the most serious gaffes I ever heard of.

Right after he hoisted the beef on board, Garibaldi learned that the Imperials were closing on him. So he had to hoist all sails and run up to Point Jesus Maria, where he was to pick up Rossetti. Well, before he started on that disastrous passage, Garibaldi never took note of the muskets someone stacked against his compass binnacle. He had to hasten, as I admit, but that's always a circumstance that calls for extreme care. Sure enough he almost ran aground as a consequence. I know right where he was, the Point at Piedras Negras, an easy passage if you maintain a check on your soundings and if your compass is true.

From Garibaldi's Memoirs: I hoisted sail without delay, and steered up the river [sic] Plata, with scarcely any plan or object, and almost without opportunity to communicate to any one that I should await, at the Point of Jesus Maria, news of the result of Rossetti's deliberations with this friends in Montevideo. After a wearisome navigation, I reached that place, having narrowly escaped shipwreck on the Point of Piedras Negras, in consequence of a variation of the compass caused by the muskets placed near it (29).

Griggs: As any real sailor knows, the main compass is more sacred than a prophet's word, especially in strange waters. A proper shipmaster, as well as his mates and helmsmen, constantly checks its condition to make sure no tackle or whatnot is stored within drawing distance to that precious needle card and those magnetic bars. So when Garibaldi thought he was sailing west, he was fetching northwest-by-north straight for the shore. He is lucky that the night was clear enough for him to make out the beach because the land along that stretch has very little rise. Not till his ship almost ran aground did he notice the clutter around the binnacle.

That sort of piloting is clean off the books, downright plow horse navigating. There isn't a junior mate out of Boston or Connecticut either who would allow such a thing to happen.

As the saying goes, good fortune smiles on bravery and bad fortune smirks on fool hardiness. I don't know where that leaves Garibaldi, but that time, luck and boldness were good companions.

Here! I begin to sound like a salt-cured Poor Richard. All right, enough of that, but one last thing. I've known a good many brave men that has gone to the bottom before their time for such muck ups.

I calculate that Garibaldi is more damnable lucky than uncommonly brave, maybe both, but I've made up my mind against sailing on board a ship with him as master, nor mate neither, even though a couple of days ago Gonçlaves named him commander of our fleet.

To the Colonel the commission is properly done, and I have no argument with him. Garibaldi has battle experience. I have none. Besides, Gonçalves has decreed that only Roman Catholics can serve as Top-rank Officers in his Government. His new Constitution calls for it, so I do not begrudge Garibaldi the honor, even though he cannot have told Gonçalves his hatred of priests and the Catholic Church in total. It's their business to work out.

I will make all our vessels fit and keep them seaworthy, but I will be responsible for sailing my own. I'm looking to transactions beyond this Revolution, and I'll not scuttle them for any two-button admiral who's given to sailing too close to the wind.

It is fine with me that he spends most of his time up in the capital conferring with Gonçalves or over at the homes of Gonçalves' sisters, where he is treated handsomely. I can see that he has his eye peeled for the ladies' favor. Last time I visited with Doña Ana, I heard Garibaldi sing songs from his homeland. He has become the favorite among the donatorios' families.

One day he asked me to accompany him along the Lagoa's shoreline on a drill in one of the smacks. He decided to combine it with an excursion for a few of the Gonçalves ladies, his real purpose, as I might guess. We took a small crew along and sailed down to Donna Ana's estancia. Along the way, we showed them our technique for skipping our vessels into the shallows to avoid Imperial patrol boats. We jumped over the side and pushed the smacks over the sand bars, with the ladies staying on board, of course. It was a likely practice for when we commenced our raids on shipping in the Lagoa, as we explained to our female guests, who, I must say, remained sober observers throughout.

CHAPTER 12

The Rebel Navy in Action/Ruthie with Griggs for a Short Stay

Editor: At the same time that Griggs occasionally accommodated Garibaldi's skylarking with the Gonçalves family, he kept his attention on the condition of the vessels for duty on the Lagoa. By the third week of May, '38 the two larger vessels were secure. Griggs had long-spliced enough lengths of rope for spare rigging to supplement what he had taken from the *Toucan*. Gonçalves had also sent some lengths of new rope down from the supply yards he'd captured near Porto Alegre. Griggs and Garibaldi had sixty hands between them, mostly foreign adventurers and a few freed slaves. Everybody was eager enough to start out, although the still largely inexperienced crews needed more drilling. Soon enough they would all test the results of their hard work.

Griggs: The ships are seaworthy at last. Garibaldi and I agree to that. Mine is named *Republicano*, about 25 tons displacement, a broad beam and a deep hold. She has a low deckhouse aft that I tidied up for storage space. I worked two gun-ports into the bulwarks, port and starb'd, not that we've cannons to fit them yet, but for bluff. I rigged smooth lengths of tree trunks to poke out as bogus six pounders. We can always use the ports as firing holes for small arms. Garibaldi's *Farroupilha* is somewhat longer and has a little broader beam in proportion, but she has a decent rake to her bow for so short a hull. We have ample room in both vessels for men and arms and for prize cargoes, too, should we take any. Since I extended the jib booms on both vessels, we bent extra canvas to catch whatever breeze ruffles the Lagoa. Now the ships will respond spiritedly enough to good handling on any waters.

I keep Procopio at my side so he can learn as much about ship-fitting and sailing as I can teach him under the limited circumstances of time and materials that we face here. He learns rapidly as always and applies his new knowledge proficiently. He'll be my first mate, has earned it for the application of his quick talents. I'll place him in charge of his own vessel when the decision is mine to make, no questions asked, especially because the others have come to respect him—that means fear him. But for now I'll want him for my own mate.

Near the end of the work day, Garibaldi came down to the galpoa, and I took him on board the Republicanoto show him how I stowed my gear. That was my only way of warning him against a repeat of his folly with the compass binnacle. I brewed maté, which I have come to favor over tea, and we chatted. That was the first time he talked about his life in Nice and Genoa, where his father sailed a ship in the trade along the Mediterranean coast.

He pressed me for the reason I joined this Freedom Campaign, as he calls it, so I told him about how I dodged the Imperial Police because I was carrying contraband to the Rebels. That set him off about Americans and our cause of liberty and justice, a bit overblown for my taste, but I could see that he heard me the way he wanted to, all about selfless nobility of mankind--too much flapdoodle. Why tell him that smuggling contraband was part of our bigger plan for setting up trade with the New Republic.

From Garibaldi's Memoirs: With courage, cheerfulness, and perseverance, no enterprise is impossible; and, for these I must do justice to my favorite companion and usual forerunner, John Griggs, who surmounted numerous difficulties, and patiently endured many disappointments, in the work of building two new launches.

He was a young man of excellent disposition, unquestionable courage, and inexhaustible perseverance. Though he belonged to a rich family, he had devoted himself disinterestedly to the young Republic; and, when letters from his friends in North America invited him to return home, and offered him a very large capital, he refused, and remained until he sacrificed his life for an unhappy, but brave and generous people. (30)

Editor: I could find nothing to support Garibaldi's knowledge about Griggs's family or the letter to which he refers. (See Appendix 2.)

Griggs: I did not need to prime him to learn about his aims. Just listened to him talk about how he threw over his boyhood studies with a young priest. His parents, obviously papists, wanted him to prepare for holy orders, it seems, but his tutor saw it otherwise and set him to reading a lot of poetry, Lord Byron and other such glorious stuff about the rejoining of all parts of Italy into one Great Republic. That is a bit of history that I know somewhat more than faintly, but it has become Garibaldi's main purpose. He joined the French Navy with a wild plan to bring about a mutiny, which French spies uncovered ahead of time. He has been suckled on risks, which sound to me somewhat short on forethought. Now he has a price on his head for it all.

Looks to me like him and these other Young Italians in Brazil are part of the same purpose. They can't fight in Italy right now, so they have adopted this Revolution in Rio Grande do Sul as training for when they get back. That's mainly how it seems to me, although they protest that they're ready to fight for justice anywhere. I won't argue the point.

I asked Garibaldi about Rossetti, who seems a different sort, more refined, not really a battler. It is true that Rossetti has little experience on board ships, unlike Garibaldi who has sailed his own ship in and out of scrapes. He assured me that I am right about that, but he insisted that Rossetti's spirit for freedom is as strong as anyone's.

Near end of May 38, I made up my mind to bring Ruthie back up here. My quarters are not as tidy or half as welcoming since she left. It's all fond memories of her but especially on lonely nights. Not easy to cast them off when I dream about her lying alongside me of nights--the way she lays her leg across my thigh. Just the recollection is enough to set off the shudders. But before I could send for her, I learned that we were about to begin action as raiders on the Lagoon, so I cooled off. I won't put her in the danger of coming on board our ships, and I sure as hell won't leave her alone with the reprobates ashore while I'm off cruising the sea lanes.

It may be no more nor wild speculation, but I have been cogitating about what life would be like for her if I took her back to Boston--just a wild notion. Nothing more, but since it is luffing around inside my head, I'll write it down here--some of it. There are Portuguese communities among the fishing ports back home. Maybe she and I could settle in one of them: Provincetown, maybe, or Gloucester or New Bedford, whose forebears has been there since before the formation of the Republic. That would give her some folks to talk to. I might even give up this merchant service and buy a trawler, cast nets off the banks. That's a faint notion but worth cogitating on. I reckon she'd soon be steady enough speaking English and taking up Yankee ways. But there's the danger she might wither once she was away from Brazil and her own kind. These are the tropics after all. Except in the high country, the weather here in the South of Brazil is different in its seasons from New England by many degrees of latitude and temperature both.

Editor: That sort of speculation seemed to fade in June, Winter of '38, when Garibaldi and Griggs began raids on the Lagoa. They captured several merchant ships, both north and southbound. Griggs was now busy with watching his own ship and fretting over the others.

Griggs: Aug-Sept 38: On the second day, we hadn't sailed more nor three and a half hours into the Lagoon when, just off the point at São Lourenço do Sul, which lies about 25 miles south of the Camaquá, we captured our first prize. She was a Brazilian cargo sloop that was transferring food and sundries to the besieged garrisons in Porto Alegre. It was still dark when we used the brisk wind to come up on her starboard side, so when the sun singed the horizon over the outer shore, she could not make us out through the glare, let alone she had no reason to expect us. Garibaldi came at her a-beam while I cut ahead and stood off her bow. We were flying our own colors, which surprised the captain. He lowered his sails without a fuss and waited for us to come aboard.

Garibaldi transferred most of her cargo into his *Farroupilha*; then he let the merchantman continue on its way. When we talked about it afterward, I reasoned that we ought to bring the prize vessels close ashore near our base instead of transferring cargo right out in a regular shipping lane. He argued that that would give them the position of one of our escape routes. He is right.

Almeida, now our Minister of Finance, sent a legal counsel down from headquarters near Porto Alegre, and he set up a proper office right there on the beach for our taking the prize cargo in the name of the New Republic. Part of our booty went to our ships' crews. I took considerable pleasure in watching the freed slaves collect their shares. The first money any of them ever counted as their own.

During the next two weeks our tiny fleet saw a lot of lucrative action on the Lagoon. Besides the benefit of prize cargoes, our ships' crews were now fully seasoned to their routines. We took seven Brazilian merchantmen, avoiding ships flying other national colors. For a short time we had the run of the waterway. Soon enough, though, our success brought a reaction.

From Garibaldi's Memoirs: After the capture of the Sumaca, the imperial merchant vessels no longer set sail without a convoy, 'but were always accompanied by vessels of war; and it became a difficult thing to capture them. (31)

Griggs: The Imperials began sending gunboats on regular patrols. We had no trouble avoiding them at first, but on our last cruise, we had just enough time to veer into the shallows and draw our ships under forested points of land until the Imperials sailed out of sight. It was becoming a tight scrape.

Editor: By August, the Imperials had begun to take the Republican raiders seriously enough to put battle sloops on regular escort duty and more frequent patrols, so Garibaldi ordered his ships to stay under cover for several days. The Imperials did not dare to follow them in close to the shore, but they could overtake the rebels in open waters. In August, the tiny rebel navy's raids slowed to a complete halt. However, the Imperials' regular patrols in the shipping lanes were a mistake because then the rebels could tell exactly when and where to expect them. Soon afterward Garibaldi and Griggs resumed their raids.

Griggs: On September 7, 1838, I sailed one of our smacks out into the Lagoa to look over the shipping lanes. Our lay-off had relaxed the Imperials. Their patrols have settled into a regular pattern. The scouting paid off, for on September 15, we took our biggest prize so far, the brig *Minerva*. She tried to outrun us but hove to when we let fly shots across her bow. The crew abandoned her and took to their boats, while the captain and his mates opened her seacocks, but we got most of her cargo off before she went down. She was filled with sundries, all salable items, for which our own crews got shares. The rest of the sell-off went to the treasury. But soon afterward the Imperial Navy Patrols shut us down again.

It looks like for now it will be the end of our raids on the Lagoa for a long spell. We continue to transfer supplies and equipment along the shore to the Republic's new capital in Caçapava. Once ashore, most of the crew loses its discipline. I can always keep the Freedmen busy. They are used to turning to at the most demanding tasks, and the Italians keep to their duties as good sailors.

Most of the rest are a bunch of scurvy dogs. They don't look for work but make off into the brush for whatever good times they can find, whores mostly. I don't know where from. Let them go at it. A horny heard of goats. Most of them will catch the pox before long, those that don't have it already, damn their filthy ways. I'd as soon most of them never came back. I caught three of them with women on board one of the ships and caned their asses 'til they all jumped ashore. Won't see that lot hereabouts any more.

Few events arouse us during these summer months. My thoughts drift back to nights when Ruthie was with me and I took the notion more than once to send for her. Something holds me back. Could be that I smell trouble close ahead. Like as not it was something told me I oughtn't to give the girl any expectations about her place in my future, for all she hints at it.

I know more than a few bachelor mates on American ships as has brought brides back from various ports in these latitudes, even now and again from Pacific islands. But I've decided I wouldn't put Ruthie through the isolation and maybe even frequent chafing she'd suffer from most Blue-nosed New Englanders, men and women alike, even though our companionship would be the coziest and she'd keep the cleanest and tidiest cupboards in the Commonwealth. But I feared anew what she would face during the long months when I put out to sea and leave her ashore to fill our shelves with berry preserves. I have no doubt now that her wellbeing is most on my mind. That's a concern I never would have foreseen but which I own up to without a shrug of hesitation.

Maybe I should do her and myself the favor of seeing her properly married to a good young man hereabouts, some sort of artisan with a steady trade. But then there'd be our farewells. When I reason so, I'll be blown if that's not when I miss her most.

I've been wondering along another tack. Maybe if things turn out in favor of this revolution I could settle into a home here in Brazil, maybe set up as an American Agent for Commerce. But that would be the reverse of asking her to settle in Boston. Who'd gain the winning or stand the losing then? Thinking such thoughts leaves me in a muddle, and so the whole cycle of cogitation begins all over again. One thing I do know: if they knew my thoughts about Ruthie, the entire Gonçalves clan would have to shift my standing among their company. I can beat her or bed her without a sound or sign from them. But even a whisper about marrying a peasant girl, Indian blood or not, and they'd cast off all lines that tie us together. With such a squall as that on the horizon, a seaman must check wind current and space in all directions for the best way to outrun it.

Late September 1838: It's a good thing I have other worries closer at hand. One of them is the way our Admiral Garibaldi tends to play too loose with the Imperial patrol vessels. He seems as ready for a chance to fight as he is for securing a prize cargo. I have had to remind him that we don't really have the crews in large enough number or inclination, nor the firepower to stand against the Imperials. But he's like a mastiff on a long leash. Holding him close to common sense begins to tire me.

Mornings and early evenings in these slack months is a good time for refurbishing our larger ships, for their timbers and planks have loosened with the shake-down cruises we've put them through. I've hauled both onto dry land, careened them, and set the crews to re-caulking below the water line. I also sailed them out one at a time to box their compasses. We have ample time. Work done with care is work done to last.

There's some might wonder why, if that is true, I am forever fussing with those cranky vessels of ours. It is a proper question, which I will answer. If anyone had seen the condition in which I found those hulks, he would have wondered how they'd ever be made to float again, let alone respond to the constant and varied strain under which a vessel sails. Well, on almost every hull, at least one rib stood bare, some so rotted that you might press a fid clear through. So there was prodding to be done on every plank and timber from stem to stern, up one side and down the other.

As for manpower, at least I have thinned the malingerers from my crew and filled their billets with dependable fishermen and Freedmen. Garibaldi has done the same with his ships to supplement his fellow Italians. The former slaves take to ship maintenance well. The fishermen already know how. They make good seamen for any battle craft.

Garibaldi does not find fault with much, but neither does he examine details all that carefully. Indeed his praise goes everywhere after the lightest examination. He has told me a number of times already that I am the person he counts on the most. I have heard him say the same thing to Rossetti and Carniglia and others, truth be known. Not for my ship maintenance but other specialties. I believe he means it every time he says it, even though at first it twangs my ears to hear the way he broadcasts his praise. Not that I have much personal investment in the man, for all that we have in common as sailors. But his enthusiasm latches onto just about anything in sight. It is more pennant flapping than I am accustomed to.

Editor: Life went slowly well into February, 1839. Griggs got news of occasional skirmishes to the north, but most of the land troops faded away to their homes in other regions. Griggs's crews stayed dependable, and the constant refurbishing went well. They also began replenishing supplies at the galpoa and continued the work for which the sheds were originally made, such as smoking meat and drying yerba leaves for maté. Griggs tried to keep his mariners busy, his as well as Garibaldi's. He knew that too much carousing was bad for discipline, especially among those who were already inclined to slack ways. When he mentioned it to Garibaldi, the admiral brought the men to attention with a spirited talk.

As for Rossetti, on September the First, 1838, his most valuable activity bore fruit with the first issue of *O 'Povo*.

CHAPTER 13

The First Issue of *O 'Povo*/The "*Moringue's*" Attack on the Shipyard

Rossetti: The effect on our comrades was joyous! At the top of the first page I printed the opening lines from Mazzini's Manifesto for Young Italy. When I presented the first copy, everyone at head-quarters shouted Bravos!

Mazzini's sentiment, noble and true, serves the International Brotherhood of warriors against tyranny here in Brazil as it will one day in Italy. The Pen is now joined to the Sword in the Just Cause of Freedom! I am glad we have this new accomplishment, for almost at the same time, our military campaign has ended in victory, except for the enemy's occasional guerilla raids against us. Meanwhile, Giuseppe and his mariners have become successful in the Lagoa dos Patos. On his first excursion, for example, he captured a huge merchant ship filled with rice and fabrics. Now, however, with the seasons changing, several cavalry officers have taken their men back home to gather herds and drive them to their estancias. That means that Gonçlaves must wait and hope that they retain their commitment, let alone their discipline when they rejoin his army.

Editor: Although he continued to issue O' Povo from his press in Caçapava, Rossetti's personal journal would go dormant until the rebels extended their territory northward to include Santa Catarina, which was still far in the future. Long before that, on April 17, '39, trouble struck the naval compound. The rebels learned the high price of relaxing their alertness, when the Imperials' most daring marauder, *Moringue* (the Marten) attacked the shacks down river from Camaquá, where the mariners were billeted.

From Garibaldi's Memoirs: I was sitting by the fire, where breakfast was cooking, and was just then taking some maté. Near by was the cook, and no other person.

All on a sudden, and as if just over my head, I heard a tremendous volley of firearms, accompanied by a yell, and saw a company of the enemy's horsemen marching in. I had hardly time to rise and take my stand at the door of the Galpon [sic], for at that instant one of the enemy's lances made a hole through my poncho. (32)

Editor: At the time of the attack, Giuseppe and about ten men were in the small kitchen shed near the forges. All the others, including Griggs, were busy gathering wood for charcoal in the forest nearby. The weather was beautiful, a proper autumn day for storing supplies and other routine activities. That was the moment at which Abreu chose to attack. In the end it was more his loss than the rebels', only one of whom was cut down in the enemy's first assault. At the time Griggs and the rest were spread out in small bands along the forest pathways, so the outcome was drastic but not disastrous.

Griggs: Here's a venture to make you calculate the worth of a man. I'd had Garibaldi pegged as a lubberly seaman at best or a downright fool at worst. That's not counting the way he comes at you in full flush as a brave breasted hero. The skirmish at the galpoa is recently over, and as I write about it, my attitude changes, not about his seamanship but his quickness and boldness in the very teeth of disaster.

I was off in the brush with a party gathering wood for charcoal. Garibaldi was staying over for the night at the compound and was seeing to some chores in the storehouse with not more nor a dozen mariners. Early in the morning before the mist burned off, my party heard shots and shouting back at the clearing. The marauders, as we learned later, had rushed in on horseback and, as it turned out, got between us and the shed. They caught one of our sailors out in the open and slashed him down. We had only axes and machetes with us. But we ran as fast as we could back toward the sheds, where the raiders concentrated their attack. We heard only the shouts and cracks of carbine fire. The smoke from the guns mixed in with the morning mist and prevented us from seeing clearly what was afoot, for we had to remain under the cover of the undergrowth. Without any firearms, all we could do was pray for our comrades under attack inside.

It was damned fool neglect on my part, leaving our guns behind, the same sort of neglect I've berated Garibaldi for. I admit to that, not that it excuses either of us. But I'll just keep on telling things as I see them and, as for myself, vow to be sharper in the future and check my faulting others as they might well fault me.

May God grant that no such serious blunders visit any of us in the future!

The fight went on for hours; it seemed, with the attackers concentrating on our twelve or so comrades holed up in the shed. *Moringue*, as they call him, was set on killing them all and in that way cripple our operations on the lagoa. Like as not, that means some traitor had got word to him about our layout, or else he has done some reconnoitering.

In the end Garibaldi saved the day. At the point in the fighting when things looked worst, we heard him and his comrades break out with singing at the top of their voices. Such an unlikely caterwauling coming out of that shed you never heard. We were as surprised as any of the raiders. It seemed such a damn fool thing to do. But who aside from Garibaldi would have thought of it? And it turned the trick. We moved in as close as we dared to watch for a chance to help, but none opened, and with few weapons of our own within reach, we were nearly helpless. It surely would not do to get in among those raiders' lances and under their horses hooves, let alone within range of their carbines.

At one point, we saw three or four of *Moringue's* men clamber up onto the roof with the notion of firing down inside or setting the thatching afire, but lance points came thrusting up at them through the roof. Those rascals did some fancy dancing then, I tell you. I don't know how many of them caught a blade, but we saw two limping off under the help of their comrades, dodging every which way to keep Garibaldi's musketeers from drawing a bead on them.

It was a terrible long time before *Moringue's* troop disengaged and scampered back into the forest, and Garibaldi's band rushed out of the shed, where we joined them in the clearing. I never saw such a lot of cheering and laughing and hugging all around. None was more excited than I was. I admitted I felt poorly about hiding off in the woods, but Garibaldi wept to see us alive and called us heroes and the best comrades he ever had for wanting to risk our lives to come back in to help him. There's no dampening his praise, earned or not.

And there's no question but that he saved the day. I doubt any one of us could have done as well. It was a glorious show of spirit, that singing and return of fire. We'd just about given up on Garibaldi and those poor souls with him. No hope, but damned if Garibaldi hadn't pulled off a downright reversal of fortune.

When it was over, we got around to taking a count and we found six of the enemy killed. Four shot in the chest and neck. The other two had been shot in the back while trying to run off, one right through the spine, which did for him in an instant. The second must have been one of those on the roof when the lances came up through, for he had a ripped thigh and a bullet through his heart.

When Garibaldi came gushing out of the shed, he pushed Procopio forward. The Black was glistening like a figurehead in a heavy sea. "This is my gallant," Garibaldi shouted out. "He fought more viciously than any of us, and his carbine is the one that wounded the *Moringue*: May the weasel serve as food for dogs!" The others shouted their agreement because they saw the *Moringue* stagger to his horse with the help of several of his troop.

Once our celebrating broke up, we turned to cleaning up the mess around the galpoa. In the middle or muddle of my ruminations, Procopio came to me and I forgot about everything else. We stood facing one another, and he beamed when I put my hands on his shoulders. No words passed between us but we knew that we were equally admiring of one another, true comrades, as we saw it, from that time on. There are those times when a body can't help showing his feelings.

Eight of our men were wounded, the three most serious died soon after, for we had no surgeons and only rum and cold-water to treat their wounds. (My Ruthie's beautiful image came to me, for we could have used a woman's touch as we set about tending the wounded. But all in all, I was as happy she wasn't there.)

Some said afterward that *Moringue's* troops numbered about 150. I don't know. If they had been that many, they didn't follow a very good plan. Otherwise, they could have rushed the shed and dispatched those inside. It would have been the end for Garibaldi. From my estimate, though, the raiders numbered forty, fifty at most. But no matter: Garibaldi handled them with rare bravado. So what price heroism now? It is a fair question to displace my earlier doubts about him.

We buried the enemy dead near the margin of the forest. Garibaldi walked off before we said prayers for their departed souls. It was the first sign of a mean spirit I saw in him and I put it to him later. He told me that he could not pray for those Austrians, which is the nationality of most of the *Moringue's* mercenary troop. "They're of the same blood as the army that holds Italy," he told me. Well, may the Lord rest their poor souls, I say. For both sides—friend and enemy alike, their days of glory are over.

In one of the shallow skiffs we carried our wounded up river to Doña Antonia's estancia where they could get better treatment and proper food. (When I saw Ruthie, I made sure to show her I was undamaged and she shed a goodly flow of tears anyway. I might as well say it, her tender feelings brought me near to tears, no doubt from high feelings built up during the fighting.)

The mariners who were unhurt stayed behind at the galpoa to clean up and make repairs. And, foolish as it now seems, we set sentries at various locations nearby. I must admit that, despite the faults I found formerly in Garibaldi's decisions and lack of foresight, I am as blameworthy as he for not setting guards earlier around the galpoa. So I say again something I already knew, none of us is without flaw or blame at some time or another.

Something else is much on my mind. Has been for some time but now it carried more of a surge than ever before. I must work out this business of Ruthie's future. I've already written a good bit about it. No denying that, and that care I've taken to set off the passages where I log in my high feelings about her. I've thought about striking them out some time before I leave this log around for others to read—my future family, as I put it, to keep from riling their feelings about me. Well, I've made up my mind. If I'm to be fair about it, Ruthie will be my family, as much so then, as now, and she should have the right of reading the way I feel about her, the here and now of it. So I've got to work out the answers to who's fooling whom; or, more likely, who is being fair to whom. For, by damn, I've tried to be honest in thought and action during my whole career. I'm not about to shift course now and be dishonest with myself. And so here's part of it. I don't know how far down the line, counting in generations, her blood goes back to Indian people. How pure is my bloodline? Those are questions I can lay aside. To the Devil with anybody else's way of seeing it, if they read this log themselves or if they have its contents told by others that's read it. OK. Enough. Settled. Back to what faces me now.

Procopio and I were fashioning extra spars when Garibaldi came by. I could tell he had something else on his mind, so I stood aside to hear him out. Procopio continued to bend over his work on the masts until Garibaldi, still looking at me, put his hand on my friend's neck and said that, after what happened in the raid on the galpoa, he intended to take him for his own ship's crew. I swear I could see Procopio shudder like a stallion shaking off a blue fly. Other than that, no signal passed between us for the rest of the day.

After our evening meal, he came to me, "I am your ship's man." He said it simply, like that. But I had to tell him that, as Garibaldi is our leader, he must have his way. We daren't start a dust-up right now. Feelings were running too high. Nothing more was said about it until the next morning when I took him aside and told him that now it was up to him to stay alert about all the details of routine on board the *Farroupilha*, especially when Garibaldi and the others were in high excitement. I let him know he has a leveler head than all the rest of them. I couldn't admit my concern for his safety in whatever adventures lay ahead for him or me either. I could only counsel him to look after himself, and that meant keeping an eye on his ship's welfare.

Soon after that, I sent for Ruthie.

CHAPTER 14

The Decision to Annex Santa Catarina/Garibaldi and Griggs Plan the Overland Transport of the Rebel Navy

Editor: Late April 1839, General Gonçalves made a momentous decision to send some of his forces into Santa Catarina, the province immediately to the North. It seems most people in high office in that province wanted to ally themselves with the new republican government. So the General decided to by-pass the besieged City of Porto Alegre and assign an army to incorporate Santa Catarina into the revolution. To facilitate the tactic, the General asked Garibaldi, seeing as how he couldn't risk sailing through he mouth of the Lagoa, if somehow he could get his two largest ships involved in carrying supplies and troops by sea to support a land campaign northward.

Garibaldi conferred with Griggs and advised Gonçalves that they might try to sneak their ships over the bar at night but only if they lightened them, which meant leaving the ships with skeleton crews and hardly any troops. That would not suit Gonçalves's strategy. Nor, even if they made it through, were there any other ports on the outer banks for taking men and materiel on board. Not to be discouraged altogether, Garibaldi, with his inclination for the grand scheme, and, knowing he had Griggs's practical skills at his disposal, made a daring proposal. Griggs records the plan.

Griggs, June 1839: With Gonçalves's encouragement, we formed an ingenious plan. We could haul our two largest ships overland across a narrow strip that separates the northern extremity of the Lagoa dos Patos from the open Atlantic. We were pretty sure that we could locate a surface up there firm enough to bear the weight of the ships and the rigs we needed to carry them. If all worked out, we would sail up the Laoa dos Patos to the Bay of Capivari and then transport the ships across to the coastal lake at Tramandai. Before hardening our plans we would have to survey the area to make sure of a suitable overland route.

So in mid-winter, Garibaldi and I sailed one of our small sloops up to confer with an engineer in Capivari sympathetic to Gonçalves. This man, Abreu, who knew the terrain, concurred in our plans and agreed to build two huge carts to convey our ships across the firmest stretch of sands to the Atlantic. It will mean a haul of nearly 100 kilometers. It's worth a try. Once Abreu finishes the carriages, we can roll them down into the water underneath our ships, make them fast, and then haul them up onto the shore. We gave him the measurements of our hulls, and Abreu will begin construction right off. Once we transport them overland, I'll inspect our ships to see that they sustain no structural damage. That over and repairs seen to, we can launch them into the open sea where we can coordinate our moves to secure Santa Catarina by land and sea. I am already familiar with the excellent harbor up there in the Lagoa de Laguna.

Editor: Abreu, it turns out, was a humble man of high proficiency. He brought experience and steady good sense to the task. With the help of Garibaldi'sand Griggs's blueprints, especially thanks to Griggs's experience in the shipyards at Bath and Gloucester, he constructed the carriages.

By June 15, 1839:In Camaquá, Griggs oversaw stowing the portable supplies for separate transportation over land: arms, ammunition, extra sails and rigging, supplementary spars to extend the masts and jib booms for efficient sailing once they launched into the open sea.

On June 30, both carriage rigs were finished. Abreu had done excellent work fashioning them. Four wheels to each carriage. Hardwood beams, one on each side, ran the length of the carriages to support the ships' keels. He laid those across two shorter beams, iron-strapped to house the carriage's axles. Each wheel measured about five-feet from hub to rim, ten-spoked, and tired crosswise with broad leather strips for gripping the sandy roadway. The saddle-ribs were fixed crossways to the longitudinal beams and lined with leather to cushion the hulls. Abreu had fixed the dimensions exactly for the ribs to catch the center of gravity for each hull.

Griggs: July 7. We received our orders and sailed north under cover of dusk from Camaquã, a tricky time of day to manage the shipping channels on the Lagoa. But we succeeded and landed at Capivari with our ships in tact and no trouble from the Imperialists. It took us a day to unstep the masts in preparation for the overland haul. With that done, we ran Abreu's carriages down a shallow slope of beach beneath our ships and cinched them fast to the hulls with a set of broad straps.

The towline to the *Rio Pardo* extended to several harnesses for the oxen, nearly fifty of the beasts for each ship. I don't know where they collected them from, but with the oxen, both crews, and a crowd of local people helping, we hauled her high and dry. Then we did the same for the *Seival*. When it was done, we all gave a hero's cheer to Abreu. After a night's rest we harnessed half the oxen to each carriage and set off across the sands toward Tramandai, some eighty miles away. Not a question in our minds but that it would work.

The transportation was glorious! (33) One hundred oxen! Along our way, citizens came out of their houses to help turn the wheels of the huge carriages, and they shared with our crews whatever food they could bring. Our hopes for success in this Revolution have soared.

If only I could fashion a comfortable locker for storing Ruthie for a snug and tidy journey to the next location. The strategy of taking Santa Catarina into our revolution bodes well—Gonçalves and the others. But for me it needs taking my own personal leave of Ruthie. We heading north but she staying south, with what chance and in what time will I be able to rejoin that sweet girl?

Editor: On July 12, they finished the overland trek. It took them only four days to cover the distance, with well-deserved rests for all at night, until the *Rio Pardo* and Seival were afloat in Lake Tramandai. After they re-stepped the masts and set the new rigging, they pushed the vessels over the bar and into the coastal lake, where they waited for a high tide to leave Lake Tramandai and breast the breakers into the Atlantic.

Griggs: With few tasks remaining before we set sail, It seems a likely time to write down some cogitations concerning the crown people have been assigning to Garibaldi. I dare say I'm not done wondering about him. Don't know as I ever will be. But here's some of what has come to me so far in both columns of the ledger.

Determination and fierceness seem to balance off against his foolhardiness or downright neglect.

If a man has a flame inside him that always responds to fanning, then Garibaldi seems to fit. But does that mean between his high points he can act like a dolt?

He is also uncommonly lucky. A neck wound during the naval battle that almost did for him--torture at the hands of the Argentines. Then they let him go free for no apparent reason. Just like that.

It is time to put all this aside and think on it. Together with the praise I myself received from Gonçalves and, let me say it, Garibaldi, too.

Right now our chores are a whole lot easier to put down than cogitations about heroes, so here's back to the day-to-day.

I have finished inspecting our two schooners. Thanks to Abreu's skills as an engineer, pattern maker and joiner, both are tight-timbered and true-keeled—literally ship-shape, as you may say. They need just a bit of fresh caulking here and there and a few pegs reset. In addition, I've fit them, with Abreu's help, bigger rudders and reinforced tillers, added rigging for the extra jibs, and I've fashioned spars to serve as topmasts. Now these vessels are ready aloft and allow for extended cruising and quick maneuvering both.

On July 14, 1839, we were soon ready to run the surf. I foresaw that it would be trickier by a good measure than anyone thought. A steep shelf lies along this stretch of the coast, where the surf runs down in like a great, ragged wall and washes up onto the shore in a tattered rush. In most places it breaks about a hundred yards offshore and sends in such a strong wash that you can hardly make headway against it.

We sent our best oarsmen in a sharp-prowed longboat to make their way out beyond the breakers. Bent to the one-inch line they trailed out was a three-inch hempen hauser fixed to the *Rio Pardo's* stem. They hauled that out hand over hand. We bent another *t*hree-incher to her stern to steady her against broaching as she entered that roiling surf. With Procopio at the *Rio Pardo's* helm and the gaff sail reefed at two points, they cut across Lake Tramadai and fought through the breakers, pitching and yawing all the way. But drenched with salt spray and sweat, they made it safely. With a skeleton crew left on board, they fought their way back ashore in the longboat, where we attached the same cables to the *Seival*. Then we wrangled her out, too, the same fight all the way.

We were four hours getting both ships through the surf to good holding ground, where they lay cradled like seaworthy babes in their true home on the offshore swells. Farewell to the choppy shallows of the Lagoa dos Patos.

Soon after clearing the surf, we transported our full crews and stowed our cargoes bung up and bilge free.

If my calculations are correct, three years plus four months have passed since I left the *Toucan* and my American shipmates.

So it feels good to have a sturdy ship rolling under me with fresh salt air in my lungs again. Pleased is a meager way to put it. After all those chores ashore and edging a vessel along the shoreline inside the Lagoa dos Patos, not quite trusting the buoys that marked the channel and constantly sounding the bottom. Now we're out here secure in the open sea.

Together, Garibaldi and I looked over the charts and synchronized our courses northward for a rendezvous at Camacho, which lies about 10 miles south of Laguna. There we will take our contingency of troops on board and coordinate our arrival with the major land force moving up to Laguna.

The colors of the waters off these sub-tropical shores make depths easy to read. They vary from royal purple to wine red and turquoise and strips of gold where they graze the sand bars close in to the ragged surf.

Just listen to my pen urging fancies onto this page! Such writing could never decorate a ship's log. It must be the glory of riding the deeps once again that puts my pen to rhapsodies. These southern seas are beautiful enough to distract a careless helmsman. How many times have I called out—or suddenly reminded myself to look toward the compass card and hold her keel on course! A seasoned sailor must stay in league with the sea's moods; otherwise, he's in danger of following those who have slid beneath her surface forever.

But give me leave for one more reverie: that of the sea dweller with ties to the shore. Them that wants not to go down in the sea but instead wishes for a safe homecoming, furling all sails to sheets and yardarms and yielding their ship's independent movement to the tugboats, thereby into a snug berth. Home and hearth means far less to a landlocked lubber than it does to a seafarer. All them thoughts affixes to my picture of Ruthie who anchors this entire revolutionary venture in place.

Such are the thoughts of true seamen, whether they speak them out or not, even laying aside my batten-brained manner of stating them.

Back to reality.

After several experimental tacks I was happy to say that the *Seival* handled well both before the wind and close to it. A western breeze prevailed and held us off shore, even though we had to look sharp to counteract those sudden winter gusts and the southerly current. So we were finally away to Santa Catarina and direct participation in this Revolution.

Two hours on our new course, and at my last sighting Garibaldi was holding the *Rio Pardo* a bit too close in to shore. I signaled him to bring her out farther. Also, she looked down by the head, even though she wasn't carrying more cargo nor I was. I know his compass is accurate, for I boxed it myself. And with his lubberly mishap back in the Rio de la Plata Estuary in mind, I myself made sure his binnacle was clear of metal debris. Also, I told Procopio to keep a sharp eye, especially to see to a tidy space around and about the binnacle. Anyway, I didn't like the look of his position and tried again to signal Garibaldi to watch for breakers ahead. I could not tell that he read me, and there was no way for me to maneuver in and lay by. Pretty soon I lost sight of him. So there was nothing for it but set the course we'd agreed on—Northeast-by-North—and hope for the best.

I have a platoon of soldiers and fourteen seamen and two extra whale boats on board the *Seival*. She is now a warship with the extra hands needed for gunnery. I've drilled my crew a-plenty and they go right to their arms and make ready like experienced battlers. Several are busy shifting cargo to put the *Seival* on an even keel. During the few days we need to reach rendezvous, I'll hold shipboard drills for swift disembarking and proper precautions to keep their powder dry, but all through these necessary chores, half my thoughts are about Garibaldi and his navigation gaffes.

CHAPTER 15

Garibaldi's Disaster at Sea

Editor: July 19: After an uneventful run with surprisingly few seasick among his crew and passengers, Griggs arrived, as scheduled, at rendezvous off the beach at Garopaba do Sul. It took some tricky negotiating to clear the bar into the Lagoa do Camacho. But he kept his crew sharp at their lines and made it over with the merest scrape of his keel before he maneuvered the *Seival* into a safe anchorage. He lay approximately fifteen kilometers south of the channel into Laguna. There, with dusk coming on, he and his crew stood waiting for Garibaldi's arrival by sea and Colonels Canabarro's and Nunes's contingency to join them along the shore.

On July 20, 1839, as if in a confused dream, Griggs was startled to see Garibaldi and a small number of his crew marching along the beach. That sight did not puzzle him for long. The worst of his imaginings had come true, for he soon learned that Garibaldi had lost the *Rio Pardo*. She had foundered off the beach not more than a few miles north of Tramandai. That was dire news but even worse details followed.

As Griggs had observed, Garibaldi sailed the *Rio Pardo* too close to the breakers without enough room to maneuver his way out against the turbulent winds that, come down from the north and tangle with the off-shore gusts. As part of that dreadful news, Griggs learned that many of Garibaldi's fellow Italians, including Lodoba and Lamberti, Mutru and Carniglia, had gone down right before his eyes. Lost also were Stadirini and the hearty Procopio.

From Garibaldi's Memoirs: At about eight in the evening we departed from that place [Tramandai], and at three in the afternoon of the following day were wrecked at the mouth of the Arevingua, with the loss of sixteen of the company in the Atlantic, and with the destruction of the launch *Rio Pardo*, which was under my command, in the terrible breakers off that coast. . . .

But our vessels lay deep in the water, and sometimes sank so low into the sea, that they were in danger of foundering. They would occasionally remain several minutes under the waves. I determined to approach the land and find out where we were; but, the

winds and waves increasing, we had no choice, and were compelled to stand off again, and were soon involved in the frightful
breakers. I was at that moment on the top of the mast, hoping to
discover some point of the coast less dangerous to approach. By a
sudden turn the vessel was rolled violently to starboard, and I was
thrown some distance overboard. . . .

A portion of the crew I found dispersed, and making every ex-
ertion to gain the coast by swimming. I succeeded among the first;
and the next thing, after setting my feet upon the land, was to turn
and discover the situation of my comrades. Eduardo appeared, at a
short distance. He had left the dead-light which I had given him,
or, as is more probable, the violence of the waves had torn it from
his grasp. . . . I rushed towards my dear friend, reaching out to him
the piece of wood which had saved me on my way to the shore. I
had got very near him; and, excited by the importance of the un-
dertaking, should have saved him: but a surge rolled over us both;
and I was under water for a moment. I rallied and called out, not
seeing him appear; I called in desperation,—but in vain. . . .

The bodies of sixteen of my companions, drowned in the sea,
were transported a distance of thirty miles, to the northern coast,
and buried in its immense sands. Several of the remainder were
brought to land. . . . My feelings overpowered me. The world appeared to me like a desert. Many of the company who were neither
seamen nor swimmers were saved. . . .

The *Seival*, our other launch, commanded by Griggs, being of a
different construction from the *Rio Pardo*, was better able to sustain itself, although but little larger, against the violence of the
storm, and had held on her course. (34)

Editor: Sixteen souls lost, Garibaldi and his survivors marched
to the rendezvous from Araranguá, the site of their disaster. It
would be an understatement to say that the survivors were in low
spirits, Garibaldi especially. When he recounted the terrible events
to Griggs, the American turned from him in disbelief. After Griggs
recovered his breathing sufficiently, he entered the events and his
reaction in his personal log. It is one of the most emotional out-
pourings we find in the entirety of his remarkable document.

Griggs: July 21, 1839. This is a hard entry for me, the hardest I
have ever put down. May the Lord keep my pen from dripping
gall. Disaster. Where to turn for comfort? Garibaldi has lost the
Rio Pardo and 16 men. A loss beyond calculation, and, as the
Heavens will affirm, a terrible waste! Lord above! Lost is the ship,

the supplies, arms, rigging, ammunition. All the work that went into her. But how can we cipher up the loss of those lives? A great, great waste. Lord have mercy on their souls. And calm my turbulent spirits enough ro get on with the duties ahead. But first of all, may the Good Lord forgive me for marking bitter blame. Garibaldi! Damn the stupidity of his judgment! All those good men. And when I heard Procopio was gone, I could have bitten clean through a ringbolt.

What was Garibaldi up to? He was supposed to have experience along this coast. He must have had a chance to examine the shoreline when he sailed down from Rio--those uneven breakers. As I look back on our departing maneuvers at Tramandai, it was just as I feared: Just what I tried to signal him about. And just what he now confirmed. Once he got drawn into the pull of that surf, there was no hope for him. That's when he began to look for a place to land but it was too late. The *Rio Pardo* broached, rolled heavily and shipped water.

What he described next, I could not believe. In the midst of that broil, he climbed the main-mast himself to look for a likely approach, some break in the surf! I don't know who was at the helm, Procopio and others, likely as not, but I don't suppose it would have mattered all that much by then because, as Garibaldi reported it, the *Rio Pardo* took one final, sharp roll and bucked him clear of the mast into that damned surf.

As he told it, a lot of gear, planks, and other stuff were swirling around when he surfaced. There he was, the captain, already in the water, hollering to his men to abandon ship!

I ask myself over and again, why did he choose to climb that mast? Why would the captain of a vessel do such a thing as that? He should have been at the helm, put all hands at the ready, set the sheets long before he put his ship into such a dangerous situation. I can taste the salt-laden death all about!

It took me half a day to get unshook enough to hear more, but ready or not Garibaldi finished his telling it. There I was squeezed between his need to talk on and my wanting to get off somewhere with my own grief and, to tell true, my anger, disgust. Mutru went down with the ship. Carniglia got fouled up in his own jacket and sank. Sixteen of his men drowned altogether, including six of his Italian comrades and my man Procopio, the strongest of the lot. Of all the things I taught him, all the satisfaction he looked forward to, I never thought to ask that brave heart if he could swim.

July 22, 1839: Again I ask the Good Lord to forgive me for fastening blame to Garibaldi. But worse than that, who among us has the right to make as if he's secure against his own destiny. I've put down words about his uncommon good luck. Well, he ran out of it in that caper. All right. Let a man himself look to the quality of his toiling. God will do the judging of it soon enough. The good ship *Rio Pardo* and its crew have gone to their reward. It's done with. What's the use of even thinking upon it further? It took me a full day before I could breathe steady enough to write this down—a hard task for me and a harder loss for us all. Truth to tell, I'll not get over it even if I was to sail clear through Perdition's Strait.

Just as well that I had little time for grieving. Our rendezvous with the army awaited, and Garibaldi and his survivors took their place in the ranks of the land army for the fast march to Laguna. I took more than my quota of soldiers on board and told Garibaldi straight out that I intended to sail my own ship into Laguna. My meaning was in my manner. He made no argument then nor since.

CHAPTER 16

Arrival at Santa Catarina/Rossetti's New Duties/The Rebel Navy's Operations

Editor: On July 22, '39, Garibaldi urged his mariners to recover their spirits and together they joined the ranks of Terceira's brigade on the march into Santa Catarina. Griggs, on signal, sailed into the mouth of the Lagoa Santo Antonio dos Anjos da Laguna. After he lowered away boats with the soldiers he carried, he stood the *Seival* off the entrance, like Horatio at the bridge. Those troops occupied the fort on the hill overlooking the channel entrance. Griggs could have held off any number of Imperial ships trying to fight their way out or in.

Thanks to his advantageous positioning, he trapped a small fleet of Catarinense vessels inside the bay with all their arms and ammunition on board. After a short battle, the resistors in the port city surrendered formally on July 23, 1839, as if by previous arrangement. The vessels Griggs trapped were of various sorts and sizes. Two were already fitted for combat. Others were mere fishing skiffs that could be used as tenders.

After they settled in their new headquarters, Garibaldi and Griggs got on with reorganizing their fleet. As a result, Garibaldi took his new crew aboard a single-gun vessel, which he renamed the *Rio Pardo* after his lost ship. Griggs's *Seival* went under command of Lorenzo, one of the few surviving Italians, and Griggs became captain of the *Caçapava*, the largest vessel left in the Laguna anchorage. Especially important, they now had a properly equipped shipyard in which to service all their vessels.

The new ship was schooner-rigged, with stubby masts, much like the *Seival's.*

It was good enough for short range cruising, but Griggs added spars to all the ships' masts, and rigged them for club topsails and staysails. They also acquired three swift sumacas, similar to New England smacks or cutters, one sloop-rigged and the others lateen. The support vessels would be the *Itaparica*, under Teixeira, the *Santana* under Bilboa, and the *Lagunense* under Rodrigues, all Laguna residents who had come over to the rebel command. TakenΩaltogether, the rebels now had a sizeable fleet, certainly one to be taken more seriously than their former company. Both Garibaldi and Griggs drilled the crews until they came to general quarters smartly.

As expected, many of the citizens of Laguna were disappointed by the Republican take-over, but most cheered and pledged their loyalty to the new government. Colonel Canabarro's first act was to commemorate the day by renaming Laguna 'Villa Juliana.' Then at the conference that followed, he wisely asked a popular leader, Don Vincent Ferreira do Santos Cordeiro, to become President of the New Republic of Santa Catarina. Other prominent Lagunenses were entitled ministers and kept in charge of municipal operations. So the newly acquired territory enjoyed a healthy continuity under its familiar and seasoned leaders.

We return now to a previous topic. Rossetti had not heard about Garibaldi's disaster until he joined General Canabarro's army for the march into Santa Catarina. When he arrived at the rendezvous he saw Griggs's ship at anchor but no Garibaldi until the latter straggled in on foot. Then he learned the terrible truth about the *Rio Pardo*.

Rossetti: I must steady my pen to write this. As I learned, Giuseppe, during the worst of the ordeal, tried to save his mariners, but alas, sixteen brave souls were lost to the Struggle for Liberty here in Brazil. Among them, seven Brethren of Young Italy, who now were lost also to the Future Struggle for a Reunited Homeland.

They will forever to be included in our Roll of Fallen Heroes.

I asked Griggs what he could tell me about the shipwreck but he was reticent to say anything. So restrained, the North American comrade, so unwilling to display his emotions. Something in the turning of his eyes suggested more than mere sadness, and I felt in him a desire to avoid talking about the shipwreck and to return to his own busy work. He was now the only Naval Commander in our forces who still had a ship.

How is it, I could not help to wonder, that Griggs's ship escaped the fate of Garibaldi's *Rio Pardo*. And how is it that Giuseppe resigned himself and his fellow survivors to a place among the land forces instead of joining Griggs on the *Seival*? I hope to have answers to those befuddling questions after we are settled among our new allies.

From Garibaldi's Memoirs: [General] Canabarro, having fixed his head-quarters in the city of Laguna . . . promised to establish a Provincial Representative Government, the first president of which was a reverend priest, who had great influence among the people. Rossetti, with the title of Secretary of the Government, was in fact the soul of it. And Rossetti, in truth, was formed for such a station (35).

Rossetti: For now, however, I must report, with some satisfaction, that Canabarro, our General in charge of the Armed Forces in Santa Catarina, has vested in me the title of Occupational Administrator of the Province of Santa Catarina. It is a timely promotion, which immediately takes up all my time and energy. In fact, next to initiating *O 'Povo*, my tenure, as Secretary-Administrator, was my most satisfying experience in this war. Only total independence from the Imperialists could be more rewarding.

At the risk of immodesty, I must point out that I am pleased by my own facility as administrator. As in my earlier task of organizing *O 'Povo*, I learned to work efficiently and expeditiously as a sort of coordinator with the Laguna authorities.

Editor: By August 12, 39, Griggs finished refitting his *Caçapava*. With the fresh supply of arms and ammunition they took in Laguna, they were ready to carry out Canabarro's orders, which were to disrupt shipping along the Atlantic coast.

From Garibaldi's Memoirs: I was accompanied by my inseparable friend, John Griggs, and had with me a chosen part of my band, which had assisted in building the launches.

The three vessels which were armed and destined to make an excursion on the ocean, were the *Rio Pardo*, which was under my command, and the *Casapava*, under Griggs—both schooners—and lastly, the *Seival*, which had come from Rio Grande, now commanded by the Italian, Lorenzo. (36)

Editor: By August 27, their little flotilla had made two successful raids, both off the Isle of Santa Catarina, about 100 miles north of Laguna. The large port of Desterro had a thriving trade, which yielded the cargoes of several coastal traders and one larger seagoing merchantman. These prizes included welcome quantities of rice, fabrics, fish, and sundries, but on their last homeward leg, two heavily armed Imperial cutters came out of Desterro to give chase. The rebels outran them but the narrow margin of escape discouraged them from risking more such encounters with Imperial ships.

On September 15, the weather continued favorable with brisk spring winds from the North. Garibaldi, Griggs, and Lorenzo had returned from a foray, this time north to Paranaguá, about half again the distance to Desterro, where they took another large cargo of rice. On their northerly leg, they swung seaward past the Isle of Santa Catarina to avoid the Imperial war ships and returned by direct course, passing the Isle after sundown. But on the next day at daybreak, they sighted the square sails of a large brigantine man-of-war bearing down on them. They made it into Laguna just before she could come within firing range. During the days that followed, Garibaldi and Griggs decided to lie low and study the Imperials' patrol pattern.

CHAPTER 17

Garibaldi Meets Anita/Griggs's and Rossetti's Reactions. Garibaldi's Distasteful Assignment

Editor: During that period of inactivity, Garibaldi began his momentous liaison with the heroine Anita. Enough direct records exist to indicate the extent and intensity of their involvement. Certainly the damage to her family's reputation would have been a serious blow to her community of relatives and friends, as we shall learn from the recorded observations left behind. Some of Anita's friends no doubt were sympathetic to her escape from the drudging life of a peasant housewife, especially for a person of Anita's energy and resources. On the other hand, this drastic shift in Garibaldi's personal status furnishes an opportunity to examine Griggs's and Rossetti's reactions, especially Griggs's relationship to Ruthie.

From Garibaldi's Memoirs: At that time occurred one of the most important events of my life. I had never thought of matrimony, but had considered myself incapable of it from being of too independent a disposition, and too much inclined to adventure. To have a wife and children appeared to me decidedly repulsive, as I had devoted my whole life to one principle, which however good it might be, could not leave the quietness necessary to the father of a family. But my destiny guided me in a different direction from what I had designed for myself. By the loss of Luigi Carniglia, Eduardo and my other comrades, I was left in a state of complete isolation, and felt as if alone in the world. . . .

Rossetti was a brother to me: but he could not live with me, and I could see him but rarely. I desired a friend of a different character; for, although still young, I had considerable knowledge of men, and knew enough to understand what was necessary for me in a true friend. One of the other sex, I thought must supply the vacant place, for I had always regarded woman as the most perfect of creatures, and believe it far easier to find a loving heart among that sex.

I walked the deck of the *Itaparica*, with my mind revolving these things, and finally came to the conclusion to seek for some lady possessing the character which I desired. I one day cast a casual glance at a home in the Burra [sic], (the eastern part of the entrance of the Jayuna,) and there observed a young female whose appearance struck me as having something very extraordinary. So powerful was the impression made upon me at the moment, though from some cause which I was not able fully to ascertain, that I gave orders and was transported towards the house. I soon received an invitation to take coffee with his family, and the first person who entered was the lady whose appearance had so mysteriously but irresistibly [sic] drawn me to the place. I saluted her; we were soon acquainted; and I found that the hidden treasure which I had discovered was of rare and inestimable worth. But I have since reproached myself. . . . (37)

Griggs: Mid-September: Plenty of whores are handy wherever the mariners settle in for their jollies, and our ships' companies are not behind times latching onto their waterfront ladies. It's foolhardiness to take any of those found about here, not knowing who-all they've lain with. I'm satisfied with letting my thoughts go back to Ruthie, especially now with all this coupling going on. Not a Ruthie among the lot of them, by my measure. I miss her tidy arrangement of my quarters, and the soft warmth of her limbs taking possession of me—an easy surrender—the sweet smell of the herbal ointments she applies to her body.

On the subject of amorous partners, I have seen little of Garibaldi during the last few days. Talk is that he spends a good bit of his time with a local woman among the houses above the Barra. All sorts of loose talk about him is getting around.

I know nothing more than I've been told about Garibaldi's woman, but to me Ruthie is an attachment to value among the highest. After the early fire of our joining, a gentle hunger settled between us. She is mine alone, a real blessing, I can appreciate now.

This woman Garibaldi has taken—I have her name now—Anna Maria Doarte—a Doña, a married woman. Lately, Garibaldi has brought her down to the harbor and invited a few of us to share supper. I tried not to be forward about studying her, but she imposes her presence clearly. They make a good match. She is young, as I calculate from her appearance, but with a seasoned show of fire in her eye. She is no loose fish for the taking. I can see that she has made up her mind not to apologize to anyone for anything she has done.

This Doña Anita, as Garibaldi insists we refer to her, is a head shorter than him but every inch as sturdy. Except for her eyes and bearing, her general appearance alone would not draw my notice. I don't know what Garibaldi has in mind for her, but I doubt she will settle for merely bedding with him. I believe he will come to know that soon enough, if he doesn't already.

It turns out she has a poor but respected family in Laguna. I don't dare ask Teixeira or Rodrigues, who are locals. But they told me openly Garibaldi has to know that in taking her, he has cut her off from her family and their community. Maybe the choice was hers. They doubt it could be strictly one way or the other. All they say is that something in each must have struck a spark in the other. I hope Garibaldi and her can stand up to the consequences. All I can say is that it's made me give more serious thoughts to Ruthie. This revolution must keep on course and settle us eventually on a campaign southward all the way to the capture of the forts at the mouth of the Lagoa dos Patos. Then we'll have safe passage up into the lagoa and snug harbors anywhere along her shoreline, including Donna Anna's estancia, where Ruthie waits for me. Then, God be willing, with her on board, what sailing far to the North until we reach the New States of America United and a home near to Boston--a house of our own, a hearth with Ruthie and a happy brood to follow.

But for now, avast and belay all desires, set my heart a-beating steady for the immediate purposes of our struggles for a free and independent Rio Grande do Sol!

After a few days, Rodrigues gave me more facts. Anna Doarte's husband is a cobbler, conscripted into the Imperial Militia and marched off to whatever destination, alongside a lot of other locals. With her husband gone and with Garibaldi presenting himself to her—I picture him the way she saw the newcomer, a glittering conqueror from faraway lands—she has flat out left her home to be with him. A mighty steep step she's taken, linking up with another man, whatever his reputation among her compatriots. Now she must cling to Garibaldi. But here's a question Rodrigues raised: what will happen to her when we go to sea again?

He is right, and I hope Garibaldi has thought it through with care. I tally it up as another of his snap decisions that ends up suiting his own fancy but bringing grief to those that count on him. No need to explain my meaning. Nobody around puts open blame on him for the disaster of the *Rio Pardo*, leastwise not to Garibaldi's face, and nothing shows that he blames himself, for that matter. "Destino," as I've heard a few of our Riograndenses justify it. But others keep long faces and their thoughts to themselves. That goes for me, too, about the ship he lost and all those comrades, as it does about this Anita of his. I can't put equal blame to her, considering what she thinks she gets in return for casting off her family and all. As for Garibaldi, stronger doubts about his restraint are out and about, as the saying goes, and will stay that way, I fear.

Editor: Rossetti, as the following excerpt from his memoirs shows, shared Griggs's misgivings about Garibaldi's liaison, although from a different angle of perception.

Rossetti: What will happen to Garibaldi's life now that he has taken the local woman? He did it with no advice from anyone, not even his closest friends. She was the one he must have, he said to my casual inquiry. She alone! A peasant girl—hardly even a woman—without the slightest refinement. Maybe that is what drew Giuseppe, the promise of a more fiery affection than the rest of us could provide, as he perceives it. "I must have someone to love me. "He told me that—I, who have been closest of all to him. I know he did not mean it as an insult. In the past when he told the others—poor, dead Carniglia and Mutru, even the North American, Griggs—that each was his most valued friend, I did not mind. It is his nature to be fervent, precipitous. Now many of those compatriots have died. And they deserve the highest praise. But I was with Giuseppe from the beginning of his arrival in Rio de Janeiro. It was I who suffered his impracticality in the management of our business, and with his impolitic, impetuous impulse to openly insult our foes, which often endangered all of us Young Italians. But his callous indifference to my reaction is especially painful. Has he even sounded my deepest feelings? Has he ever tried to appreciate, penetrate my restraint?

Some of the things I have done for him he will never know about. It was I who kept his records in order when he was assigned to collect taxes from the citizens of Laguna, a task he accepted reluctantly, to be sure. And it was I who softened our commander's irritation with him when Giuseppe proffered constant, unsolicited, contrary advice. Also the grumbling that followed his punitive expedition against Imarui for their counter-revolutionary uprising.

Editor: Here Rossetti refers to Garibaldi's expedition up the north shore of the lagoon to sack the town in reprisal for their disloyalty. It was a distasteful task, especially for him because by impulse he wished to be a friend as well as a leader to all.

From Garibaldi's Memoirs: I wish for myself, and for every other person who has not forgotten to be a man, to be exempt from the necessity of witnessing the sack of a town. A long and minute description would not be sufficient to give a just idea of the baseness and wickedness of such a deed. May God save me from such a spectacle hereafter! I never spent a day of such wretchedness and in such lamentation. I was filled with horror; and the fatigue I endured in restraining personal violence was excessive. (38)

Rossetti: Certainly several of his mariners acted badly on that expedition, destroying more homes than they had to, and the raping and general brutality that civilized men detest. Of course Giuseppe was right to threaten to punish the brutes under his command, but they had behaved according to their own habits. Most had never served with him before and did not know his high moral compunction, as if they had the right to measure his life by their own gross motives. I always treated him with the highest gentility, even tenderness. What those unruly brutes could never comprehend is the abiding delicacy of Giuseppe's humanity. The agony, often transformed into physical symptoms, he suffered when others, especially those under his command, but whom, for the moment or at the occasion, tormented, tortured other human beings. I have reported his emotional reactions to random acts of inhumanity that I observed in the streets of Rio de Janeiro. Those occurred when he was a dissociated observer, and even then I had to place a touch of comfort on his brow, and as often, had to restrain him from wreaking vengeance on the spot, even to the point of endangering both of us. But this sacking of Imarui occurred under his tacit command, when, that is, he was supposedly responsible for the actions of his troops. When he reported his men's actions to Canabarro's and received an indifferent response, he retreated into the burrow of his own helpless agony. It took days of patient and tender care to retrieve him from the edge of insanity. That depth of despair, that battle with depression, left him exhausted and perhaps that gives reason to his resorting to the companionship of this woman, Anita, and away from the rest of us.

As for my mention of Canabarro's irritation with Giuseppe's insubordinate criticism, it is true that the General had an entire army to maintain at a time when restlessness was spreading rapidly in Santa Catarina. No wonder the General began to question Giuseppe's dependability to carry out necessary and even distasteful orders. But I argued energetically for my friend's irreplaceable skills and unshakable commitment. Giuseppe will never hear about such pleading in his behalf.

And so this Anita. He needed a woman. All right, I can understand that. But this Anita was already with a husband. A terrible sin, adultery, but for her to break her vows and go to live with Giuseppe. None of that mattered in the face of Giuseppe's dependence on her willing show of affection. When I asked Griggs about that, he said," I have always avoided ties with the shore. "That is all. Connection to women left behind in port makes problems. That is certainly true. But she is one who will not easily let go of Giuseppe, especially since she has cut ties with all others ashore.

I agreed with Griggs then and still do, especially now that the woman goes everywhere with Giuseppe. Such boldness at least, I admit, makes her a likely companion for him. In truth, she may prove to be as fierce a warrior as he is. At first I imagined she was simply infatuated, a person whose passion awaited him at the end of each day. But now everyone talks about her bravery. Still, Griggs is right. Ties with the shore indeed. That is what Giuseppe took for himself. But how does his attachment to her affect his respect for the rest of us, his affection? She is fiercely jealous of any attention he gives to others. Now will she make him forego his obligations to free his Homeland, too, to unify it once more? I pray not.

I cannot refrain from including that concern here in my private thoughts. I may yet express it openly to Giuseppe himself when the time is right. Is she truly a proper match for him? Can she even write her name, let alone read—a letter, a newssheet, a book? Giuseppe is somewhat cultivated. Too impressionable philosophically, impatient of analytical thought. But he can respond enthusiastically, even if mainly to the lyrical ideal, heroic love in the large span of dedication to humanity, in both the collective sweep and the individual sympathy. But of what commitment is this Anita capable? She will make of Giuseppe her entire universe, I fear. Will she also close him off from others who love him equally?

CHAPTER 18

Anita's Conversations with Doña Feliciana Begin

Editor: At this point we make our next major shift in focus and begin Anita's account of her association with Garibaldi. Although it comes after Rossetti's expression of skepticism, even resentment, we will see that he eventually shows he is fair-minded about certain of the same heroic qualities in Anita that he celebrates in Garibaldi, just as, in the record of her experiences and attitudes, we will see Anita's fair-mindedness about Garibaldi. We also will see her appreciation of Griggs's sympathy and modesty. Of Rossetti, she has little to say

I remind the reader of the peculiar circumstances under which Anita's accounts originate. That is, as I state in my preface, Anita could not have written her own memoirs. For their existence we must thank Doña Feliciana, of Montevideo, and trust her fervent insistence that she recorded as accurately as possible everything, just as Anita had spoken it. This feat, remarkable in itself and most fortunate for us, attests to Doña Feliciana's earnest intentions as well as her appreciation of the importance of Anita's story.

As token proof of her accuracy, I refer the reader also to Anita's subsequent interviews with Fra Lorenzo, in which his representation of the vocabulary, tone, and rhythm of phrasing of Anita's additional ventures are practically identical to those in the documents that Doña Feliciana passed along to him. What we now read, is their rendition of Anita's own voice.

I have omitted most of the obvious question—indicated by a line of asterisks—that Doña Feliciana and Fra Lorenzo asked, by which they prompted Anita to disclose her experiences. I have, however, omitted the asterisks whenever Dona Feliciana and Fra Lorenzo express their occasionally spontaneous, emotional reactions to Anita's disclosures. Finally, we are indebted also to Father Lorenzo for preserving his notes as well as those Doña Feliciana turned over to him, for, in addition to his obvious fascination with the substance of his notes, he recognized their importance as a legal record of his advice respecting Anita's marriage to Garibaldi.

Doña Feliciana Garcia Villigran, Montevideo, Uruguay
Her Record of Conversations with Doña Anita Garibaldi
Given over to the Possession of Don Zenón Asiazu
Curate in the Church of San Francisco de Asis

Anita: I measure my real life from my first meeting with José Garibaldi, who came to me like a bright vision out of a Golden cloud. Everything he had, as he told me, he would share with me, beginning with his undying love. That is the treasure that Destiny intended I should share. José did not know then to tell me how much that would be. So in answer to his appeal and promise, I fled from my home and my family to be with him. Yes, from my husband, too.

I was only a girl. Now I am not that girl. I have birthed José Garibaldi's child, our baby Menotti. I rode here with that child on my own saddle when we left the Revolution in the Rio Grande do Sul. All the way from São Gabriel to Montevideo behind that herd of cattle. Was it the right thing for me to do, my union with José? I don't know. Fleeing to an unknown home in Uruguay, José was not afraid any more for our little Menotti or for me. Besides, he knew he would hear something here about his family in Genoa.

To tell the truth, I knew the second was his biggest reason for coming. In Montevideo. So how could I say no? That our duty was to stay with General Gonçalves and his ragged soldiers in Rio Grande? I could say that. But if we stayed there, the only hope we had was in President Gonçalves's victory. He vowed to free the slaves who fought in his Revolution. In Laguna, I was like one of them, you know, given away like a slave to marry Manoel, to sit with other wives, stitch together old pieces of clothing, throw bits of fish into a pot?

Now, to my family far back there in Laguna, I am already dead. That is no longer my home, not even a place for me to be buried, in a hole in sanctified ground.

* * * * *

Anita: Maybe you are right, Doña Feliciana. One can never lose family. I pray you are right. But now I must let Destiny decide, for I am farther from Laguna than I ever dreamed to be. It's a harder journey to go back to one's home than to run away from it.

* * * * *8I am sorry. Yes, I believe that hope is a powerful helper. But I don't believe I will ever return. For our comrades the revolution continued. It kept their hope alive. When José brought us to Montevideo, for us the Revolution in Rio Grande do Sul was already over. José told General Gonçalves he would return from Uruguay after he got news about his family in Italy. But I know he never will go back. We had 900 cattle—that's what the General gave us as our pay—I saw it as our final payment—and he assigned six gauchos to help us. I didn't even bother to learn their names. José trusted those gauchos to do what is right, only he didn't know as I do that first they do what is right for themselves. He paid them in cattle before we left São Gabriel, you see. He expected fairness. So foolish. So they let many of the cattle die. They pushed them too hard, didn't give them enough rest. And half of the herd drowned when we crossed the Rio Negro. Half of 900. Finally only three hundred were left to us. A mistake. Can you imagine? So we slaughtered them and took only their hides the rest of the way to the frontier.

From Garibaldi's Memoirs: I took up the business of a cattle-drover, or trappiere. In an Estancia, called the Corral del Piedras, under the authority of the Minister of Finance, I succeeded in collecting, in about twenty days, about nine hundred cattle, after indescribable fatigue. With a still greater degree of labor and weariness they were driven towards Montevideo. Thither, however, I did not succeed in driving them. Insuperable obstacles presented themseles on the way, and, more than all, the Rio Negro, which crossed it, and in which I nearly lost all this capital. From that river, from the effects of my inexperience and from the tricks of some of my hired assistants for managing the drove of animals, I saved about five hundred of the cattle, which, by the long journey, scarcity of food and accidents in crossing streams, were thought unfit to go to Montevideo.

I therefore decided to "cuercer" or "leather" them,—that is, to kill them for their hides; and this was done. In fact, after having passed through indescribable fatigue and troubles, for about fifty days, I arrived at Montevideo with a few hides, the only remains of my nine hundred oxen. These I sold for only a few hundred dollars, which served but scantily to clothe my little family. (39)

Anita: The gauchos! It's in their blood to take advantage. I know them. How many of them among the Riograndense soldiers left the army as soon as their homes were out of danger? How many ran to join the Imperialist enemies when the other side looked to be victorious? Please understand me, Doña Feliciana, I do not blame them altogether. They live always with great risks, the weather, the stubborn cattle, the unknown wills of wild animals. They must take their advantage whenever Nature and chance allow. So the Gauchos, all people who live near to the soil and the sea, must imitate the animals they are so close to.

But even though he saw that, José could not change, even after it was too late. He has much faith in people to help each other in a common cause. Brotherhood, an idea he believed in. Too much. So others cheat him. How has he kept his faith alive this long? It was a question that stayed close to my mind. And poor Griggs asked me that same question many times.

Doña Feliciana: This was the first time I heard Griggs's name. Anita mentioned him in passing and promised to tell more about him because he was obviously an important friend to her, so I was sure I would not offend her by asking about him. She spoke his name with such warmth, such sympathy.

Anita: Ah, Griggs. A comrade, one of José's Marine Officers. A Norte Americano. A special man. I met him the day after José found me in the house of a friend. But I tell you first about meeting José. You see, on the way from Rio Grande do Sul to Laguna, José lost many close comrades in the sea and needed someone to share his grief, to give him comfort. How far away is that from love?

That was his condition as he looked up into the hills from his ship and saw me. It was our Destiny, good to us at that time! But you know that Destino always makes us pay something back for her favors.

When I first saw Giuseppe in the dim light, the way he stood in the dark doorway of my friend's house, I swear to you, I could feel the heat of his love. He told me many times since and I have heard him tell others how he saw me from the foot of the barra. He recognized me as the woman he was searching for. Can you believe it? I tell you the truth, at that moment I was not searching for him. But you see how it has turned out. When he went to my friend's house to ask about me, I could understand only some of his words, but I could tell what he meant.

* * * * *

Anita: Yes, I felt it at first. "Such a love as that is not carried by words, and I am fortunate to have that experience." But Doña Feliciana, it pains me to tell you that since then I've seen him look at other women. It makes me feel such shame. He swears no. He is true only to me, but I see that he is too free with his eyes. "My feeling of fellowship goes everywhere," he tells me, "to all men and to all women. All people. It is different than the closeness you and I share." That's his religion; he told me. But how can a woman believe that? "My deepest love is for you alone!" he says. What am I to think? I don't believe he really tries to hurt me. But he seems to make me wait my turn, for only after he sees my bitterness is he tender with me.

Doña Feliciana: "Certainly, Anita," I told her, "he means not to hurt you. How can you stop a man from looking at other women? They are like wolves with their eyes always tuning sideways." You see, I felt somehow that I wanted to protect her emotions. Give her assurance. She was such a child in her innocence. I did not care to justify Garibaldi, even though it might seem that I did. But in these circumstances, he was nothing to me compared to this incorruptible girl.

Anita: All right, Dona Feliciana, but he must not forget that he came to me when he needed someone. His friends he lost in the sea. He was in a strange land where people didn't trust him. Me he chose, and I have shown that I can do more than help his loneliness. You will understand that, if not now, when I tell you more, believe me. Of course, our first days together on the ship were wonderful! I knew nothing like that before. In Laguna when I was little I went in the canoes with other children. We paddled in the rivers and around the sandbars and marshes by the shore of the lagoa. But the men in Laguna never let us go out on the fishing boats, not even the prostitutes, so certainly not a girl like me from a respected family. But when I joined José, I refused to be left behind. I went everywhere with him.

Doña Feliciana: I had not known about the ships. That I could not imagine. A young woman alone on a ship with so many men? "What did your family say about that?" Immediately I felt ashamed. The question simply came blurting out. But she responded without irritation, as always, this remarkable young woman.

Anita: Ah, my family. Yes, you may ask me what became of the respect I had in my own family, in the whole village. Not that I thought about that at the time. Now you will see, I left them for him. Yes. You may well cross yourself, Doña Feliciana. How could anyone think to separate me from my mother, my dear sisters? Leaving my husband, God forgive me, was easy, but the rest of it, May God forgive me!

* * * * *

Anita: No. I knew only love then. Only love for José! The fear came later. I still have it, to say the truth. But at that time, I felt nothing but our passion, each for the other. What my family felt at that time, I knew very well. I had friends who still dared to meet me secretly where the ships were moored, to plead with me to return. Yes, I knew the suffering they felt. I felt it too, but, Doña Feliciana, may God forgive me, I knew also that they must be a little jealous. Destino! You can see that, can't you? I need someone to see it, that even with all the pain it caused others, I had to stay by José's side. So when Colonel Canabarro ordered José to sail out of Laguna and attack the Legalistas ships, to take what they carried, all the men tried to keep me from going along. But Colonel Canabarro and the others, soon enough they learned who I was, what I would do to be with him. So none of the officers, not anyone tried to keep me from going with José.

I lived with him in the ship or in a room we had near the shore. I cut myself off, you see, from the will of others, their advice, their feelings of what is proper.

* * * * *

You have asked me to tell you everything, Doña Feliciana:. Everything, you say. What is this everything? You must let me decide that. And please, Doña Feliciana, ask no more questions. Do not try to force me.

* * * * *

Anita: All right, ask if you must, but I will answer as I choose.

Editor: At his point, Doña Feliciana attached what we may consider a sub-introduction addressed to Father Lorenz before she handed her notes over to him, which, as I indicate earlier, he fortunately kept as part of the record.

Doña Feliciana: It was easy for me to catch Anita' voice because I put down my recollections after each meeting. I have done my best and hope that by what I have written here, Father, we may help this precious person in her travails. I swear to you that what I write down here is the way Anita expressed herself. I have earnestly done the same throughout, but in this part and those that follow, Anita's words, the language of this humble peasant girl, became like a poet's, at least to my ear. How this could happen struck me as a mystery, for suddenly she changed into a person of, what can I call it, eloquent sensitivity.

Editor: Later, at the point where Doña Feliciana's notes end, Fra Lorenzo takes up his conversation with Anita under much the same responsibility. Both of Anita's confidants obviously appreciated the unique value of the manner as well as the substance of her delivery.

I should observe also what the reader has very likely already wondered about, and that is the task of exact translation. Griggs's log and Dwight's translation of Garibaldi's memoirs aside, I have been put to the task of transforming into English the literal meanings and quality of expression of these different persons: Italian and sometimes French from Rossetti, and then Spanish from Doña Feliciana and Fra Lorenzo. Luckily, Doña Feliciana saved me the task of translating what must certainly have been Anita's rough mixture of Spanish and her native Portuguese, although, thanks to the necessity of my earlier research, I can claim a decent command of both.

Now, back to Doña Feliciana's notes.

CHAPTER 19

Anita's First Sea Battle/Griggs about Anita

Anita: Good, Doña Feliciana. I have wanted to tell someone what my life was like before I came to these little rooms in your city. Other things I will try to explain later. For now I will tell what I shared with José. I will go back to the first time I went with him into a battle, our earliest times on board the ships in the ocean outside the Bay of Laguna.

It was hard for me at first in the *Rio Pardo*, when we sneaked out of the channel at night. Three ships under José's command. After us came Lorenzo, the Italian, in the *Seival*. Then came João Griggs, the Norte Americano—you heard me name him—in the *Caçapava*.

All the ships were in a line. The sailors were quiet as stones. I didn't know what to do to help, what ropes to pull. At night I couldn't see what the others did so swiftly. They opened up the big sails and swung them this way and that as we twisted our way toward the open sea. I told José I wanted to help, but he told me just to watch what the crew did.

Beyond the channel the ocean was black but full of white streaks of foam. I heard the sails snapping in the darkness above the deck. Then we were in the open sea. I could see Griggs's *Caçapava* roll and jump from wave to wave, and I heard the sea crash against the side of our ship. When the sun first began to come up, I can never forget what the sea looked like. Whatever danger I faced, I never wanted to leave the picture that was forming, changing with the growing light, and the sound of the sea, like giant broom strokes cleaning away all my painful doubts. And the freedom, with the ship rolling like a wild horse that I had to master! Let me try to tell you the way I saw it on that morning.

The shore was far away, a thin golden line, bright from the rising sun. The clouds over that coast, clean, blinding white, like rolling mountains rising toward heaven. The sky was blue behind them. Like a crystal lighted from inside. Soon we were even farther out from the shore. Then for the first time in my life I could not see any land. Only the ocean. The waves were like rows of hills torn from the sea, rising up and then falling away. When we rushed down between them into the valleys of water, the other ships vanished from our sight until we climbed up to the top of the next wave. Then there they were. Amazing! I didn't care that I was the only woman on the ships. We were all comrades, you see, in this ocean without boundaries, so powerful and so patient to accept us as long as we respected her strength and handled our ship by her demands. I could feel it. A new surrender I made, as all sailors must. What I express to you now is a brotherhood of seafarers.

Doña Feliciana to Fra Lorenzo: You see what I mean, Padre? This was not the quiet Señora Garibaldi I knew before. So don't be surprised at the change in her voice. I am still earnest about my determination for reporting her own words, their feeling, to you. "Yes, this is my voice," she cried! It was as if she read my mind. "Many eyes have seen what mine have; but no one else can tell you what this heart carries."

Anita: We sailed for a few days up the coast, I don't remember how many, our three little ships in a line. José told me we were near Santos. What that meant to me! Before then I never was away from Laguna. Now we were far to the North, near São Paulo. For years I only heard others speak of it.

Suddenly one of our sailors saw an Imperial Brazilian ship of war. I looked where he pointed. She had so many sails. They were piled to the clouds. It looked more important than our little ships. Dangerous. Striding like a giant toward us. But when Giuseppe commanded us, we spread our sails and fled away, back toward the south.

At the end of the next day we lost the Imperialist. Then on the next sunrise we turned back toward the land, the Isla do Abrigo. There we met two sumacas. Small, harmless boats. Fishermen. We took nothing from them and let them go. Some of our sailors shouted insults at them and showed their guns and sabres. I was embarrassed for those men in the sumacas. Simple people, like the fishermen I knew in Laguna. May God forgive me, like my husband Manoel. They were surprised and frightened but José was gentle toward them and kept sailing past them.

Later we met three large trading ships. One was full of rice— good food for our army. That's how I felt about it, our army, you understand? I was beginning to feel like one of the sailor warriors, sharing their boldness and their fate. José put a few of our own men on those captured ships to command them, and we all sailed south for Laguna.

We had a few days of easy sailing. By then I knew how to help sail our ship, to hold the tiller, help with the ropes for the sails. Sometimes I cooked for the crew. In a little galley even smaller than the little kitchen I share with the other wives in this house. Even while I prepared food, I had to stay alert, but I'll never forget those beautiful days and nights.

Editor: On the return leg of that foray out of Laguna, Anita had her first experience in battle. As the rebel ships approached the Isle of Santa Catarina, near their home base, the large warship they had sighted earlier began to overtake them. Griggs's ship had vanished during the night, leaving only two rebel vessels.

Accounts of Griggs's absence from the fighting vary, by the way, but on November 6, 1839, nearly a week later, Garibaldi and Lorenzo returned to Laguna with no prizes. Here is what happened.

When Griggs had lost touch with them, they were heading down the coast with the three prizes under crewmembers from the *Rio Pardo*. Somewhere near Santa Catarina Island the Brazilian *Andorinha* took up the chase and bore down on the rebels. Although she was a boxy brigantine, she showed eighteen guns, which was more firepower than anything the rebels could withstand. So when Garibaldi saw there was no chance to outrun her, he and Lorenzo turned and took her on. They easily outmaneuvered her but had to withdraw their prize crews and abandon the two smaller prizes.

That took some precious time before they broke off the engagement and ran south with the biggest captive still under their control. After the *Andorinha* secured the two smaller vessels, however, she came after them again. So Garibaldi had to abandon the last prize and put in behind a little point of land that forms a sheltered harbor near Imbituba. Hastily, Garibaldi took the only cannon off the *Rio Pardo* and set it up on a high point of the shoreline with Manuel Rodriguez in charge. Then he set up a hasty bulwarks for cover near the inlet and waited. That's all they could do.

Griggs's ship, as it turned out, remained out of sight far off to seaward, having lost contact with Garibaldi and Lorenzo during the night, so the rebels still had only two ships to hold off a powerful enemy.

After they dropped their anchors inside the bay, the crews, to Anita's amazement, took time to prepare supper, after which most of them went to sleep. To her they acted like carefree fishermen after a day's work. Some tried to explain to her that they had plenty of time before the enemy reached them, but she could not relax. José tried to calm her but she kept fretting about what was to come on the next day.

In the morning, not one but all three Imperials together came down the coast toward the bay where the rebels had taken refuge. The fighting lasted the better part of the day, but the Imperials abruptly disengaged and sailed off, after which Garibaldi and Lorenzo returned to Laguna. Both sides suffered a number of dead and wounded. None of the ships was seriously damaged, however. Here is Anita's account of the struggle.

Anita: Most of the crew of the *Seival* had taken positions on shore, up on the barra where José made them carry our only cannon. He called to the men on both ships to be brave. I felt his strength, as I knew the others could. He ordered me to go on shore until the battle was over but I refused. I could not run away and hide in a safe place while he faced danger. It was the first time I showed him my desire to fight. Don't think I was brave, Doña Feliciana. I did it for myself as much as for José. When the fighting first began, believe me, I struggled against my wish to hide, but it was Destino that held me in place.

The noise, Doña Feliciana, that was the worst thing. I could not know before what it would be like. The smoke and the fire were terrible, the splinters flying everywhere. The stink of gun powder puffing into Hell's flames. That stays with you afterward. But the noise is the worst, like it would never stop, crowding out everything. It was like nothing else I heard in my whole life. Somehow underneath the high shrieking and the cannons pounding you can hear smaller noises coming through. I mean the crackling from the carbines and muskets and the creaking of the ropes. And through it all, the men kept screaming. I couldn't tell if it was from their pain or their anger, or sometimes, I swear to you, it sounded like they were laughing, bad spirits taunting each other in that piercing inferno. Terrible what your mind does to you. And sudden little stammers of silence close off all that noise, like your ears have too much to take in.

Donna Feliciana: "You poor girl!" I couldn't help saying it. But something else I cannot help writing here. My suspicion, may God forgive me, that this young woman was, how shall I say, inventing or exaggerating. That's how it came to me. That maybe she was inventing these adventures. It was all too much to take in without such doubting, a person of her background to report so vividly everything, all the fantastic sensations going on around her. Why would she not exaggerate, even make up such stories? Could she not have a motive to create a special reaction, a respect in people's eyes, feelings? That could be a motive, not so?

So I was tempted to doubt her. That is possible, too, you see. I want to be honest about all this, to hope also somehow that I would some day learn that I was wrong. I want to be honest about that, too. Despite my suspicions, maybe because of them, I try to show, forgive me, I'm not sure what. Anyway, even in all the confusion of my feelings, you see, I tried to show sympathy. But she would not have it. Maybe I should rub out all these thoughts, for as soon as I said, "My dear girl!" she continued, "No! Not girl! I'm trying to make you see that!" And right away my doubts vanished. Like magic. Her tone. The honesty of her impatience with me wiped out all my suspicion.

Another thing, forgive me for breaking in here again, Fra Lorenzo, but I also want to explain how I managed to write so rapidly and, I assure you, accurately. The ciphering and records I kept in the emporium where I worked with Sr. Garibaldi. All of that I learned in convent school where my parents sent me. That is how I got the job. I put down everything Anita told me. I was surprised, yes, and I admired her and surprised by her vivid descriptions of her first voyage with Garibaldi. The sights, sounds, taste of saltwater breezes, crystal clean sea air, the odor from sea, from the tar and wood and rope of the ship. Anita told me and I was able to get it down, especially her description of the battle, all the sensations. You may suspect that I made some of it up, just as I suspected her truthfulness, but I wrote it all exactly as she told it to me before any of her words evaporated between us.

Editor: Before we return to Anita's narration, I should point out what we have when Fra Lorenzo refers to Anita's natural gift, in the record he keeps of her extraordinary observations and analyses to him. Therein he suggests his reaction. The following segment illustrating Anita's indomitable spirit had to rout any of Donna Feliciana's and his skepticism.

But first another brief passage from Garibaldi's memoirs: We had resolved to fight to the last; and this resolution was increased by the Brazilian Amazon on board. My wife not only refused to land but took an active part in the engagement. (40)

Anita: I was a comrade with those men, leaping into that battle with them, helping them in any way I could. Looking this way and that for a way to help. Soon I began reloading their emptied carbines for them until finally I aimed one myself at a man, an Imperial sailor on the ship closest to us. It was good to see an enemy, I tell you, one person on the other side. An enemy, a real object that you can strike at in all that chaos. That was the biggest change for me. Don't think me proud to say this, but I knew then who I was. I don't know if I hit him, that man I shot at. Too much smoke, water flying, and the passing ship making us rock up and sideways, like a wild pony. But I kept shooting with the men at my side. Don't you see, Doña Feliciana? Do you understand? Don't look away. Please. Listen, I was ready to die, as long as I could share death with my beloved José and our loyal comrades. That was all.

I don't know what happened next, but suddenly I was trying to stand up. I felt someone tugging me. It was José. Through a mist, I felt him carry me to the space below. Then his face was close to mine to see if I was alive. He was satisfied, for he rushed back up to the main deck. When I was over my dizziness, I looked around and saw some of our mariners, five or six, I can't remember, huddling in a corner. I became like an animal, insane. I spat at them to go back up and fight. Pigfish and jellyfish, frightened girls, I called them, to hide there in safety while the others faced death on the deck. I kicked at them and screamed. "Think! Think what you will feel like after this is over." Until, like shamed mongrels, they followed me, yes, a woman, to do their duty. Together we joined the others and fought off the enemy. I don't know how long it took us. Until the sun was high above us.

From Garibaldi's Memoirs: At length, after several hours spent in active fight, the enemy retired, on account, as was said, of the death of the commander of the *Bella Americana*, one of their vessels. We spent the remainder of the day in burying our dead and in repairing our greatest damages. (41)

Editor: The record shows that, suddenly, inexplicably, the enemy disengaged and sailed away. The rebels, amazed and surely relieved, watched them leave. When they had collected their breath and looked around, they had no idea how many of the Imperials they had killed. After a safe spell of waiting, they took count of their own comrades. Five were dead and many others had serious wounds.

That was Anita's first exposure to the misery that follows battles. But José did not give any of his comrades time to think about their sorrows. Once all the survivors were back aboard their ships, the crews began to clean up the carnage. Some rowed the dead ashore to be buried. Anita and the others helped the wounded with whatever they had at hand. Clean water they saved for the wounded to sip. Some wounds had to be cauterized, and mercifully the sufferers fell unconscious under the searing blades.

Anita: Few complained. Some died, already too weak when the pain tore their souls from their bodies. Poor, brave comrades. I'm sorry to upset you, but you understand, before now I have told no one these things. I don't choose to tell you now, but you said you wanted to know. No, Doña Feliciana, make no mistake. It is a good thing you did, for now, God be praised, all the tiniest memories rush from me and lighten my burden of pain.

Editor: Amazingly, Donna Feliciana was able to recover her composure enough to get the complete account onto paper. Before their next meeting, she filtered through everything Anita had told her, during which process it occurred to her that Anita had omitted any mention of Griggs in her account of the battle, whether he had taken any part in the actual fighting at Imbituba.

Anita: You listen well, Doña Feliciana. No, he was not with us in the battle, it is true. We started with three ships, but Griggs was separated from us in the night. Once we returned to Laguna, we found Griggs's ship already at anchor, totally unaware of our fight with the Imperials. When we rejoined him in Laguna, he knew nothing about our battle. It was not his fault, you see. He tried to find us. Don't mistake it. Griggs was a brave man. He proved it later with the sacrifice of his own life.

CHAPTER 20

Griggs's Absence from the Sea Battle

Editor: At this point we break from Dona Feliciana's report to clarify Griggs's absence from the battle north of Laguna.

Griggs: By mid-October, the Imperial blockade vessel sailed off and Canabarro ordered us to start new raids in the shipping lanes. Garibaldi told me to see to the readiness of the *Rio Pardo*, the *Seival*, and my *Caçapava*. No need to tell him that it was already done. I also laid in fresh provisions of food and arms all around, and the crews turned to distributing stores among the three ships. The prospect of action has brought even the worst of them back to attention.

November 2: Just before we set out, Garibaldi had a row with Anita but it was settled that she would sail with him. Nobody liked it, not Canabarro, not any of us, but there was no putting her off. She's not the most placid woman in the world. We all feared having her with us. It was not going to be easy for Garibaldi once the fighting started. Still, I can see it her way. She's better off splicing her fate to his. What would she do ashore while we're out? And if Garibaldi didn't make it back, where would she turn then? It's different for the rest of us who don't have the same personal stake in this Revolution. Any one of us can shut himself of the whole thing and make for home. But what could that mean to Anita? She could return to her family, beg them to take her, acknowledge her again. But I can not see her in that role of asking forgiveness. Never. So now her home is wherever Garibaldi goes, and if he dies in battle, who can say what she might do to herself? Without him her life is a void—neither port nor portal. A terrifying prospect.

So now, Anita included, we all sailed north on the night of November 3, up the coast to the vicinity of Santos. After passing by some fishing smacks, we took two small coasters and one big merchantman with a cargo of rice. They surrendered right off. The engagement put little strain on us.

But on our return leg we sighted Brazilian warships cruising the area, so Garibaldi ordered me to lower some of my canvas and limp off the seaward flank to draw the Imperial's after me, while he and Lorenzo stayed in closer to shore with their prizes. I hoped not too close. Apparently my show of helplessness didn't work as we'd hoped, for the Imperials ignored me and continued to pursue Garibaldi and Lorenzo. I lost sight of the lot during the night. Come morning, I sailed in closer to the shoreline and looked for them the better part of the day but failed to sight them. So I made my way back here.

Editor: Griggs's account agrees with Anita's, but he goes on to record the subsequent consequences of that battle and tests his observations about Anita against his own relationship to Ruthie.

Griggs: That battle ended in a big forfeiture on our side, nine lives and two prizes lost. I did not see nor hear a bit of it or I would have come in from seaward and threatened the enemy flank. My failure to do so put a heavy weight of guilt on me, I must admit. I said as much to Garibaldi, but he dismissed my apologies, hugely on account of his lost mariners and all. Four killed in the actual fighting, five died of wounds shortly after, and five more badly wounded who survived.

We'll be safe from the larger Imperial blockade in here unless they decide to bombard us from offshore, so all crews are on special alert. I have set regular watches and put most of our sailors to regular maintenance, greasing blocks, replacing frayed lines and reef points on the tattered sails. The shipyard workers stay at their tasks, but keeping the sailors busy is a separate chore when there's a lull in the fighting. There are too many hands for ordinary maintenance on a man-of-war, and slack ways or downright idleness are always creeping into the routine. I would have careened the larger vessels to check their bottom planking, but with the Imperials possibly returning at any time, that operation was best postponed.

I'll say something now about Garibaldi's woman. After her experience in the battle at Imbituba, she took to roaming more freely among the ships. She shows a lively interest in what I've been doing to keep our ships at the ready. Watches everything closely, which surprises me. Not that it bothers me. At her own request I showed her how to do an eye-splice and bend a few knots, which she took too quickly with her strong hands and forearms. She tells me to address her as Anita, simply that, instead of Doña Anna. She told me straight out that she had given up her right to that title, her *titulo de propriedade*, as she put it, a high formality for such a little renegade, but that's the way with her, considering the proper status she forewent by tying up with Garibaldi—*propriedade* indeed!

She surprises me with her frank talk about the fire she feels for Garibaldi, the attachments she had cast off to link up with him. She needs to get it out in the open. That's clearly her reason for staying close to me. I could see that right off. I think it best to let her air it as she needs to. So she seeks me out as a regular comrade now, her *companheiro* and *confidante*. It's something she has a hunger for. I am cautious against appearing to judge her.

She has taken to asking me about my role in this revolution. My being a North American has set her to wondering, as it has most of the other Brazilians. She tells me that Garibaldi thinks I am the most reliable and wisest of his officers and that I am his inspiration. I don't tell her how many others I've heard him address in the same way. Some day she may count them. But that is not what she needs to hear at this point in her life.

Whenever Anita talks about herself and Garibaldi, Ruthie eases into my thoughts, her and the Gonçalves family. I cannot avoid the memories. Back when I first arrived at their estancia, the sisters sent Ruthie to me, although they hinted, with some covered smiles, it was by her suggestion. However it came about, I took much comfort in her company and she in mine. But it didn't stay centered in the heat of passion between us once that began. Ruthie is sweet and bright. Once we put aside our pretending and began to share a bed of nights, she and I talked a lot while awake. She is a wonder at making love! Putting any early resistance on my part far beyond my resolve. But I set a high value on our mutual affection. A sort of calming companionship.

She took such care for my feelings, with her worrying at first that maybe I had a wife and children in Boston. I thought maybe she wanted to know if I was free to marry her but I came to appreciate it as her forthright fretting that I might feel guilty about being disloyal to my family at home. Soon as I understood her, I assured her that I had no such attachment, actually that I had few immediate family at all aside from uncles in trade together with their own families.

Then I did a thing that still feels mean. I told her I still had no plans nor did I feel ready for marriage. Well, at the time that was my honest belief, whereat she silenced me and once more gave her passion freely, her sighs and murmurs softer than any melody I'd ever heard before, always watching for my response, a kind of giving that has me wondering what more I could feel for her. Affection of that sort is always chafing against my intentions to hold off any attachments. Think what you will but I was still fixed to the primary expectation of a favorable trade with the leaders of this Revolution. I never felt backwards about fixing national ideals to the main chance for steady profit in a good business.

It's such ideas as that—honest as they may be—that make me circle back to my cogitations about Garibaldi's treatment of Anita, him being the noble one as his Italian comrades proclaim, a hero who ought to give weight, as we expect, to his concern for others' lives. Well, I must ask myself, who's the better of us, after all? Can I claim to be better than him, using Ruthie the way I do? Whose aims are the more selfish? What leeway have I to doubt his proper intentions for Anita compared to mine for Ruthie?

I jot that note down just to show that I'm not entirely dim. These are my own ruminations. I write them down here but I don't air them freely with others around here. I will allow no one to get close enough for such confidences. And there you have it.

CHAPTER 21

Anita about Griggs

Editor: I return now to Anita's memoirs, whereby we can compare her evaluation of Griggs's with his own. Doña Feliciana, by reintroducing Griggs as a topic, prompted these ruminations in Anita.

Anita: Of course. He was one of José's and my most valued comrades. His sailors respected him, even feared him, but with me, he was always calm, *tranquillo*, as you may call it. He died a hero, you know. After his last battle I didn't even see his body, a great pity to me, for I would have served his memory a proper honor. As it turned out, his ship became his funeral pyre. That was José's tribute.

* * * *

I think you are right, Doña Feliciana. I have been close to some true heroes, even though I am sorry to say that they have not always brought happiness into my life.

He was different from José, this Griggs. He used no words more than he needed. But he always understood what to do. No shirt cuffs stayed stainless. Griggs knew how to work on humble tasks. He was the best skilled to fix our ships. Very clever in that. He worked fast, finished everything quickly. About that and other things, he never gave us his thoughts, but I believe he never felt passion for the Revolution like José.

Oh, yes, and to his Braziliera companion, Ruthie. She was a nice young woman from the Gonçalves household. Part Indio. I could tell from her color, her hair and eyes. She was very mild. She cared much for Griggs. Maybe she was the reason he was so polite to me. I think he would present her if she stayed with him longer but he never spoke of her to me. I believe because he did not wish to embarrass me—or her, or himself. I never asked.

You would believe he felt no passion for anything, so serene, so *simpatico*, until you think of his Ruthie. He kept his life with her private, protected. I never forced myself into that, never asked any questions, even though I believe she could make a good friend and companion. But you know, she was not there all the time. She came and went as Griggs bid her. That was part of his protection. I heard from others the same thing. She was not a secret companion but private.

Anyway, soon after I joined José in Laguna, I learned that Griggs was the only person I could talk to like a friend. I didn't trust the Riograndenses and especially not the Catarinenses. Most of them were polite because I was with José, but they knew about my past. Many were rough, very cruel with their looks and their mumbling when he was not near me.

Doña Feliciana: Anita could see that I was somewhat embarrassed by what she said about herself, but she told me simply, "Well, as you know, I left my family." With apologies I feared right away that I had interrupted her confidence because she protested, so I urged her to try to understand. I wished to respect our agreement not to ask many questions, but I was restless about what she said about her family not wanting to see her when she went with Garibaldi. To cut her off so completely, and she responded forthrightly.

Anita: Maybe the fault was mine. But I felt proud. Some might say too much pride. Stubborn, you could say. So even if they wanted to talk to me, I could not let them think I was the one who needed it. I know that my best friends in Laguna wanted to see me but maybe they didn't want to shame their families by coming to me. For myself, I no longer cared. It is true. Other kinds of women came there to mingle with the mariners but not respectable women. Not for me to befriend.

Another thing, even though I felt equal to the other officers' families, I never mixed with any of them. Besides, not many came to stay in Laguna. If they did, they wouldn't speak to me, anyway, I know it, even though José said he was sure they would, even the family of General Gonçalves, who José said were the most gracious and democratic people he ever knew. Yes, they were that way to him, but no, I don't think they would talk with me. Anyway, they lived far in the south of Rio Grande do Sul, so it didn't matter.

* * * * *

Griggs was the only one I cared about. When I found him doing some work, I talked with him in a way that could not bother him. I knew he blamed me for nothing. And I knew I could trust him to tell no one what we spoke of. Giuseppe told me Griggs was wild. When he was angry, he said, the curses rushed from his mouth like Satan's oaths. But when I was near him, I heard nothing like that. To me he was respectful, always serious. Most of the time he seemed to have deep thoughts about something: Maybe sad thoughts about being far from his homeland. But he could laugh at crazy things that happened, sometimes even when his helpers made serious mistakes he would only puff out his cheeks, like this, and then smile. That way, his workers were not embarrassed--unless they were drunk or disrespectful to me.

I talked to Griggs about other things, of course. He was some-one who listened to my thoughts, not like José, who talked always about his own thoughts. It is my duty to listen to José. But Griggs did not need anyone in that way. That's why I liked him, to have him listen. José angered me, mostly when I saw him looking at other women, even the prostitutes who came to the ships. He called to them, jokingly. They laughed with him. But not when they saw me!

After all that I gave up for him, to show so little sympathy! When I scolded him he would say, "No, Aninha, it is nothing. I like to make jokes with everyone, to be cheerful. I cannot change what I am. "Such foolish ideas he had—respect for all people. Pleasantness. When he talks like that he seems like a stupid man, blind to my feelings, my sacrifices. Then to tell me he respects those women who love for money! I don't wish to embarrass you, Feliciana, with my frankness. After all, we are not children, you and I.

Well, to tell the truth, I talked about such things to João Griggs. He listened, always to everything I said and didn't stop me. But about José he would say, "Ah, Senhora Anita, Captain Garibaldi likes to joke with everyone except the enemy."

One time I asked him if I can trust Giuseppe, you know, to be faithful. He said, "Yes, in my mind I believe that you can trust him." I know he believes what he told me, but even today some times I burn with anger and jealousy. I know they are terrible sins, but who am I, after all, to resist them? One time, when I was a girl, long before I met José, I told that to our priest about how I was guilty of those terrible sins. He only said that I must try to avoid them and to follow what God tells us through the Church. Well, all right, I know what that means, but it is hard for me to keep my thoughts away from jealousy. When the cause is right in front of my face: Who is guilty?

CHAPTER 22

The Editor's Thoughts about the Comrades/Griggs Learns about Anita's Bravery

Editor: At this point in my arrangement of these documents, I began to wonder about the essential nature of my task. That is, I acknowledge admiration for biographers, the complexities, ambiguities, even contradictions of the problems they faced in presenting their subjects' motives. People who are at all worth writing about, I learned, are laden with inconsistencies, much like the characters that any worthwhile novelist might design. That was an unsettling discovery for me, my responsibility to all four of the persons who had drawn me into their lives.

Garibaldi, although I include few of his own words, remains the focus of what all the others think.

Rossetti's ambivalent struggle to maintain his equanimity in the face of Garibaldi's neglect, and his barely hidden resentment of Anita were evident.

Anita, although indisputably volatile, her honesty, forthrightness, the inherent logic of her analyses. We can measure the stages of her development as she discloses more of her feelings about Garibaldi.

And Griggs, as sensitive as he was to Anita's plight, keeping his own counsel about his relationship with Ruthie, and his ambivalence about Garibaldi and the revolution.

I come back to the substance of this intrusion in my concluding remarks.

Now back to the primary sources, this one from Griggs's log, which begins with Colonel Canabarro's commission to punish the counter-revolutionaries at Imarui during the annexation of Santa Catarina, obviously a distasteful task to Garibaldi.

Griggs: Garibaldi is off to Imarui, a small village bordering on the upper lagoon. Colonel Canabaro sent him up there with a troop of mariners to punish those townspeople for turning coat on their alliance with the Riograndeses. As I saw it, their joining the revolution was never all that secure. Given the fierce independence of these people, they must have resented giving up their sovereignty to satisfy the Riograndense revolt. Maybe they already heard that the Imperials would be sending a large army and a good part of their fleet down here to shake us loose from Santa Catarina.

Anyway, Garibaldi unequivocally commanded Anita not to accompany him. A good thing, too. So this is a good enough place to repeat some reports I'd heard about her part in the other battle back at Imbituba where the Imperial ships chased Garibaldi and Lorenzo. That's where I was separated from them. When I asked Anita right out about her part in the fighting, she would only say that she fought alongside Garibaldi because there was no other place for her to go and no place else she wanted to be. But later I heard the full story from the crew of the *Rio Pardo*, how during the hottest fighting Anita was on deck loading carbines for the men and then firing some herself.

At one point Garibaldi ordered her below deck. She obeyed him, but the men I talked with said when she got down there she rousted out some cowards who were huddling in the ship's hold. She changed those slackers into a pack of battlers, shamed them with her curses, until they went back up on deck and stood fighting alongside her. Then a shot from one of the Imperial's cannons exploded right next to where she was standing. Miraculously the explosion killed a crew member on either side of her but merely knocked Anita against the bulkhead. The other sailors said they were astonished to see her get up and go on fighting. That's the picture left printed in their minds, and that's what convinced me she's the right and only mate for Garibaldi. No question. Anyone would have to admit also that she shares his uncommon good fortune.

CHAPTER 23

Griggs's Temptation to Abandon the Revolution/His Thoughts about Anita and Ruthie/Final Entry in Griggs's Log

Now I must own up here something about my thoughts when I was far off shore and Garibaldi and Lorenzo were battling for their lives. I took to reflecting on that carefree cruising I enjoyed back in my days as mate of the *Toucan*, running in easy, southern waters and earning a steady profit. Now here I was, separated from Garibaldi, thinking he was on a trouble free course back to Laguna with his prizes. Out there all by myself I dreamed about just bringing the prow of the *Caçapava* about and sailing right on up the coast, all the way back to Boston. I knew my crew would be happy to go along with the change of course. But along came conscience telling me that such an escape, inviting though it might be in itself, would mean veering off from the pride and duty I was raised to respect. I knew that even if nobody else ever heard about it, I would never be able to get past the guilt of desertion.

Besides which, truth be told, the *Caçapava* was a mite too small for the entire journey—that and other practical considerations. I wasn't afraid the crew wouldn't be up to handling her in a bad blow. So, even with some problems, we could have made it all the way—but, not without putting in at ports along the way to take on water and provisions. Then there's the question of paying for provisions without a cash cago, which would be trouble for us to take on with questionable registration papers. I must admit to all those problems a-weaving through my calculations, as they must for any practical sailor. But still topping all those was that nagging question of loyalty.

That last thought hit me with extra force when I learned afterward about Anita on board Garibaldi's ship with all those carbines and cannons firing off rounds about her head. What would she have thought of my cutting and running? (And while I'm at the task of setting down all these reasons, what rasped at my conscience as much as anything else came from putting Ruthie in Anita's place. What would she think? If she ever linked herself to some other man afterward, what would she tell her children about me?

There are more twists in this life than supposing brings about, where thoughts harden and take on the feel of reality with little enough comfort in them. So, with all that uncertainly, I kept my helm on course to join up with my rebel comrades in Laguna.

Editor: More restless thoughts about Ruthie and Anita lay ahead for Griggs. Although quiet times had set in at Laguna, tension was in the air. No one talked about it but everyone had heard the rumor that the Imperials would soon descend in full force on the rebels. Locking his thoughts away, Griggs fell to his regular duties. He moved about examining item after item but saying little to the crews. Ironically, had he sailed the *Caçapava* back to Boston, as he had fantasized, he would have avoided death in the imminent Imperial onslaught on Laguna.

Griggs: November 12, 1839. I don't trust the mood. I am getting my small arms and ship's cannons greased. Hope I can count on our crews to stand to their posts when the Brazilians come at us, which will surely happen. By damn, I wish they were all like Anita. She is a firm one. Her quick thinking and good sense have come through handsomely in the short time she has joined her destiny to Garibaldi's, poor girl. Or maybe not so poor, she being one of the few hereabouts with an iron bound commitment, if not to the revolution, then to him.

Today, when we were at ease, she talked to me for the first time about her girlhood, which does not go that far back in years, for she is still only 18. Down here, the sturdy peasant stock matures early.

Her family members are shut of her, officially, that is, and all but a few friends avoid her. They have to because she has as good as foresworn her marriage vows, which is the same as standing against her faith. If I understand the talk going around, her mother sneaks a word to her now and then. Sad business, but Anita has made her break openly. No pretending with her.

She worried plenty about Garibaldi's commitment to her and talked to me about it. I knew what she needed to hear so I told her that she can count on him. No sense in telling her otherwise. And frankly I have no reason to question his loyalty. She has too much at stake here, so I put it to her straight out that I have seen Garibaldi acting the gallant around women all the time I have known him, which is not that long, but none with the devotion he shows her. I also told her what I think his plans are for One Italy Free and Sovereign. When this war is over, she has to be ready to cross the ocean with him. I can't see her letting him go on without her.

I reminded her of what she once told me, that Garibaldi called me his most valued comrade. Well, I wanted her to know that I have heard him say that to a number of others. That is his way. I wanted her to know finally that at the moment when he says it to any of us he means it. Whenever he's close in with one of his comrades, he says it in the same confirming manner. But I told her as firmly as I could that there are only two things I have never heard him swerve from. One is a Free United Italy, and the other is her. I know it was what she hoped I would tell her and I am happy I could. She is a brave soul with strength that will have to carry her through some lonely times, I venture to predict. I am sure she feels remorse about her break with her own family but she will never betray her trust again. I stake my life on it.

She tells me now and then as best she can about Garibaldi's ideas, his *filosofia*, as she calls it. Pretty much the same he's lectured me about from that book he carries everywhere. A lot about unbridled companionship, as he calls it, but which seems to me to translate into free love. That's also what she's picked up on, which sets the rest of it to souring her spirits. She is not about to share Garibaldi's love with others, especially women. No met-today tavern maid, this Anita. So Garibaldi had best look to his behavior, especially his breezing among the women hereabouts. She has asked me again—not for the last time, I reckon—if I believe Garibaldi will remain loyal to her. If she'd seen him carrying on back in the early days when I first met him, making eyes at all the women of that Gonçalves clan, she would not be encouraged.

In a way, she is trapped by her own strength--something about these peasant women, something in the blood. But Anita gave up her own sworn husband and her family for Garibaldi. Maybe she'd been watching for the main chance to dig herself out of that dull life for something better, more passion and surely more adventure.

Anita and Ruthie. Their feelings. As I've already put it to words, it's not the sort of topic I figured to include in this log, but I'm trying to parse this business out. Anyway, there's no turning back now for Anita or for me and I would guess not for Ruthie, if she has her way. Something special burns inside each of them. A man looks for a woman who'll hold to him fiercely no matter what trouble he finds himself in. I'm thinking Ruthie would hold to me no matter what comes, who will never give me up, once I say so.

I wonder sometimes if Anita believes she has a choice, the will to resist attaching her fortunes to Garibaldi's. I think not, but in her way of seeing things, she allows Garibaldi no choice, either. She's locked him into place like an eye splice to a ringbolt.

That's my calculating the difference betwixt her and my Ruthie, who's soft in soul, sweet in temper, and yielding in her willingness to let me decide about us, like a slip knot that holds firmly but is easy to undo.

I'm not sure which of the two types brings more comfort, the one who waits on your will, giving up her own, or the one who presses your will into hers forever. No man can have both, like different wives, one dutifully awaiting you at home port and the other who accompanies you on board your vessel, even if it sails through perdition. Should I count myself better off for having one like Ruthie or should I welcome the strain of Anita's iron will? Garibaldi seems unaware of Anita's way of reckoning. Well, if he forgets, she'll remind him.

But I need be honest about comparisons. If I calculate things right, I have to admit that Garibaldi is more committed to Anita than I am to Ruthie, for I am still not sure of how she may fit into my plans over the long haul.

Editor: Fortunately or not, Griggs's quandary about Ruthie remained unresolved, for he was compelled to take up more pressing concerns, which share space in the next final entries in his personal log.

Griggs: November 13, 1839. I've just read back over what I put down yesterday. I don't know if I can keep up that sort of cogitation. Too much strain trying to get it right.

It's a good time to turn to some action, tasks outside myself. And there's no lack of them. Truth to tell, with the Imperial campaign to retake Santa Catarina heating up, I come back to my notion about weighing anchor and setting a course for home. It's the same reverie that came to me when I lost sight of Garibaldi, Anita and Lorenzo off Imbituba. But duty still has its grip on me.

So I am going to leave it the way that makes me feel best right now. I can still take some comfort in the notion that when this rebellion is settled, one way or the other, and I'm free to turn my prow homeward, I will take Ruthie with me. That much is settled now, for there's no sense in playing loose with a girl who is mine completely. There it is. I've put that in place for good. I'll go back soon and cross out the awkward passages in this log that would turn her face red as well as mine.

So, back to the tasks at hand.

Editor: A few days earlier, Colonel Canabarro received word from agents in the North that a big army—cavalry, artillery, infantry—was moving south from Rio. A fleet of Imperial warships also. Griggs believed that he and Garibaldi could keep enemy vessels from sailing into the bay, but they feared that the Imperials could still bombard them from offshore and then force their way in, especially if they coordinate with their army. And once that force moved in by land, the tiny rebel navy would not count for much.

Griggs: Confirmation is at hand. The enemy is in our neighborhood, on land and off shore. In any honest measure, we can't hope to hold them off for long. So over all, it sounds to me like a good time for our people—land and seafarers alike—to pull out and move south.

Which is just what Canabarro has told us to get ready for. Our main vessels are prepared, but we should not wait too long, unless the General commands us to abandon our entire fleet and join his land troops. That, I believe, would be a mighty waste of all our work. Still, even if we could make it to the open sea, I don't know where we'd sail to, for there's no decent port between here and the mouth of the Lagoa dos Patos. We aren't welcome here and we sure as thunder won't be welcome there. I know of a few bays to the North and South of here that we might slip into. But that would do us little good for long. It's a tight spot we're in.

Despite that, the arguments on strategy keep swinging back and forth, mostly between Garibaldi and Canabarro while the rest of us stand by and count the precious minutes away.

From Garibaldi's Memoirs: I had already sent information to the General that the enemy were preparing to force the passage of the bar, having been able to discover the enemy's vessels while I was effecting the transport. Having reached the other side, I satisfied myself of the fact. The enemy had twenty-two vessels, all adapted to the entrance. I then repeated the message; but either the General was doubtful, or his men wanted to eat or to rest. I asked Canabarro for men to continue the battle; but received, in answer, an order to destroy the vessels and retire, with all the remainder that could be landed. (42)

Griggs: Garibaldi is for keeping our fleet in tact and staying on here to fight the Imperials. I hope he does not keep Canabarro arguing over it too long. He must learn to put his idea in and then yield to those who best know the over-all strategy. If we are to load up and get our fleet safely away, we must weigh anchors soon. If Garibaldi holds us up with his stubborn arguing much longer, I'll have to put in my druthers.

Editor: Griggs's personal log ends there. His life ends soon after, leaving only Rossetti and Anita to Garibaldi.

CHAPTER 24

Rossetti's Account of Griggs's Death/Retreat from Santa Catarina

Editor: We will read a more detailed account of Griggs's death in Anita's memoirs, including the verbal skirmishes between Canabarro and Garibaldi that may have stranded Griggs and his crew at anchor. Cause and effect remain ambiguous. It is possible that Garibaldi kept his disagreement with Canabarro going too long, thereby giving the Imperials time to disrupt an orderly withdrawal of the small rebel fleet that Griggs had thought to preserve. To that extent, the American's apprehensions were borne out. Not only did Imperial war ships gain time to station a blockade to prevent the rebels' safe departure, but they sent several shallow-drafted vessels through the channel to blast the ill-prepared rebels, both those tied to the shore and those still at anchor, thereby killing Griggs's who, with his crew, was still aboard the *Caçapava*.

But first, we return to the section of Rossetti's journal, in which he also reports the fatal battle that Griggs had apprehended, as well as the Riograndenses' retreat from Santa Catarina.

Rossetti, Villa Settembrina, Capital City to the New Republic, June, 184: Now with this respite between campaigns, I take time to record my life during the War for Independence from Imperial Brazil.

The significance of my life lies solely in the shadow of those true heroes who have made greater sacrifices than I could possibly conceive, some of them, now sadly drained of their precious life's blood. My beloved fellows in Young Italy: Mutru, Carniglia, Stadirini, and to those let me add the American John Griggs. May the Great Architect of the Universe give them tranquility in the Shining Edifice in which they have so clearly earned their places! Thanks be to the Grand Maker that my Valued Friend, Hero of Heroes, Giuseppe Garibaldi, is destined, soon I pray, to be the Hero of All Italy, our Homeland, which we will restore according to Her Historical Vitality and Dignity, to the Glory she once held Above All Other Nations on the Earth. Giuseppe, whose Heroism, born abruptly into our Movement, as if by a miracle, has become, in this remote region, our Man of the Field, our Leader of the Soul's Own Command!

Because Giuseppe's career plays so large a part in this venture, permit me to point out that—as I do not deny that my own feet are composed of clay—no hero, including Giuseppe Garibaldi, is free of the flaws that mark us all as mortals. If I were to hide evidence to the contrary, then my trusted readers would be fully justified in rejecting outright the words that follow.

I have returned to my duties as editor of O 'Povo. Our troops hold Porto Alegre in siege, for it is still held by the Imperialists as their Capital City of Rio Grande Do Sul. The men I trained so well are still the real operators of the press. Neiton and Paolo. Let no one say that the Blacks, even those born in benighted lands, cannot learn the mechanical skills necessary to operate the complicated machinery. I am proud of my accomplishment of training these people, and I still bathe in their gratitude. If the truth be known, after I organized the transfer from Caçapava and oversaw the re-setting of the printing press here in our Northern Headquarters, all they need from me are my hand-written dispatches. With those in hand, Neiton sets the type and together with Paolo runs the press. I am more than ever free to serve in whatever other way the Revolution needs. Bravo!

Sad to say, the Province of Santa Catarina is no longer ours. For the second time we were forced to retreat from there. No longer am I administrator. The capitulators in Desterro and in Lages, our former comrades among the landowners, rejoined the Imperialists as soon as they heard General Andrea was moving toward us from the North. Cowards! Shivering at the thought of his approach.

In truth, his massive army was too much for us to engage. But I still have faith that victory will come to us finally and that my duties will expand once more. I have made notes for my next issue of O'Povo, praising our carefully organized retreat from Laguna, even though we were pestered with ambushes all the way down the beach from Tubarão to Torres.

Still, we have showed them our front sides, when we turned and faced them. We had our great victories in Vacaria, and at Taquari, at Santa Vitoria, and again at Lages before we were forced to retreat from Santa Catarina. (43)

Our failure against the Fortresses far south at the opening of the Lagoa dos Patos, was costly. But the populace, the real people of Rio Grande do Sul who live away from the fortifications, I know that they appreciate the value of a Free Republic! So, in that spirit, that faith in comraderie, we will prevail again as soon as our gallant vaqueiros have regained their resolve to reunite as a single, formidable army. Then we will march again, north and south and speed those glorious words again—Liberty! Humanity!—to all of this vast country.

Editor: Rossetti obviously intended segments of the preceding anthem for a general introduction to his memoirs, a job of editing he never had the opportunity to complete. Indeed, several such flashes of rhapsodic verbiage appear throughout his document. After the above, only two more segments of Rossetti's memoirs remain. In the first he expands on the final campaign in which he participated, to the southern tip of the Lagoa dos Patos. For the sake of comparison, I place his report on that campaign before Anita's account to Doña Feliciana, which appears eighteen pages below. In Rossetti's second—and last—we have the entry in which he prepares to transport his printing machinery along the treacherous route of the rebels' final retreat, an ill-fated project interrupted by the guerilla attack in which he dies.

For now, however, we return to Anita's recollection of the circumstances of Griggs death, in her view the death of a true hero, although Griggs would not likely agree with her assessment.

CHAPTER 25

Anita about Griggs's Death/
The Retreat from Laguna

Anita: Griggs was the only one like that I ever met. He had a warm heart, *muito simpatico*, but now he is gone. May his soul be at rest. After the battle when he died, it was the first time I felt real despair.

* * * * *

Yes, his was a heroic death. In Laguna when we were finally trapped by the advancing Imperialists on land and from the sea, he did not abandon his ship.

I survived, yes, and José, too, but too many died. And the ships were lost to us. There was terrible confusion, you see. I tell you how it was.

José hurried back from his expedition to punish the people in Imaruí. I think those people got word that the huge Imperialist army was coming to attack us, and they wanted to be on the winner's side. To tell the truth, I knew how they felt. What was the revolution to them? Whatever army was victorious, they took everything from the peasants, anyway, to feed and satisfy themselves. That is how it always will be. Liberty, revolution! The poor people care nothing for such ideas. They only want to protect their families, keep their children alive.

So as for me what did it mean, that struggle for a Republic's freedom? José was my freedom, carrying me farther and farther away from my other life. Now who knows what is ahead for our own little family?

Doña Feliciana, I know that you will help us here in Montevideo. But after Montevideo, then what? Maybe those who have died before us are the lucky ones. Like poor Griggs with his quick, strong hands and his quiet eyes. Telling you how he died re-opens a wound, Doña Feliciana.

Soon after Garibaldi came back from Imariú, General Canabarro came down to organize our retreat from Laguna. The Imperialist army truly was moving swiftly into Santa Catarina from the north. We worked hard to get the soldiers and horses to move to a safe place, even though Garibaldi hesitated. He was sure we could fight back the Imperialistas, you see.

So while we were all busy gathering whatever supplies we could reach, José climbed to the top of the barra and came running back. All at once, he told me, like a bad dream, like a surprise storm, the Imperialist ships were close to the channel. José sent a soldier to bring some of Canabarro's troops back so they could fire on the enemy and do large damage to them, but Canabarro sent back only one firm order: bring all of the equipment you can collect from the ships to the shore and set the ships on fire. His order left no choice.

By the time the messenger returned from Canabarro, the Imperialists were already approaching the channel. I was busy unloading the boats when one of the sailors on our ship fired his carbine. When I looked up, I saw the first Imperial boat inside the channel. I could not believe it. We expected only large ships that could not cross the sand bar and would remain outside. But they released several gun-boats, like our sumacas—too many for me to count—and they were full of soldiers with muskets and carbines, and moving fast with oars and sails before a good wind.

Our mariners who were still on our other ships out at anchor were calling for us to come out to help. I had little time to worry about that because the first Imperials were already aiming at us. The small cannon on José's ship was not yet unfastened and lifted ashore, even though our ship was tied to the dock, so I pushed it around and called for help to load it. As soon as it was ready I aimed at the first enemy boat, low, the way José taught me, and fired. I could not tell from the smoke and flying water if I hit it. Maybe. But others came on, one after another. Their shooting was so thick that we had to crouch down behind the bulwarks. One of our men crawled over to help me with the cannon; then another joined us. I let them load and fire the cannon while I took up a musket.

When all the enemy ships were crowded inside the lagoon, I still couldn't tell how many. I could see it was the end. We could do nothing but shoot back at them with our few small guns. But not for long.

From Garibaldi's Memoirs: I had sent Anna with the message, directing her to remain on shore; but she returned on board with the answer, showing a coolness and courage which excited my astonishment and highest admiration. To her boldness and exertions

was due the saving of the ammunition, which was safely landed.
(44)

Anita: I could not see José. Then suddenly, like a spirit, he was
with me on the ship with some other mariners. The enemy was
shooting in bursts like thunder. José had to scream to make me
hear. "Go ashore. Run behind the wall to the camp where Canabarro has his troops. Bring instructions." I knew he wanted to get
me away from the battle, so I clung to him. But he shouted, "Aninha, you must go. If I send another, maybe he will not come back.
You go. Now! Bring some more warriors if you can!"   So I
crawled over the side onto the pier. Before I left, I could see only
one man still alive at our cannon and thick smoke coming from our
other ships still out at anchor.

I jumped across the dock to the other side of the stone wall and
ran with my head low, to the other side of the hill. There I saw Canabarro sitting on his huge horse, like a calm mountain. He told me
that he would send a man to tell José to hurry and take everything
valuable from the ships. I shouted to him that I would go, that the
men were dying there with no one to help them. But he was firm.
"They must leave now and burn the ships behind them." He sent a
soldier. "I need you here, Senhora ," he told me, but I freed myself
and ran back to the ships.

When I reached the beach again, I saw in the little time I was
gone how much damage the Imperialistas made. Only one mast
stood up from any of our six ships tossing and swinging on their
anchor cables. My first thought, I was afraid that I would not find
José alive. Some of the mariners huddled behind the wall on shore
and I roused enough of them to help row three boats out to save the
mariners still at anchor, but when we got out to Griggs's ship, José
was there. He wouldn't let me come on board. He had to be the last
one from the ships, he told me. I could see his strain so I didn't argue. Later I understood that he did not want me to see what was
left of Griggs. Still, the enemy kept firing like they wanted to destroy every piece. After we made it somehow miraculously back to
the shore we stacked everything we could carry on the other side of
the stone wall and waited for José.

From Garibaldi's Memoirs: Captain Enrique, of the *Taparica*,
from Laguna, was found shot through the breast with a grape shot;
Griggs, commander of the *Casapava*, had been cut in two by a
shot, and his trunk was standing against the bulwarks, his face re-
taining its natural rubicund look, so that he seemed as if living. A

few moments afterwards their bodies were sunk in the water: those victims of the empire were lost to human sight. (45)

Anita: I don't know how long it took but finally he came back with a few mariners. No Griggs, no Enrique. Once more José went back alone, and soon I saw the flames rise from Griggs's *Caçapava*. José climbed onto the pier alone. Then I knew that Griggs was dead. When the same happened to the *Itaparica*, I knew that Enrique too was gone, that their ships were their funeral pyres. That is how José told me afterward, and my breath came like a knife in my throat. When José climbed onto the beach he was pale. I asked him nothing. In silence we helped carry the guns and ammunition to join the retreat. That is the way we left Laguna, left Griggs, my dear companion, behind forever.

Yes, gone, our Griggs. José used to say that his was the greatest heroism, to die fighting for another's homeland. Both of us gave up our homes, as you say, for a cause that would profit us nothing. The brave and quiet Norte Americano, who did so much to keep our little navy afloat and ready to fight. No cross will mark his place. Nor mine either when my end comes. No, Doña Feliciana. I know it well enough.

Back then I had little time to think about my fate. The retreat south from Laguna along the beach was sad for all of us. We could not forget the evil day that took the lives of so many comrades. José tried to cheer us up. War does not leave much time for grief, he told us. But I knew that we must take some time to mourn even a little. Most of our comrades were hard men who could brush away the sting of a soldier's death like a mosquito on their skin. Women, I think, carry the grief longer.

From Garibaldi's Memoirs: Among the many sufferings of my stormy life, I have not been without happy moments; and among them, I count that in which, at the head of the few men remaining to me after numerous conflicts, and who had gained the character of bravery, I first mounted, and commenced my march, with my wife at my side, in a career which had always attractions for me, even greater than that of the sea. It seemed to me of little importance that my entire property was that which I carried, and that I was in the service of a poor republic, unable to pay anybody. I had a sabre and a carbine, which I carried on the front of my saddle. My wife was my treasure, and no less fervent in the cause of the people than myself; and she looked upon battles as an amusement, and the inconveniences of life in the field as a pastime. (46)

Doña Feliciana: I had no choice but to join in her thought. But what she had gone through! I could not force her to tell me everything, so I asked her to stop for now. She agreed but insisted that she was glad to tell me, for my sake, too. "It's my only way to keep it all because I can't write anything to leave for others to read." She confessed that, as if she of all people needed to apologize. Without telling her at the time that I was already saving everything she told me, I assured her that we would do it together. "Let us see what happens," she answered.

I could not go back to her house for several days. I had to wait, to recover my spirit before I could hear more of her experiences, but I also felt that I wished not to insult my dear, new friend. So, after those few days of taking care of my own affairs, I called on her again.

The dear girl responded as if I had not been absent at all. So strange how vital I felt to be with her again, even after a short absence, for in a way, Doña Anita's trials had become the center of my own life. So I picked up where she had left off when we last spoke, about the retreat from Laguna. She recited simply and directly their long and arduous journey filled with danger at almost every turn, leaving nothing out, as far as I could tell, not even the most routine details.

Anita: Two weeks we marched south from Laguna before we reached the border of Rio Grande do Sul. But even there we had little time to rest and little time to think about going farther from my family and friends. My breast felt empty, like someone had torn my heart from my chest. But soon we learned about a new Imperialist attack against our inland stations in the high country to the West. General Canabarro told José that his mariners were now soldiers. He saw José's disappointment and assured him that soon enough we would need a navy again.

CHAPTER 26

Battles along the Retreat from Laguna/Anita Becomes Pregnant

From Garibaldi's Memoirs: We reached Torres, the boundary of the two neighboring provinces, where we established our camp. The enemy contented themselves with being masters of the Lagoon, and did not proceed beyond. But, in combination with the division of Andrea, the division of Acunha advanced by the Serra....The Serrans, overwhelmed by a superior force, asked assistance of General Canabarro; and he arranged an expedition for their aid, under the command of General Terceira. I, with my companions, formed a part of it and, having joined the Serrans . . . , we completely beat that division at Victoria. (47)

Anita: So the General attached us to the Army of General Terceira. No one said so, but I included myself among those soldiers.

We brought our guns and ammunition together with whatever food we could gather, and we followed the river—I think it was called the Caminas—up from the beach to Praia Grande. But we could not stop there either for more than a short rest. So right away we mounted the steep trails toward Vacaria far up into the forest, through many steep ravines and twisting trails. I had never been in such a high country before. A tiring climb and with all our equipment, but very exciting for me, I must tell you. A new and strange country. That was early in December [1839] and already hot. José tried to make us feel excitement about the battle ahead.

When we reached the plains above the coast near to Vacaria, we were met by more messengers to tell us that the battle was even further north at Santa Vitória on the Rio Pelotas. It was in the middle of December when we reached Santa Vitória. I thought about Griggs. Not one month passed since he died, his burnt bones scattered in the waters at Laguna. But I had little time to pray for his soul, even if God would listen to me now.

When we were in the District of Vacaria, General Terceira sent José in command of a troop to attack the enemy from the side.

You see, Doña Feliciana, there was no time for resting, but José was always ready to fight without it. I would have joined in with him, right away, but the general ordered me firmly to stay away from the battle. Never mind, I thought, I will keep my horse. And so I helped the wounded comrades when others brought them back to our camp. Our army captured more than two dozen enemy soldiers, and they all pledged to join our army. But we knew they would stay loyal only until the next battle.

On that night of victory José was proud. The next day we would chase the Imperialists back north, he told me, "We will take back Santa Catarina and you will be home again, Anita, in your own free country!" On that night of glory we formed our first child. I know it! Our night of love lasted until near dawn. But I was not weary. Pardon me, Doña Feliciana, if I embarrass you. That passion! I'm not ashamed to tell you about it.

* * * * *

Ah, may God help me for making you think that I no longer loved him. My love for him can never die, even now in the times when it seems like a curse. You have found something in what I say, for sometimes I fear that I love him more than he loves me. But that goes away when we are alone together, when the rest of the world is shut out. José is a kind man—only different when he is in battle. But when he is back with us, he asks nothing for himself. Truly everything is for the baby and me, and his sympathy is for all innocent people. So if I say that sometimes he doesn't show me that he loves me, I know as well that he has never shown me anger or even coldness.

But let me go on. The next battle came soon after Vacaria. It was at Forquilhas, further to the north, near where the Rios Canoas and Marombas meet. I know these places mean nothing to you, Doña Feliciana, but they are important in my memory, and I must pull them out to test myself, you see.

Doña Feliciana: I could find nothing to reply except to praise her power of recollection, which I truly meant not only as a compliment. So I had to show her that nothing she told me could leave my memory, either. She told me once about an accident with her horse, and I asked if that was where she fell.

Anita: That wasn't important, except it separated me from José. But I found him soon afterward.

Editor: In her conversation with Fra Lorenzo, we learn why Anita was reticent to say more about that incident and the terrifying spiritual struggles that followed it.

Doña Feliciana: She pushed that question aside, but I understood that other, more serious troubles fell upon her, troubles that she wished not to tell at that moment. "You pass such things so easily, Doña Anita," I complained. "You see, those are the things I wanted to hear about, your own sacrifices, escapades." But she excused herself." Maybe I go too fast. But telling about those things now is not like living through them. I have told them to no one. So please, they have been inside me, kept in silence for so long. Now when you ask, they rush out."

I told her I understood what she said. But she felt we had come to a good place to rest for now. I could still not help myself feeling that she was holding something back, so I pressed her the next day when I returned.

Anita: I found José again on the trail that leads down to Vacaría, toward the headquarters of our revolutionary government in Viamão, where we stopped for some rest. That is a long journey, more than two hundred kilometers from Forquilhas to Viamão. Once again I was with other women and their families. In the past I wasn't anxious to be with them. Truly, the few officers' wives I met were polite, but still, I could feel that they weren't comfortable with me. And the few soldiers' women, some with children, were shy of me. My name meant something to them, you see. But when I knew that the child was growing inside me, I welcomed the friendship of other women near me, any of them. In the end they gave me advice, very *simpatico*. So my life soon became like family with friends, almost like before I met José. But of course, there was the baby inside me.

When we were getting ready for the battle at Taquari, I was growing bigger and knew that I could not fight. That was in February [1840], late in the month. General Gonçalves himself heard about my condition and let me travel with José, but he gave me no place in the battle.

A large number of our troops formed a huge army. The excitement was high, especially because Gonçalves himself was going to command us. It would be an important struggle, maybe the one that would bring total victory in the revolution.

When we were getting ready for Taquari my strength was huge, more than I ever knew before. I knew women back in Laguna who worked hard until near the day they gave birth. I was from that kind of people, the strongest of them. The General knew about my strength. None of the other women of the officers' families ever went into the battles, never even near. But Gonçalves was a *cabalheiro* in the way of tradition. For him women had no place in a soldier's work. Families followed after the battles to take care of the fires and make food for their men. Even that he did not like to see. But he couldn't stop it. That was tradition, too, as you have said. You can imagine the feelings that ran among us, both hope and fear, we women who had to wait for news about our warriors.

So I rode along with José's troop. We were with Colonel Canabarro again, a long and hard march, very slow because we had almost one thousand men. When we started into the mountains, we had to travel in a line all the way along the steep Trail of Pareci, wild and thick forests up to the edge of the River Cai and then to Pinheiro in the District of Taquari. There we were joined by Netto's army. They told us that the Imperialists had many thousand infantry and cavalry, also artillery but they could not move the big cannons up along those trails, only some of the smaller ones.

Doña Feliciana: I had to interrupt again to tell Anita how much I admired her memory. Actually, in addition to my fascination with her ability to recollect so much, I needed to slow her down in order to keep up with her account. "You recollect all the details, the places, the terrain. And in a strange country of wild forests and ravines in such terrible conditions."

"Well, I have had enough of troubles at each of those places to mark each one in my mind," she explained to me. "And remember, Doña Feliciana, "that was my entire life."

I wanted to argue that few people could be so keen of recollection as she was, but I saw that she was not comfortable with such compliments, so I apologized for my interruption. She turned aside my apology and went on.

Anita: On the way to Pinheiro we already had some small skirmishes, you see--Ambushes. José was worried about me and the baby. Our future, he said, was inside me. He told me that General Gonçalves said no one was braver than me in the battles, not the other officers, not the Black Lancers, not José himself. You can see how proud that made me. But he still told me to stay back with the rear guards.

When José went into the battle without me, the general did allow me to have a horse but kept me near himself. From our high spot overlooking the field I saw much of the fighting. Not all of it. There was so much going on, you see, in other copses and behind far ridges. You have to watch carefully many places at once. Others are completely out of sight. That is why I admired the generals so much and wanted to be as alert to everything as they were.

The battle started with Imperialist cannons. They shot at us from near the River Cai. Canabarro sent his cavalry of freed slaves, the fire-eyed Lancers, to charge. They knew how to keep their mounts under control. The officers that led the charge also were the most daring. The whole cavalry moved with great dignity, no shouting. They started to gallop up to the nearest enemy, faster and faster. Now with their long lances tipping straight forward. Then they spread out and attacked the side of the enemy army. Such strength in their arms and shoulders, leaning forward, and in the horses' flanks. I know what that galloping feels like, to trust your mount even on rough ground, to be just another part of the animal. The Imperialists had to retreat from such an attack, back across the river. On the other end of the line, our foot soldiers moved into the forest ravines toward the river, but I could not see them there. The fighting took a whole day until darkness.

The next day, after the sunrise melted the mountain mist, the enemy was gone, running away from the battlegrounds. When José came back he tried to convince Canabarro that we should chase the Imperial army and destroy them.

It was always his way—never to stop fighting for long: So fiery, and so stubborn. But the others told José that it was not wise to spill too much blood, and right then I was ashamed for him. It made a bad feeling between us, too. I will tell you how.

He complained to me later when we were alone, about Canabarro's refusal to follow the enemy, but I told him that this was a war between Brazilian brothers and he was a foreigner, after all. His vengeance at such a time was not wise.

If I slashed him with a whip he could not be more surprised and hurt. I read in his eyes that he believed I stood with the others against him. But, you see, he asked me and I had to tell him what I thought. Maybe he was surprised that I had my own ideas, that I felt the strength in myself and the pain as much as he did. So he walked away, and I saw that he struggled with his anger.

When he came back, before he took the food I made for him, he kissed my hand and told me that he thought about my words and apologized to Canabarro. I was surprised. I felt a new excitement in my love for him. This was a true man, I discovered, Doña Feliciana, one who could hear others and say he was wrong himself. So he gave me a new reason to love him, now even more.

It was such a beautiful moment for both of us, my dear friend. If only it all stopped then. But now I know, when I saw the enemy from that hillside near Pinheiro, that even if we beat them in that battle, I knew that, in the end, the Riograndenses would not win. The Imperialists had so many men, guns, even many more horses than us. The other officers saw it, too. It didn't matter who was the bravest, the more fierce.

I knew that many of our soldiers would finally agree to accept a pardon by the Imperial Government. Only the biggest land owners from the oldest families, like Gonçalves, those with the biggest herds of horses and cattle, wanted to be their own government. Most of them, anyway. So only those highest leaders wanted to go on fighting. The smaller owners did not care. I heard the other women, their wives, talk about it in that way. So some of them must have heard their husbands talking. When such talk reaches the women, then you can begin to take it seriously.

For a while, things changed with José and me. How could they not? At first I wanted to make him proud, nothing else. We loved. He was still tender with me, but after Taquari I began to fight another kind of battle inside myself, separate from José.

Back then, in Laguna, before I was married to Manoel, before I met José, whenever I was on a horse, no one was a better rider. I can't say that now they were jealous of me, those other women, the soldiers' wives. Maybe they were. I know I could see that they didn't know what to feel about me. When danger was near, no one was more happy than me to meet it. Even the men were nervous about me acting so bold, especially José. Doña Feliciana, we all believe in destiny. Before, when danger came, before I was with my child inside me, I fought without care for myself. I knew Death could come to me at any minute. Only two things mattered—being near José and the chance to show that I could be his true mate. I did not ask for death, but I did not care if it came.

Then after Taquari, my baby was inside me. So the end of that battle was the beginning of my new life. Many of the same things continued the hardships. Those I could stand. But I didn't want to go any more into battle with José. I was happy to be out of the forest ravines and get back to Villa Settembrina, more people, more houses with other women, and food for us all. So it was a calmer time for me, different between me and José.

That is where we rejoined Rossetti. A good thing for José, he had long talks with him about Italy, and I listened to their plans for a future outside of Rio Grande do Sul. After Taquari, we had two weeks, maybe a little more to rest. Enough!

But soon we were busy again with the Revolution, and the Commanders sent us down to São Simão, far down on the outer banks of the Lagoa dos Patos, to get ready for a new campaign. Now you will hear about dangerous times that even I did not expect.

CHAPTER 27

The Campaign to Capture the Mouth of the Lagoa dos Patos/Rossetti about Garibaldi, Anita and the Rebel Cause

Editor: Before we read Anita's account of that campaign in the South, we shift away from Doña Feliciana's notes to pick up Rossetti's account of the very same unsuccessful attempt to capture the forts at the mouth of the Logoa dos Patos. It is Rossetti's next to final journal entry, which combines his unembellished honesty and his unswervable faith in ultimate victory. In her parallel account, Anita will tell of some of the same ventures but her account, which appears in Fra Lorenzo's interviews, are attached to other, more momentous developments that illustrate her incredible fortitude and resourcefulness.

From Garibaldi's Memoirs: The enemy . . . had partly garrisoned with infantry . . . .San Jose del Norte. . . .That place, which stands on the north shore of the outlet of the Lake Dos Patos, was one of its keys; and [our] possession of it would have been sufficient to change the face of things. The town was taken, and [our] Republican troops gave themselves up to pillage and riot. . . .[That] greatest triumph was changed, towards noon, to a shameful retreat. . . .Good men wept with anger and disappointment. The loss [for] the Republicans was comparatively immense. From that time [our] infantry was a mere skeleton. A few cavalry belonged to the expedition, and they served as a protection [for] the retreat. The division marched to their barracks of Buena Vista, and I remained at San Simon with the marine, which was reduced to about fifty . . . officers and soldiers. (48)

Rossetti: The retreat from the mouth of the Lagoa is finished, the saddest I have been in since Garibaldi and I joined this Revolution. General Gonçalves confidently led the main mass of our armies south all the way from Villa Settembrina to gain control of the entrance channel to the Lagoa dos Patos. That would have given us rule over the entire province, excepting the capital in the northern city of Porto Alegre. But with the entrance to the Lagoa secured, that city would soon surrender. Garibaldi could have easily enlarged his navy and transported men and supplies anywhere along the shores of dos Patos. All the foreign consulates in San José do Norte and Rio Grande would transform their official representation to serve our New Government, secure in the claims of our Revolution and in our alliance with the Unitarian Colorados in Uruguay. Then the Imperialists would be forced to capitulate to our terms for peace and treat us as we deserve—a Free and Fraternal Republic under the Leadership of Don Bento Gonçalves and a newly elected Legislature.

That was to be my recital of details for *O 'Povo*. What a glorious declaration it would have made. I had already written it in bold headlines for an essay of burning eloquence. The words had resided in my head for weeks, throughout the planning of the campaign.

But, alas, we did not succeed. Although our spirits were high until the final days, our supplies for a siege were insufficient to exhaust the power of the fortress's guns and the Imperial Navy. After that disappointment, we made the march back north, all the way up here to Villa Settembrini and our diminished glory.

Editor: Rossetti failed to note one nasty incident to the discredit of the rebels and for which Garibaldi suffered terrible remorse. (49)

Rossetti: Now even the siege of Porto Alegre is ineffective. Now, too, the Imperialist Army will not rest, and we will hear their horses' hooves again. Even now they send massive expeditions, under General Caixas to confront us, and no doubt Colonel Abreu, the rogue marauder, to sneak around and prick at our flanks.

Yes, The *Moringue* will continue to nip at us until one of our companies destroys him. I hope the task falls to Giuseppe. Since The *Moringue's* sneak attack upon our Naval Base back in the early days at Camaquá, Giuseppe especially wishes to engage him and his detested Austrian mercenaries, whose arrogant brethren divide our beloved Italy.

Here, I must say something that has occurred to me about Giuseppe and *The Moringue*. It is, I hope, a fair-minded assessment.

One reason for Giuseppe's ambition to defeat this Imperial Guerilla, I believe, is his begrudging admiration for The Marten. I admit this is my own interpretation, but some of the things Giuseppe has said have forced me to this conclusion. In a way, I think, each, Garibaldi and *The Moringue*, is a counter-self to the other, as if some One of the Fates had determined that they should join in battle, like mutual Nemeses.

Giuseppe argued to me that *The Moringue's* success inevitably follows his sneak attacks, by which he really means the tactic of surprise.

"That devil knows that the one way to insure victory is to choose your own time, the best opportunity, but you must be given the freedom to lead your troups into quick and sudden thrusts at a time you choose, and to be left to fashion your own tactics. Instead of being locked into the manual of some general's formal strategy, you must be left free to win or lose on your own account. That is the sort of fighting I believe I too am meant for. My own timing, my own plan. Hit quickly and suddenly, and just as abruptly disappear. Guerilla fighting. It is always guaranteed to do some damage to the enemy and always to be feared, a threat."

That is what he told me. And I can see in every way that it suits Giuseppe best.

I wanted to put that observation down while the idea was still fresh, to show that I do not study Giuseppe for nothing. I hope that whatever glory he earns comes by his own devices, his independent tactics, which he directs always for the good of all his compatriots' cause. (50)

Editor: The following is another unique segment that breaks into the chronology of Rossetti's memoirs. It is about Anita. He obviously added it either as a sort of reluctant afterthought or in response to his apprehension about the perils that lay ahead in the final retreat of the rebel forces. I should point out that, without effacing the actual text, he had drawn a single, diagonal line—for which I substitute brackets—through the following entry, deciding finally that he could not in fairness exclude it. It is ironically a tribute to Rossetti's fair-mindedness, despite his inclination to neglect Anita's exploits. He felt compelled to acknowledge that she was as intrepid as any of Garibaldi's fellow mariners, more than most, in fact.

[Rossetti: Not long afterward, when the Imperials invaded Laguna by land and sea and forced our retreat, Anita, right under the enemy's deadly onslaught, helped to vacate the ships caught in the Imperial barrage. She bolstered the courage of her comrades and made them return whatever fire they could against the enemy, while at the same time salvaging supplies from the ships. That was the engagement in which John Griggs, our North American comrade, was killed. Anita was unaware of that loss until the battle was over. In the same display of fortitude, at Santa Vitoria she refused to leave the battle area. And most amazing of all, she kept fighting at the Forquilhas in Curitibanos, where she was finally captured in the Forest Mortandade. From there she made a daring escape under the very eyes of her captors.

Heroine, Canabarro and Terceira called her, even as high a person as General Gonçalves himself, although he finally forced special rules upon her when she was with Giuseppe's child, and especially after she bore their son.

Who can help but admire such a woman? With the infant not more than a few days after its birth, she fled with him on horseback from an attack by that devil, *The Moringue*, the same man to whom I compared Giuseppe. A new mother rising from her bed of birthing! Yes, a heroine, I admit it. I attest to it.]

Editor: Following those interjections, Rossetti's regular memoirs continue.

Rossetti: Now to get back to my responsibility, I must rebuild the spirits of these Riograndenses for the Noble Cause to which we all have committed ourselves: the Struggle for Justice and Reconciliation to the deaths of our Fair Comrades All. May the Universal Spirit Empower my Words.

No one should forget Taquari, where we broke the Imperial army's attack. Now the enemy will come again, send their best. By the time they arrive, our troops once more will be an army, organized and ready, I pray, to rally for Bento Gonçalves. My hopes rise whenever I see the formidable Black Lancers— Slaves once, now Freed and Noble—who, in past encounters, have left the enemy corpses strewn upon the battleground. I shall muster all my skills to raise our spirits. I have already drafted some appropriate passages: "In shreds our foes will fall. Then *they* truly will become the Ragamuffins, as they, in derision, have labeled us."

I thank God my printing press is securely packed and ready for transport to the high interior plateau, where we will be safe in our own territory and I can print new issues of *O 'Povo* without the need to move again until, God willing, we seat ourselves in the Official Government Chambers at Porto Alegre. Until then, our grief for the souls of Carniglia and Mutru, their sacrifice remains a silent prayer, and for the North American, Griggs, cut down at Laguna. But for the living we must be grateful.

If we could reverse time to when Giuseppe and I first met, I wonder would we have stayed in Rio de Janeiro during those restless months after we went to see Zambeccari in his prison cell. Our return to Italy is still our hope and intention. Garibaldi swears that we will yet stand among the ranks that re-unite the States of our Homeland! Soon, he says, it will come. His hope is unquenchable. It sustains us all, as it has from the beginning of our great venture together.

CHAPTER 28

Anita and Garibaldi Settle on the Outer Banks/Anita's Confinement and Garibaldi's Campaign to the South

Editor: At this point I include Anita's account of her adventures during the army's campaign to capture the mouth of the Lagoa dos Patos. Except for the interjection of Rossetti's final entry, twelve pages below, hers will be the only voice of the three memoirists left to us.

Anita: Following Gonçalves' orders to prepare for the coming campaign, we traveled across the Rio Capivari and south along the sand dunes between the sea and the eastern bank of the Lagoa: a flat, low country where the winds never let up, winter or summer. They bend the trees to the ground. In that season constant cold rain swept us along. We marched near the shore of the lagoa, where the water was a little calmer. But we still felt the winds from the ocean that crossed the narrow, flat strip of land.

From Garibaldi's Memoir: My object in staying at that place was to prepare some canoes, (boats made of single trees,) and to open communications with the other parts of the lake; but, in the months which I spent there, the canoes did not make their appearance; and for the reason that they had existed only in idea. Instead of boats, I therefore occupied myself with procuring horses, there being an abundance of wild ones, which furnished much occupation to the sailors, who became so many knights, though all of them did not manage their steeds with dexterity. (51)

Anita: José was allowed to take ten of his mariners back under his command. A small band of hardened sailors, most he trained himself. They found some sumacas to move supplies and to support the coming battle down at the mouth of the Lagoa.

All the time I was getting bigger with the baby inside me, like a balloon. Oof!

From Garibaldi's Memoir: . . . San Simon is a very beautiful and spacious place, although at that time destroyed and abandoned. It was said to belong to an exiled Count San Simon, or his exiled heirs, who had left home because of opinions different from those of the Republicans. There being no masters there, we strangers fed on the cattle and rode the horses. (52)

Anita: In São Simão, part of the way down the shore of the Lagoa, José found us a small house on a quiet bay. No other houses were nearby. But soon we found friendly people in the Village of Mostardas. It was only a few kilometers away. We were comfortable there for nearly one month. A paradise for me!

In the first days of July, General Gonçalves himself came with a large part of the army. Down to where we waited. José finally found several canoes and fashioned them into double-hulled and out-rigged sailboats for ten or twelve men and their supplies each. By then I was almost seven months with child.

Before José and his mariners sailed down to support the army, he moved me to Mostardas to be with a family, the Costas. They became good friends to us. I can never forget their kindness.

* * * * *

Yes, of course, while he was gone I was afraid for José. I lived in fear for a whole month while the army fought the Imperials.

They were unsuccessful, you know. When José told me about it, he was discouraged. Gonçalves thought that they would surprise Saõ José. He even formed a siege when they came to the fortress. But Imperial boats could still reach the residents with food from the Atlantic outside, so our army could not break the will of the people in the fort. Besides, the Imperials fought battles against our men all the way down to São José do Norte. During those attacks, slowly our army lost many men and used up much of their ammunition.

After that failure, the Army had to march back up the same sandy road. It was a sad withdrawal. From the army that rushed down there, only a small part came back. I could not believe what I saw. Most of the men had no guns; they were tired and hungry. Gloomy faces, but I was relieved that José was not harmed.

When they came back to Mostardas, the General told José to settle there with me, for my condition. The rest of the war meant little to me then, you see. All I thought about was that now he would be with me when the baby came.

We agreed that I would stay with the Costas, to have an experienced mother to help me. José settled into our little Estancia of São Simão, but he came every evening to eat with us. He was still supposed to fix more canoes for travel to other parts of the Lagoa. But Imperial patrols sailed all over the waterway. All the boats he prepared before were lost in the last campaign. And he found no other boats of any worth. So he and his mariners took care of the cattle they brought down from Capivari and those they found in the region. When he came to the house of the Costas in the evening, he brought milk and meat for all of us. Even in that terrible winter with the rain that never stopped, we were satisfied. He told us about how he and his mariners were fixing our new home for our family. The Costas, such good people, were happy to keep us nearby.

From Garibaldi's Memoir: At that place our first child was born. . . .The young mother, although so short a time before united to her martial husband, had already passed through many trials and dangers. . . she had accompanied me on the marches, and even in the battles . . . , and had endured great fatigue and hunger, and had several falls from her horse. During her stay at the house of an inhabitant of the place, she received the greatest kindness from the family and their neighbors. I shall be most thankful to those good people all my life. It was of the highest importance that she had the comforts of that house and those friends at that time, for the miseries suffered by the army then rose to their height, and I was absolutely destitute of everything necessary for my wife and little son. (53)

Anita: I needed José near me, and he never stopped showing me his love. But the weight of the child was tiring me. I had to make myself stop moving around so much. I was not used to that. I wanted to do things. I kept begging José to take me to the house in São Simão. Of course he could not but I kept at him. Mrs. Costa was surprised that José never lost patience with me.

But he thought all the time about the war. He told me about any new plans because he knew how much I was a part of it. He told me about the messages from the Imperialists offering to make peace in the provinces. José hoped that Gonçalves would continue to fight. I must tell you, that made me angry. I told him, people like our friends, the Costas, would gain nothing from a change in the government. What mattered to me, I was carrying my child and his. That became more important to me than the entire revolution of the Farroupilhas.

Sometimes I even wondered just how much the freedom of Rio Grande do Sul meant to José. I do not say it became unimportant to him, but it was always a question I asked myself when Rossetti was with us. José always talked with him about Italy and the Revolution that would take place there. That idea went far beyond Rio Grande do Sul or Brazil. To me Italy was less than nothing. I could not tell him that. I know that he suffered much for this New Republic ever since he left Rio, but it angered me when Rossetti made him think only about Italy. At first, you see, I liked Rossetti. But as I told you, I could see that he did not think the best of me. He thought of me only as a woman for José. I know it. When he was together with José, he talked to me very little. Even though he talked about equality for everyone, I don't think he meant common women like me.

What I wanted most of all was a peaceful time for our family. That was my hope. That Gonçalves would stop the fighting. And then José and I could live in the estancia at São Simão in a little farm with our own small herd. It would be a new life for us. Accepted as honorable neighbors with people like the Costas. With the Lagoa dos Patos open to us. To travel easily, without fear to other places. The wind blows hard there in the winter, that strip of land facing the sea. Much colder than in Laguna. Still the ocean is nearby for us to use in our own pleasure.

But even those good dreams were mixed with bad ones, dreams that peace would never come for us, that we would wander forever, always out of one danger into another. Sometimes I dreamed that José left me behind, that he and Rossetti left Brazil without me. Sometimes when I woke up from such a bad dream, I wished that I could climb to a high cliff and jump, with my child still inside me before the baby came into this world to suffer. May God forgive me for such thoughts! I could not stop them. Then I woke up and I was glad that no cliffs lined our shoreline.

Doña Feliciana: You can imagine how much that shocked me. I begged her, "Please, Anita, try not to have such thoughts, but if you must say them, for your sake and the soul of your child, cross yourself." You should have seen how she answered, without hesitation, stronger even than her words.

Anita: Doña Feliciana, please be calm. Those bad thoughts ended in the days before Menotti was born. Did I tell you his birthday? What I went through to bring him alive into this world? September 16, in 1840! And such a birth! I felt like the little animal would claw his way out by his own strength. Señora Costa was my savior. The birthing was easy, she told me. How could I know that? But I am glad Doña Costa knew everything to do afterward. But to me, no battle in my life was as hard or as full of pain as that in the Parish of São Luiz do Mostardas. I remember the name for my child's sake. Not even the battle at Laguna was as fierce.

José came afterward to the bed. He was gentle. Every minute that he could, he stayed with me.

Doña Feliciana: Talking about that experience excited her but gradually it put her in a tranquil mood, so I asked the question that had been on my mind for a long time.

"And did you baptize the child since then?"

She answered openly, frankly and again without hesitation. But it was an answer I was not calm about, one that I feared to expect. "No, Doña Feliciana."

So I pressed her without hesitation. "Anita, excuse me, but why not then? How long afterward?"

"José named the child Menotti," was her simple answer, although an indirect one. "Menotti was an Italian hero who was executed in the name of freedom," she explained. "It seemed right to me that our tiny child who already suffered from the conditions of battle should bear the name of such a hero."

That, of course, made sense in its own way, but I was still restless. Obviously I thought it was important in a way that maybe she did not. "Is that the name you wanted for him? No one in your family, even his second name? A saint's name?"

She said, this time more abruptly, "I let José choose." She must have thought me stubborn, indeed, because I kept on about it, at the risk of her growing impatience. "Well, did you baptize him then? I'm sorry to ask again, Doña Anita, but it is important, not so?"

And to that she replied more calmly, as if at last she was freeing herself of a great pressure, like childbirth itself. "No. We could not. There was no priest in Mostardas."

There was the answer I truly feared to hear. Forgive me but from then I pressed more freely, for I knew she was beyond being angry with me. "But, Anita, it was still all right for you to baptize the child. Senhora Costa would know that. Didn't you know the prayers? Later you could go to a priest, a church."

Yes, she knew that.

"So now, my dear girl, the child's eternal soul, must be protected, after all. You took a terrible risk!"

She looked at me wearily. I shall never forget how wearily. "Please, Feliciana, so many questions! I'm sorry, but try to understand. The place, the dangers. We had too much to think about.

And we had little even to cover the baby's body. To get such things in a few days, not even one week, José went far north to Viamão to collect equipment that we didn't have. Soft cloth for the baby and clothing for me. Those were our first concerns. True, we should have taken warning, for everything seemed to favor us."

So, despite her reasoning and excuses, at last I could work out the answer to the question of Menotti's baptism: José was a non-believer. And Anita may have doubted her own standing, since she had denounced, in a way, her own marriage vows taken back in Laguna, and with it all the features of the faith that she was born into. There was no need for me to force her to answer, for it was the source of one of her greatest agonies. She had committed herself to Garibaldi with a love that weighed more than the safety of her own soul, more even—may God forgive us all—than the soul of her own child!

I let her go on with her recollections, unwilling to interrupt her for long. She sighed at my extended silence, poor girl, collected her thoughts, and asked me, "Should I continue?" I could only nod and remain silent, knowing that she wished to move away from the topic.

CHAPTER 29

Anita's Narrow Escape with the Infant Menotti/The New Family Moves North to Capivari

Anita: Just as we should have expected, terrible troubles found us out. Not one week after José left, The *Moringue* attacked in the area of Mostardas. Can you believe it? He must have learned where we were. First he surprised the estancia at São Simão. A lucky thing I did not move back there with Menotti. Some mariners rode over to warn us that *Moringue's* troops were coming toward us. The Costas offered to hide us in a shed outside their house.

From Garibaldi's Memoir: …my band of sailors…were obliged to take their clubs and go into the woods, taking my wife with them, who mounted the saddle to avoid the enemy, with her infant, then only twelve days old, although it was in the midst of the storm. (54)

Anita: You talk to me about risks to our baby's soul. Now consider this. I wrapped the baby in warm cloth, flannel. Senhora Costa wept and begged me to let her husband hide me, but she saw that I paid no attention. She blessed me and the baby—maybe that counts for a baptism? I put a shawl around the clothes I wore, our men put me on the extra horse they brought, and we galloped through the forest north of Mostardas.

The rain fell hard, but I held Menotti to my breast. That was his first training in war. That bitter day! He was so good, the tiny baby, not a sound from him where we huddled in the cold rain among the bushes and dripping trees. Believe me, Feliciana, even then I thought about the baby's soul, as you have said. But I thought more about keeping Giuseppe's baby alive. If I said a prayer it was to Garibaldi to destroy *The Moringue*.

Maybe the wind and rain saved us. That day was miserable for the enemy, too. They marched right near our hiding place on their way back to the South. But they didn't find us. I don't know how long they searched in the village. I give thanks that they didn't bother the Costas.

After the raiders were out of sight, the small troop of soldiers and I still couldn't tell where *The Moringue* was. Maybe still in the village. But the rain forced me to look for better shelter. For the baby, you see? We started for the house in São Simão. On our way near the edge of the woods, José found us and led us back to the Costa's house.

When he saw the danger we were in. He decided right then that we must move closer to the headquarters far north in Villa Settembrina. Then like an answer to his thoughts, orders came that our troops were to travel north—exactly what we had planned. They gathered the horses and drove the few heads of cattle with us for food in our new home.

When we arrived there, I was among other wives. Other mothers. Their comforting helped. We were closer to the things I needed for the baby, flannel, linen, even soap and oil.

Our parting from Mostardas was sad. Those brave members of the Family Costa. They proved themselves our most valuable friends. That was a time when most people were afraid to show sympathy to us. I had to leave without saying farewell to them. Can you tell how sad it made me feel? José rode to them on the night before—he promised to do that—and pledged our friendship forever. I never saw them again.

On the next morning we moved north through the marsh grass and low forest, under whatever cover we could find near the road. But now it felt good to be on a horse without hurrying, feeding my infant from my breast as the pony trotted along. I knew that he would be a fine horseman one day.

Our new house was on dry ground. It was on the edge of the Rio Capivari. Right away José was busy to settle us there. And he became a mariner again. He found two large canoes to use on the Lagoa and some smaller ones for crossing the river. He and his mariners fixed the canoes and crossed to the other shore of the Lagoa—that was near the Gonçalves' land—for supplies for our army. But in Capivari I had the company of other wives--a safe place for us.

We had almost six weeks in our new home before we had to leave. But in that time much happened to our cause of liberation. José tried to keep his feelings from me. To be a happy father. But I saw that he was worried and I made him tell me about his worries.

What he explained to me I could understand but I must be honest, I could not decide about it. The Imperialists wanted us to give up the fighting and let the land owners keep their territories, go back to their peaceful lives. They could keep their cattle and horses and sell meat and hides as they wished. The big land owners and their followers, everybody would be left in peace, not punished like the revolters in Paraná or like the poor slaves we heard about who fought for their freedom far away in the Northeast. The Imperial Government in Rio told Gonçalves that General Caixas was now in charge of the Imperial army. He was their greatest general but he would make a treaty with us. If Gonçalves refused, Caixas would march against us to finish the struggle. No guarantees.

We saw what was happening. Our troops were tired; the cavalry and foot soldiers had little ammunition, fewer supplies. We had no Navy to carry us across the Lagoa to safety. The Imperialists had everything. Their ships came into the Lagoa with more supplies all the time, and José was helpless to stop them. He only sneaked his little boats back and forth across the Lagoa at dusk or before dawn.

He did not discuss with me these terrible problems. I felt more lonely and trapped. Whatever he decided I had to respect. If he goes to fight, I keep Menotti with me and wait for him to return.

Doña Feliciana: I remained silent for a long time, Fra Lorenzo, as you can see. I was not worried about keeping up with her speaking because, as I told you, I developed a way of writing down her words and phrases in a short form so that I would not fall behind.

By the way, after the first few days of our conversations, my husband saw me at our dining table after we had eaten, where I translated my notes into complete—what shall I call them?—versions. I explained what I was doing, and he retorted that, if anyone could keep up with other peoples' gossip, I could do it. That was all right. I did not argue with his teasing.

Anyway, after Anita paused in her last, long report, I felt that now was a good time to allow my dear friend to rest. I wished to relieve her mood somehow from recollections of her exhausting trials. I was sure she felt the sorrow, for her child's sake, at the least. In that spirit I told her, "But, Anita, you must have hoped for peace." As it turned out she was not finished reciting her terrible adventures, and with such convincing authority, I must admit.

Anita: Ah, peace. Yes, I knew how that would be. The locals who were loyal to the Imperialists would make peace with the defeated rebels, even the common soldiers and their families. The owners of the big fazendas would still have their land, yes, even have places in the government again, but what about us? José didn't even belong in that country, and I was a fugitive from my own. We had no land, no house, no family except ourselves. How were we to bargain for our safety?

When I saw him come back from his secret voyages across the Lagoa, carrying messages and small supplies, I saw how much his life changed. He was not the golden sailor who climbed the barra in Laguna to find me. Many times I wished for those days to return, when our freedom and all our friends were still with us.

In the middle of November the message came from Gonçalves. No surrender. But even before and after he said so, many of our former comrades decided to quit the war and settle on their own terms with the Imperialists. They just went back to their homes, picked up where their lives left off. Once brave comrades, they became men who wanted only to live in peace with their families. Who can blame them? Gonçalves told them to do what they must. He did not accuse them. He was right. Many stayed with the General because they chose to, but only the freed slaves had to go on fighting. Like us, they were the only ones who could not turn back to their old lives. Back to slavery! Never. They would run off into the forest and make their own communities, some of them told me, like the Indians in the high hills beyond Piratini.

When our army was weakened and discouraged, the Imperialists threatened us more. Again José decided that we must leave our comfortable house, this time in Capivari where we had food and sunshine. Menotti was healthy, a miracle, and now I had ample milk for him, soft bunting, and a way to keep our clothing clean and still take time to play with him: A baby of barely three months to come through such troubles. But the worst was still ahead. Believe me, the chill is still in my bones from remembering the terrible journey we made after Capivari.

You cannot understand it. I know that, Doña Feliciana--only if you were there. But I will not tell what you do not wish to hear. Good. You wish to hear everything. I do not doubt you. Listen, then to what it was like when we left our little house. We took our few horses and two of our cows. It makes me laugh, or cry, to think about it. We did not know what was ahead. The other families were divided among the troops. All the other wives wished to stay close to their men. Even though we retreated with an army smaller than ever before, we felt some hope that we could still find a place to rest.

CHAPTER 30

Final Entry in Rossetti's Memoir/
The Rebels Retreat to the High Plateau

Editor: With apologies, I must break into Anita's narrative once more. I wish not to cause an arbitrary break in Doña Feliciana's remarkable record, but with Garibaldi about to accompany Anita and others on their painful retreat up through the ravines to the plateau above Villa Settembrina, I think it opportune to report on Rossetti's fate. His name resurfaced briefly when Anita told Doña Feliciana about the terrible journey into the forest-covered hills. At the staging point, she soon became the sole survivor of the three special companions to Garibaldi because Rossetti never made it out of Villa Settembrina. What follows is the last passage in the memoirs he had begun far back in Rio de Janeiro.

Rossetti: Villa Settembrina, November 1840: Preparations for our withdrawal into the high country is underway. The journey ahead is perilous, as I have heard from our comrades who know this country to the West. In fact, they tell me that I will never get the heaviest equipment up through the ravines and across the countless streams that rush down through them. They suggest that I find a place to hide the printing press here until we can come back to retrieve it during a calmer season. My apprentices simply look to me and await my decision, and I am determined not to disappoint them. I don't know whether the others whom Garibaldi has assigned to help us will be as loyal, even though they promise to do as I wish.

Surely it will be a difficult terrain with so many people and supplies to arrange for. Let alone the families of those who flee with us. Wives, mothers, some with little children: How the innocent must suffer, caught in the ventures of these warriors. Believe me. I look far back to those days of my seasickness when we sailed out from Rio on board the little *Mazzini*. That stands in idyllic contrast to what we have been through since and the unknown troubles we have yet to face. When I approached Garibaldi to ask his advice, he acted as if the problems did not matter, only solutions for their own sake. Typical!

Editor: That ends Rossetti's journal. He never got to extend his account of the retreat. Near the end of November, he and several of his comrades fell during a surprise attack by none other than the intrepid *Moringue*.

From Garibaldi's Memoir: At that time died Rossetti an irreparable loss to the army, and especially to myself. Having been left with the Republican garrison of Settembrina, which was to march last, he was surprised by the famous *Maringue*; and that incomparable Italian perished fighting bravely. Having fallen from his horse wounded, he was called on to surrender—but he sold his life dearly. There is not a spot of ground on earth in which do not lie the bones of some generous Italian, for whose sake Italy ought never to cease from the struggle until free herself. (55)

Editor: That is the last of Garibaldi's excerpts I include, for soon after he and Anita reached Montevideo, he becomes involved in the civil war in Uruguay.

News of Rossetti's death reached Garibaldi, only after the rebels were in the middle of their cruel ascent northwest of Villa Settembrina. It came as a disheartening shock. More of that later. For now, we re-enter Anita's memoirs at the same time and place as Rossetti's final one.

Anita: In Settembrina, near to Port Alegre, we saw Rossetti. He was getting his printing machines ready for the move. He had some mules and horses to carry everything but we couldn't wait for him to pack, so we went on ahead with one of the several retreating companies.

The first march to São Leopoldo went well. The trails were not so steep. I stayed close to José. I didn't wish to follow with the other women. Too many kept complaining. I wanted to keep my own spirits up.

But outside of São Leopoldo, the first ambushes started. We thought we would be safe from them, but attacks by guerillas kept surprising us. They shot at us from the forest. Then they ran away before we could make a defense and fight back. Some of our people were wounded. Not many, thank heaven, for we always reacted swiftly. We shot back but we could not chase the attackers because that would spread us out, as they wanted. All we could do was watch carefully every step ahead.

After São Leopoldo the trail became steeper. That's where our real misery began. It became worse each day when the early winter rains began to fall. Very cold. The ravines rose quickly--steep and thick with brush. I never was on such trails before. Even in a dry season these would be hard to climb. Now the higher we went, the wetter and colder we became. I tried to keep everything dry for Menotti. José gave me a good cloak before we left Capivari, but we didn't have enough heavy clothes against the cold. We couldn't carry much, and when the rain soaked what we had, they became heavier for us and our horses.

The rain never stopped. That's why our guide lost the trail several times. I can't blame the poor man. Any path in this season becomes a gully, a rushing flood. The crossings kept getting steeper. I could not believe it. With the rain, every little stream added to the next. Soon two or three made a wide torrent. We had to get down from our horses to lighten their burdens, and we struggled to stay on our feet because we walked on the slippery banks next to the rushing water, sometimes right in it.

When we crossed streams people began to let go of some things they carried. Some stubborn people at first tried to carry all their large bundles, but finally they surrendered and watched them disappear into the rushing water. Some were swept away with them. Some tried to throw their possessions across the swift stream. But soon they lost strength for that, too. Then their will vanished in the rain and the mist. I think back on what I just told you and know it seems cold blooded, like I didn't care. But each of us struggled to catch the next breath. Just to keep breathing in that soaking undergrowth was all we could think about, to keep ourselves alive for the little children.

All of us took the most care with the children. We carried them across the streams one after another. I see now that a tiny baby like Menotti was easier to carry. It wasn't so easy with the larger children. Most of the horses could make the crossing, leaping and bucking, but the children were too little to hold on by themselves. Sometimes we had to cut bundles away to keep the horses from drowning. We struggled to stay on our feet in those torrents—sometimes for most of the day in water up to our hips. Even to think about keeping the children dry was impossible. When the rain stopped or fell thinner, the wind shook the trees and more water fell down from them in sheets. Everyone became exhausted. Only José was patient, like a miracle force. He called to his soldiers to help us, and bless them all, they always watched out for us. Many times I was close to giving up hope. But I knew I could not stop. Never!

We were ten days and nights in that Hell. What do I say? All that endless rain, the rushing water would put out the flames even in Hell! Yes, it was like an inferno but in the other way. Which way is worse?

Always we had higher to climb. In good weather, we could reach the first ridge of the serras in two, maybe three days. But with that endless strain our lungs were stretched. Each time we reached an easy place for a rest, we had to push those ahead of us to move on, or we had to make room for those coming after us. And the guerilla bands waited with ambushes in the best places for us to settle down, waited to spring on us. Only one good thing about the rain: the Imperialists were miserable too. So their attacks became fewer.

Already by the end of the third day we began to leave women behind. When I think back, I can not believe we did it. They were exhausted, clinging to their possessions, helpless to follow us. Each day more fell behind. Mothers begged us to carry their children when they were too tired to move. We tried to make them keep up. In our group eight women gave up. Some had small children, two, three years old—too weak to go on. Most times their men stayed with them, to protect them, from what? Hopeless! Each time that happened, I felt like a piece of my own flesh was torn from me. I did not count the children. But each of us thought the same thought. Save our own. Don't weaken. Even pity gives way to that. I have said blessings for their souls many times since and begged forgiveness. Whatever good it could do them, coming from me.

I still say prayers of thanks that Menotti was so small, too small to know about these things. The little baby had pain enough. Not a dry cloth for me to change him. For hours he had to stay wet and dirty. I nursed him as I could, and I held my cloak over him even after my arms wanted to fall from my shoulders. At my breast at least he could be warm.

In my mind I tried everything to keep from weakening. When I was girl, I liked to ride in the forest in the rainy season. I tried to think about those good rides, to pretend I was a girl again. But I could not make that pretending last long.

I know that José watched me--every step. So I tried to see how long I could go before he had to help me. One time he tied a kerchief around his neck for a sling to carry the baby against his chest to give me a rest. There he kept his poncho over Menotti and blew his warm breath on the little baby. After I saw that, I carried the baby in the same way.

The soldiers were good to us, too, those without children of their own. They brought food for me and Menotti. Whatever they had, even when they were hungry themselves, the food I took gladly to keep up my strength and to keep milk coming for the baby. José kept sending soldiers with berries when he found any along the path. I could see in his eyes that he grew very tired. Still, he did the things others could not keep doing, like leading the pack mules over the worst places, a terrible labor.

At night we had to set sentries. The soldiers couldn't grumble about staying awake because not many of us slept at night under the tarpaulins, anyway. José joined me when he could to try to keep us warm, even if he couldn't keep us dry. I could see the way he arose in the morning, that his terrible rheumatism in his shoulders tortured him. But I know that he also suffered for the people we had to leave along the way, the poor women who weakened and could not be helped, especially the children who could not be carried along. He tried to help every one. But after the first few days, even his strength began to vanish.

Not many whole families made it to the top of that gorge. When we got there, we did not wish to count those left behind.

Ten days of struggling, every step taken twice, up the sides of steep cuts and down the other side with always a new scramble waiting ahead. We grabbed at trees, pulled horses by their halters, slipped back sometimes more steps than we took forward. Our lungs always tried to reach for more air. We tried not to think about getting to the top. Then we fought to think about nothing. Ten nights without rest. In the daytime we did not dare to stop for more than a few minutes.

CHAPTER 31

The Rebels Reach Safety in the High Country/Doña Feliciana's Concern /Anita's Mystical Identities

Editor: When the survivors finally reached the plateau, the worst of their struggles were over. The sun shone strong and the companions at last had dry wood for fires to warm their bones and dry their clothing. Also food was easier to gather. The land was flatter with better visibility for the sentries to look out for enemy attacks. Best of all, Menotti was still healthy. He had a terrible rash from the dampness and infrequent changes, but he recovered soon, much to Anita's relief.

At the top of their climb the troops settled and waited for the rest of their comrades to catch up. The last were led by General Gonçalves, himself. They came slowly in small groups, reporting that they had suffered more than the people in advance from attacks by *Moringuue* and his bands. But they had lost not one person. Even better, they had retrieved several of the families, who had fallen behind.

As soon as they had settled to rest, Gonçalves gave his terrible news to José. Rossetti was killed in a raid by *Moringue's* guerillas just before the rear guard left Villa Settembrina. He and Neiton were loading their printing press onto their packhorses when they fell.

Anita felt Rossetti's death keenly, perhaps because of the suffering it caused Garibaldi.

Anita: Poor José. If Rossetti knew how hard the trail would be he would never try to pack his machinery and he might still be alive.

José's grief was like a terrible weight on his heart. For the whole journey ahead to Cruz Alto, he stayed close to me and the baby. I was like a mother to them both, and I prayed for José to recover his spirits. His agony was worse now than when Griggs was killed because at that place he had no time to grieve for the North American.

But, praise heaven, after a few days rest in the warmer weather even José's spirits were stronger between his bouts of sad memory.

Editor: The retreating rebels could not stay long in Cruz Alta. They were so numerous that food became scarcer and they needed fresh horses. Colonel Canabarro announced that they would have to continue all the way to São Gabriel, 200 kilometers farther south before they could feel safe. "We can let the sunshine separate the aches from our bones as we go," he told them. Anita reported to Doña Feliciana that it took three more days for her to stop shivering.

In all those early days of mourning for Rossetti, Garibaldi never neglected his wife and son. He kept searching for the things they needed, a store of food, extra shirts and soft wrapping for the baby, who was now more than two months old and already a seasoned trooper. Everyone fought for his attention. The soldiers especially. A smile from him was a real prize. The winner boasted to others about it. José was proud, of course, but already he was thinking more about other things, such as moving on from this campaign. He complained to Anita that, for him, retreating before the enemy was difficult to accept. Earlier, as chief naval officer and later when he led his own cavalry, he was always first to risk his life. We do well to recall Rossetti's speculations about Garibaldi's enthusiasm for independent guerilla warfare, which was his preference all along. But now the whole army moved slowly in retreat, like a lame mule, and no one could leave off looking for food.

Anita: Everyone was tired and sad. José wasn't worse than the others but not better. Before, I always saw him with a high spirit, strong enough to make all the others brave. Now he talked more and more about Italy. I didn't blame him. His family is in Nice, a place I know nothing about. Since our tiny hero was born, I had thoughts about my family, too. But I could not think about going back to Laguna.

I thought many times about sending news to my mother. But what good would come of it? What is Menotti to them? In truth I could say that my child is from a marriage—a family, anyone would say—better than any of my friends. May I be forgiven for saying what is in my heart.

And my baby has a father. Not like those poor girls who had the babies from the strangers in Laguna or from the men in our village who ran away and would not admit their fatherhood. We all knew about them. My child's father is a true hero: A warrior who loved me from the beginning. He is honored among his compatriots. Destiny toys with us with both hands. For my sins, I will pay, as all of us must. More, I think. But I still rejoice in the family that she brought me.

Editor: Even though winter approached, the nights were warmer. The rebels made their next camp in Cruz Alta. They stopped there because the cavalry advised that it was a good place to capture fresh horses.

When the time came to move on, Anita was sorry to leave that beautiful village in high, open country, where they had plenty of clean water. She knew that no other girls from Laguna had ever journeyed so far or under such circumstances. But she knew from Garibaldi's changing mood that they could not stay in Cruz Alta. Try as he did to hide them, his thoughts were already far ahead.

The retreat continued to São Gabriel, which took almost one month. It is a smaller town than Cruz Alta but below the rugged mountainous terrain. It rests among lower hills covered with grass and plenty of cattle and horses roaming the sloping grazing lands. Anita and the others were welcome there, for most of the residents were sympathetic to the revolution.

Anita: After our long march to São Gabriel we rested for a day. Soon everybody became busy building barracks for soldiers and houses for the families. It felt good. We could settle there until the revolution gained new strength. I thought that my wishes about settling down as a family might came true here. The people in the village helped us. José even met an Italian settler. Francesco Anzani. His family made a place for me and Menotti. But José built a simple hut for us. "Our own four walls," he told me. That was better.

With the Anzanis I felt again the distance that grows between José and me when he speaks to another Italian. He talked to Francesco about the baby and me, but in Italian. I could understand quite a few words. I know he said proud things, but often when José held him so long the baby reached for me. José and Francesco laughed. I just took the baby back. I did not like that joking. José sees it. I am not a wife to stand and smile at everything.

Somehow I cannot blame him, but I did not let him forget his real family. No one, not any Italian or anyone else stands over us: Me and my son.

The Anzanis were happily settled in São Gabriel. They had no plans to return to Italy with José, but even after José finished our little hut, almost every evening he went to the Anzanis. I knew that Italy was getting bigger and bigger in his thoughts.

He told me about coming here to Montevideo, Doña Feliciana. I felt no surprise. He always talked about many Italians he knew here. Also, he wanted to get some news about his family. So I was ready when he said he wanted to leave São Gabriel.

Doña Feliciana: After so long a silence I felt that this was a good time for me to speak again, to say something to raise Anita's spirits, a compensation for her having to leave San Gabriel. As for me, I could never settle in such a small, remote village. As humble as her little home here in Montevideo seems to her, it is still worlds above such a primitive place as that. But who is to say? After all, the circumstances count for a lot. Still, for Anita's encouragement, I had to say, "My dear Anita, I count it a fortunate decision that Garibaldi brought you here."

Anita: Thank you, Doña Feliciana. I am lucky to be here with you as a friend. But back then I knew nothing about this place, what to expect. We faced hardships to get here. As I told you, Gonçalves allowed us to gather a herd of cattle as our pay because his revolutionary government had no money to give us. In Montevideo we believed we could sell them. A good plan. But it was hard work to keep so many cattle together on a long voyage.

I had to take care of Menotti so I could not help to herd them. José is not a gaucho, so he had to learn quickly how to control everything. But he grew more tired every day, and we had a journey of almost 500 kilometers. The baby grew bigger every day and needed more than my milk. I had to stop to clean him, to get down from the horse to rest my legs, my back. If I fell behind a little, I wasn't worried. I knew I could find my way back to the others. Sometimes I even rode ahead. That way I could take care of Menotti and rest while I waited for the others to reach me. I hoped that when we got to Montevideo we would find friends, a good place to live. Who could blame me for worrying at night while José and Menotti slept? Before you came to see me, I though my worst dreams were true. You have changed my life, Doña Feliciana. I can never repay you.

Doña Feliciana: I could not answer her right away. I knew that sooner or later my emotions would overcome me. So be it. When I could speak again, "Anita, my dear, dear girl," I answered her, "Just listening to your ordeals tears my heart apart. But why do I call you girl? Yes, of course in years you are far younger than I am, but in the things you have seen, what you have suffered, I am the one who feels like a child."

Anita: Doña Feliciana, I don't tell about the things I have seen to make you feel like that towards me. You asked me, you see? So you helped me to speak, even in my simple way.

Doña Feliciana: Can you imagine her saying that to me? I protested that she is gracious, not simple, not at all a simple person. Then with apologies I came back to the most important question still on my mind—in Santa Cruz or in São Gabriel, was there a church, a priest? And without going round in circles, I told her straight away about christening Menotti.

Clearly, she remembered, so I pressed her to tell me if she saw to it. "The boy's soul--I am thinking of that!" I told her. "He went already through so much danger. Suppose, may God prevent it, something should happen to him, Anita?" She answered still somewhat shaky, "Yes, the child's soul, my soul, and José's, too!"

"Well, then, my dear?" I ventured to ask.

Anita: Doña Feliciana, you are my friend. All these days, whenever you can, you come to talk to me. You listen to all I tell you. You write it down. It is a big thing in my life, what you are doing, but I don't tell you everything.

Doña Feliciana: "My dear Anita. I have done little. I sit and listen, ask a question here and there at the risk of annoying you. I have heard your own voice change from a shy girl's —Yes, you are a mother, and I am barren, childless. That is God's will, but still to me in many ways you are my daughter. I have listened while your voice changed from a girl's to a true heroine's. You don't boast. Not once. You tell me everything, simply. Don't you see? It is an honor. I have not said it before, but to me it has been a great honor." I think it was the longest speech I made to her. Maybe not. But everything I said carried the truth of my deepest feelings.

Anita: Well, well, that is so. But about christening Menotti, I let José name him, as I said. As for the baptizing, when he was born in Mostardas, I knew the prayer. I tried to say it, but I could not make it leave my throat.

Now, Doña Feliciana, I will tell you a thing that may make you wish not to come here again. You know I left my family to go with José. I left my mother, my brother, sisters. But more. A husband. I left my marriage behind.

You asked and now I tell everything.

Doña Feliciana: It took me some minutes to find my voice again. What had I forced her to confess? What pain had I caused her to tell me?

"I'm sorry, Anita, I did not wish to shame you, but believe me, if there is any shame, it falls on me. Let me tell you the truth. I will never turn from you, no matter what happens, whatever you choose to tell me. Somehow I knew there was more to tell, some explanation for your hesitation." That is what came out of my mouth finally.

Anita: Ah, yes, explanations. Always reasons. Let me try to show you how this could happen. Then you will understand that before Garibaldi came I was a thing only, another poor girl, married too early to a man sixteen years older than me. I do not complain, not even about him. My family gave me to him for my own good and, of course, so they would have one less mouth to feed. At least he had a trade. Besides, I was not a calm daughter for them. I admit I made trouble. It was in my blood.

The old men of our village joked with me. "You Mameluca," they called, "what Indian tribe did your father steal you from?" My father would tell them to stop teasing me. But he smiled, too. I think that he was proud of me a little, for my wildness. The men meant no harm, and they stopped before their jokes insulted my mother. My father was a gentle man. They respected him. He was a hard worker and honest. But they never teased the other girls that way, even before I showed them that they should not laugh at me.

I see that you wonder about that. Let me explain. A young girl, Feliciana, in a poor family is always in danger from the men: The touristas in Laguna, even men from our own village.

Doña Feliciana: "I understand," I could tell her honestly. "May Santa Maria protect us all!"

Anita: Yes, I prayed for that protection. But I also learned how to protect myself. More than one time I had to do it.

The worst came when I fought off one of the villagers, a brute, but no more than the rest of them. My friends knew that the men watched us when we bathed in the stream. But he made a mistake about me. One day he waited by the road. Right away his arm was around my neck. He pulled me to the ground.

I don't remember how I fought him. I only know that quickly I had his whip in my hand. I struck at his face, his arms, at anything. He tore my dress, you see—but I saw the blood on him from the whip strokes, and I heard him scream. It was from the whip across his face, his eyes. He screamed without stopping, and I kept whipping him until I was on his horse. I pulled up on the reins, to make the horse rear and kick, you see. But I did not have to.

It was a long time before he returned to the village. And he still wears a patch on that eye. When he dies, may the wild pigs feed on his carcass! Pardon me, Feliciana, for saying such bold things. (56)

Well, the men in Laguna teased me a different way after I rode back on his horse with his whip in my hand. "Mameluca!"

They meant no harm. They respected me. Maybe I am a half Indian. Why not? I can ride my horse like the best vaqueiro even now, better than José, my golden hero from Italy! Every horse I ride knows my thoughts. I am like the Empress Leopoldina, who was herself a great rider. I can ride the most fiery horses without fear.

That Leopoldina, yes. You have heard of her? The wife of the first Dom Pedro of Brazil. Maybe her love for simple Brasileiros entered our soil, mixed with the blood of Atiola.

Doña Feliciana: Atiola? Her I did not know. The Brazileiros have their own special myths. Her name, this Atiola, sounded like an Indian, and I was right.

Anita: An Indian Goddess from the earth in Santa Catarina. She gave the people manioc. That came from the old tales. Her blood nourished the earth, you see. I heard the old men tell it, laughing, that I am the new Atiola.

And there was the other, the heroine in the Bahiana revolt. You have heard about her, maybe? Maria de Jesus. Her name is the same as mine. Her brother was called to war but she went in his place. She was captured and executed in the same year I was born! So you see, I am a daughter of Destiny! (57)

CHAPTER 32

Anita Accedes to Doña Feliciana's Concern

Anita: I believe it! Their spirits are in me. Why not? A lot of magic comes with those names, and a lot of mystery. More than a few men stayed away from me. So I cannot blame my mother for wanting me to marry Manoel. The look in my eyes, she told me. "Be careful, Aninha. You have the spirit of men's longing in your eyes. "I will never forget it. I was fourteen years. And my poor father by then in his grave. So I married, and she thought I would be tamed, safe. But now I have given her worse than she ever expected.

Did she know when I was a baby what was ahead for me? Now does she think all her pain and trouble worth it? Too late. I was a woman eighteen years old, four years married. I would have lived my life on the edge of Laguna, watching my husband fix shoes when he had the trade, or sailing his fishing boat back into the lagoon. Maybe someone will understand what I felt. The four years before José came to me, I had the duties of a wife. I hated it. I tried everything to stay away from Manoel's desire. "Wait, Aninha," my mother told me, "you will learn patience." Patience!

He was a nice man, Manoel, but weak. He expected things from me. I knew that. He tried to order me but he couldn't control me in everything. I think he was sorry he married me, and I thank the saints that I never had to carry one of his children. God forgive me! That would have been the end for me! He complained to my family and my mother begged me to be a respectful wife. "Be grateful, Aninha." That's what she told me. "You are a fatherless daughter. You are lucky to have a good man with a trade, one who desires you and provides for you."

My poor Mama. What did she know about desire? José gave me that hunger. He filled it, too. No one else. I'll tell it. From the beginning he was so patient for my pleasure. I still can't hold back my passion for him, even when he makes me jealous. I must tell you that in making love José is no brute. I nearly faint from the fire he makes me feel. Such fire from the first time even until now!

But Manoel. He was a dull animal, an ox who fell between my legs and pushed. Uh! Uh! Uh! Like punching stitches into shoes. Uh! Uh! And then he rolled off me, leaving me with my secret prayer that no baby would start to grow in me. God forgive me! That was life to me before José came to Laguna, after Manoel was taken into the Imperial Militia. (58)

And how eagerly I went with José. I could not stop myself. Away from my own husband without saying goodbye to my mother. Only one friend saw me depart, Maria Fortunata. My best friend. One quick embrace. I left her my little scissors to remember me. She said that she would pray for me. What a sign it was. Her prayers and my little scissors, for sewing, to fix her husband's blouse or to snip threads from the patches on her children's clothes. A little pair of blades, too dull to hurt the skin but sharp enough to slash me from my family, my friends, the Church, from everything. Destino! I left my husband for José, my family. Everything for his love! (59)

Now, Doña Feliciana, you decide if you still wish to be my friend.

Editor: As things turned out, the reverse was true. It was Doña Feliciana who had to admit her own doubt that Anita would still accept her. She confessed that she had taken steps that Anita might well consider interference of the boldest sort. She told it during their final recorded meeting together, just before she brought Father Lorenzo into their relationship.

She acknowledged that, by now, Maria had broken too many of God's commandments to hope for a union sanctioned by the Church, especially given Garibaldi's distrust and disrespect for all priests.

Still, Doña Feliciana suggested that some priests might sympathize with the Riograndense Rebels.

Anita still wanted to know what these political complications had to do with her marriage and her child. That is when Doña Feliciana's admission came tumbling out. She knew a priest, she said, a young curate, who might be willing to speak with Anita. In fact, she admitted, she had already spoken with him, strictly out of her concern for the baby Menotti's eternal soul and of course Anita's and Giuseppe's, although she assured Anita that she had mentioned no names to Father Lorenzo. It was clear by now, however, that whatever Doña Feliciana had written during her last few entries were meant for Fra Lorenzo's eyes also.

To this, Anita insisted that she could not meet with him until she talked with Garibaldi, only to learn that Doña Feliciana had already done so! Doña Feliciana added hurriedly that Garibaldi told her his belief that Anita wanted a marriage and that he did, too, especially for when he would take his little family to his relatives in Genoa, so she would be respected there as she is here. "What I did, you must believe me, it was for your sake, yours and the child's. But to come between you and Señor Garibaldi, never! I would never wish that. For your souls, you see! I did it for your everlasting souls! Still, if I was wrong, you may never wish to see me again."

To all of that rush of words and rationalizing, Anita's response was succinct.

"Bring the priest.

CHAPTER 33

Conversations with Fra Lorenzo Begin

Editor: Before handing her notes over to Fra Lorenzo, Doña Feliciana asked if he would be willing to read them and, knowing all that
they contained about Anita's and Garibaldi's union, help them in
any way he could. Fra Lorenzo listened carefully and, without taking a moment to consider, reassured her of his willingness to read
what Doña Feliciana wished to give him. He also acknowledged
the urgency of her concern for the family's status in the eyes of the
Church. To which purpose he, following Doña Feliciana's example, recorded the following.
Conversations with Doña Anita Garibaldi:

I, Father Lorenzo, Curate in The Church of San Bernardino in
Montevideo, Uruguay, record here, at the urging of her friend and
confidante, Doña Feliciana Garcia-Bellegas, conversations between myself and Doña Anita Garibaldi, which follow my perusal
of a document of approximately one hundred pages of interviews
between Doñas Feliciana and Garibaldi.

I attest that I have recorded, directly after each meeting, according to my honest recollection, the exact words by which each
of us expressed ourselves.

Furthermore, the substance of the conversations recorded here
falls within my function as counselor, prior to and separate from
any formal Confession or other Sacramental procedures for which
I am licensed by The Holy Roman Apostolic Catholic Church.

I wish to add a concern here for Doña Feliciana. That at an early point in her interviews with Doña Anita, she, Doña Feliciana,
understandably had doubts about the young woman's veracity. I
had to tell her that, from what I had already heard about her, Doña
Anita might seem perhaps at least to have embellished the truth. I
had to assure her, however, that I was in no position to judge the
Braziliera. I had made that clear. First, I had not heard or read
enough of her disclosures to measure the veracity of their substance; second, any judgment about her veracity, even if she were
to confess as much, must be directed by God's Will.

To this, Doña Feliciana, conscientious woman that she is, told me she feared Doña Anita's suggestion that she might have some Indian blood and, more serious, that she was an incarnation of an Indian Earth Spirit and—Doña Feliciana was less certain about this—that Doña Anita might also be in some way an incarnation of The Brazilian Empress Leopoldina and also—here she crossed herself, poor woman—of one Maria de Jesus, who went to war in her brother's place.

I gave her my assurance that such assertions were not so much superstition as symbolic inventions, and that I would have ample time to weigh their earnestness later. For primary purposes, such suspicions bear much less importance than my responsibility for her as yet un-christened child.

So now, to my best ability, I convey Doña Anita's and my conversation.

Doña Anita: Yes, Father. If that's what Doña Feliciana has told you, then you know about me, my problem. Can you help me?

Fra Lorenzo: That is what I am here for. As to my helping you, we will see. First tell me about your legal husband, his name.

Doña Anita: Manoel Doarte de Aguiar.

Fra Lorenzo: Do you know where Don Manuel is?

Doña Anita: No. He went in the Imperial Army, when the Riograndenses came to take charge of Santa Catarina. He joined the Imperials or somehow they took him away to fight.

Fra Lorenzo: Have you seen him since that time?

Doña Anita: No.

Fra Lorenzo: Not once?

Doña Anita: Never.

Fra Lorenzo: Did he write to you?

Doña Anita: I can't read, Father. Manoel, maybe he could read numbers, to count money, or some words about shoes, leather, awls, and such. He was a cobbler, but I never saw him write.

Fra Lorenzo: So when he went with the Imperial Army, that was the last you saw him?

Doña Anita: Yes. Some men from my village said they thought they saw him among the troops, but only rumors.

Fra Lorenzo: How old were you when you married Señor Doarte?

Doña Anita: I was fourteen years.

Fra Lorenzo: And how long were you married when you met Señor Garibaldi?

Doña Anita: Four years.

Fra Lorenzo: You had no children with your husband?

Doña Anita: None.

Fra Lorenzo: Now you have a son, so you are not barren. Did you consummate your marriage to Señor Doarte?

Doña Anita: Father?

Fra Lorenzo: You did not withhold yourself from him?

Doña Anita: No, Father. But I couldn't make believe I was pleased about that, you know?

Fra Lorenzo: Well, you were married in a church. Do you remember its name and the priest who blessed your union?

Doña Anita: Yes, Father. Santo Antonio dos Anjos in Laguna. Vicar Manoel Ferreira da Cruz heard our vows.

Fra Lorenzo: You remember well, my daughter. Everything. I have met Señor Garibaldi. He too is a likeable man and a hero by reputation, but no one has told me much about you before Doña Feliciana. There, there, my dear.

Doña Anita: Forgive me, Father. I haven't cried in many months. I couldn't stop myself.

Fra Lorenzo: Your tears are justified. Take it as a good sign of your contrition. Be assured, some things I can do for your child. But I am concerned about all of your souls, not only your son's. That is what we must consider. Whatever is within my power by the authority of the Church, I can, I will do. For now, try to be tranquil. I will ask Doña Feliciana to come back to you. You should be grateful for such a friend.

Doña Anita: I am, Father. I am.

End of first meeting

Second meeting between Doña Anita Garibaldi and Fra Lorenzo.

Fra Lorenzo: My daughter, the things you told me are you contrite about them?

Doña Anita: I don't understand, Father.

Fra Lorenzo: Are you truly sorry for what you have done?

Doña Anita: For which things, Father?

Fra Lorenzo: You try to tell me.

Doña Anita: For disgracing my family, for bringing pain to my friends, for insulting Manoel.

Fra Lorenzo: More than insulting him, my daughter. You made promises to the Church about your love and your duty to him.

Doña Anita: For breaking my vows, for doing peril to Menotti's soul, to José's soul.

Fra Lorenzo: And do you wish to save your soul?

Doña Anita: Menotti's first of all, and José's too.

Fra Lorenzo: But yours?

Doña Anita: Father, if I don't try to save their souls, how can I save my own?

Fra Lorenzo: We are not here to satisfy subtle arguments, my daughter. Nevertheless, you are right. But, as for saving souls, that is not up to you alone. You can only help by saying that you wish it. Now you have admitted everything, and you have told me that you truly wish to make amends, to do penance as you need to?

Doña Anita: I am honest when I say I'm sorry about hurting every one. But Father, I still can't say that I'm sorry I went with José. I go back and forth about my love for him.

Fra Lorenzo: What are you saying? Do you mean that you have had other men?

Doña Anita: What? Never, Father, never!

Fra Lorenzo: I warn you, Doña Anita, if you do not tell me everything truly, I can do nothing for you. You are not now in formal confession. But that must surely come later, and if you hold something back, tell me now so that I can judge your worthiness for absolution. What do you mean about your uncertainty?

Doña Anita: Nothing like what you said, Father, I promise you. But sometimes, José has made me doubt him.

Fra Lorenzo: Do you mean you doubt his fidelity to you? If you have evidence of it, then I sympathize, as a human being. If he is guilty, that is a sin he must atone for. If you are jealousy for no good reason, then, you must beware of that. But understand, none of that can mean much at this point. Now I ask you one final time, have you anything more to tell me? Think carefully, my daughter! Be true! Consider all that lies ahead for you. . . . All right, if you cannot speak now, let your tears cleanse your heart. I will come back tomorrow. Be ready to answer in truth the question I put to you one last time.

End of second meeting

Third meeting between Doña Anita Garibaldi and Fra Lorenzo

CHAPTER 34

Anita's Most Drastic Confession

Fra Lorenzo: Now, Doña Anita, are you ready to tell me of anything more that troubles your soul? Remember, although we are not now in formal confession, I am here to counsel you for the time when you will be, that time when you must indeed tell all. For if you do not; then your soul will face the gravest dangers.

Doña Anita: I'm ready, Father. But I must begin with one thing that maybe led to my worst sinning, the one I haven't told about, not to any one before.

Fra Lorenzo: Take as much time as you need.

Doña Anita: You know that I was with José in many battles.

Fra Lorenzo: No one has told me about such things. Really, you must let me hear all about them, as much as you remember, and let me judge your behavior.

Doña Anita: This one battle I must tell you about, the most important in its way. It happened far in the North near to Santa Catarina, my Province.

Fra Lorenzo: I know the area. Go on, please.

Doña Anita: The Imperials formed a huge army in Laguna and pushed us back into Rio Grande do Sul. We were still strong but smaller. So we made a march north toward the Marombas Pass and Curitibanos to meet them. It is a wild country. We marched as far as the fork of the Rio Canoas and set guards all around for the night. In the middle of the night, the Imperialistas attacked. I stayed close to José all the time watching where I could help. We fought so hard that the Imperialistas ran back across the river. Our soldiers chased the enemy to the high plain above the gorge. But when they were almost up to the plateau, the enemy fired on us from both sides. An ambush, you see. Six of our brave men were cut down.

Fra Lorenzo: You remember all such details?

Doña Anita: Yes, Father, you told me to omit nothing.

Fra Lorenzo: That is quite amazing, Doña Anita. Go on. I listen to you with full confidence.

Doña Anita: How could I forget such things? Before I met José I could never dream of such adventures, to be in them, not to watch them from far away or hear about them afterward.

Fra Lorenzo: You are right, my dear. As I have said, I do not doubt you. Please go on.

Doña Anita: We galloped our troops to a small stand of woods and made ready to fight. There we piled our ammunition and extra guns. José ordered me to stay in the middle of the copse with the soldiers guarding our supplies. He and his troop moved to the other side and began to fire on the enemy to bring them away from our soldiers trapped in the ambuscade. If I knew what was to happen to me, I wouldn't let him go far from me. I have reason to remember it well, as you will see.

I did not like to stand on the ground with all the fighting going on near me. So when some horses from fallen cavalry ran past, I caught one and rode back to our station.

Fra Lorenzo: You were able to do that?

Doña Anita: Of course. I was brought up with horses, wilder than those trained for the cavalry.

Fra Lorenzo: Well, well. Please go on, my daughter.

Doña Anita: The Imperialists soon found us in the copse and cut us off from José's cavalry. There were many enemies and they fired as they came without stopping. The bullets flew around us like bees in thick swarms. My hat flew from my head. Then I was on the ground climbing free from my fallen horse. The poor beast already lost its first rider and then its own life. I got to my feet and called the men to form a circle. We shot all our muskets at the enemy; then we had nothing but our sabres. When they formed a second circle around us, they pointed their muskets and bayonets and we had to stop fighting. I didn't know where José was, not even if he was alive.

I expected bad things from our captors. We heard many stories about the way the Imperialist soldiers treated our people—especially the ones who were far from their own homes. But nothing like that happened. A few of our captors taunted us, made fun of me. Then they took me to their commander. Colonel Melo Albuquerque. He surprised me. He told me in front of his officers that he knew my name. He said the things he heard made him respect me. Can you believe that?

Fra Lorenzo: Yes, my dear, I can see why. Of course!

Doña Anita: That was the first time I was set apart with my own name, you understand, Father? He was a gentleman who treated me like an honorable enemy. Believe me I was sure he was making fun of me, but I couldn't think of that for long, for soon I had a worse thing to remember. That is what I tell you now.

Fra Lorenzo: Don't stop, please. Doña Feliciana told me that you suffered much in the war, like any soldier, but I did not understand her completely.

Doña Anita: She is the first person I ever talked to about it. But this battle, Father, I didn't tell her about it. The Colonel told me that José was dead. His soldiers reported it to him. "Your husband fell in the battle not far from where you became our prisoner," he told me. "I am sorry to tell you of this, Senhora Garibaldi. "I heard him but I couldn't keep his words in my head. Now I remember every one.

The next day he gave me permission to look for José's body. On that field of death, it was like I went down into The Pit. Hell itself couldn't be worse, Father--all the fallen bodies. It was a place of wandering souls. No, please, Father, let me explain. You see, in my own heart I was already mourning José. Those people said he was killed. So I turned bodies over, pulled stiff arms away from faces, wiped mud from those faces with my hands, my skirt.

If I knew before what it would be like, I don't know if I could have the strength. But I had to find José, to know if in truth he was dead. I crawled under bushes, dragged bodies from ditches. They were already stiff, many had flesh torn away by bullets and sabers. Each one I turned I wondered if José would lie like that, alone, his soul searching for a place to rest. Again and again I had to stop, to stand up, rest my back and see where I had already looked, where else I must search. And each time I paused, I wanted to stop looking. But I still moved from one body to the next with the hope that I would not find him. Do you see, Father?

Fra Lorenzo: Yes, I understand, Doña Anita, why you could not give up that terrible searching, what was at stake for you.

Doña Anita: But, Father, my feelings were twisted around. (60) Such searching is work that wants to be finished, do you understand? Then the evil thought came to me. That is finally what I must admit to you, as you said to me. I wanted to find José's body and let him lie dead where he was! May God forgive me for saying so. My confusion. I swear I couldn't help the bad thought that came again and again, no matter how hard I fought with it. I kept thinking, if I find José's body, I can run away into the forest. I will know that he is dead, but I will carry my own name alone. Colonel Albuquerque, my captor, showed me that I already had one. I knew that I could take care of myself, steal horses, find food, whatever I needed. May God forgive me, even if I don't have the right to call on Him. I wanted to find José dead. No more living like his shadow. I could be a person with light to make my own shadow.

That was my hardest time, Father, the sin I wanted to keep from every one. I knew I should beg God's forgiveness for listening to those bad spirits struggling for my soul. But I tell you now that, even with those thoughts in my head, I kept searching. May you find something in that to save me, even though I can't say that I willed myself to keep searching. It was an action that went on by itself. Oh, Mother of God, I felt such pity for those fallen soldiers! I went to the far edge of that circle of death until I could find no more bodies. So many dead, our comrades and the enemy's, all warriors, but not one of them victorious.

Fra Lorenzo: Well, my dear, at least those whose souls are at rest.

Doña Anita: From my sleep that night back in the camp I jumped up again and again, seeing in my dreams another body behind a tree, in a ditch, bodies I didn't see before to turn over, another and another.

That is what I wanted to tell you about. Even now the guilt troubles my dreams.

Fra Lorenzo: I understand, Señora. This is a most remarkable experience. I mean I appreciate your anxiety. But, please, we will come back to that. For now tell me what happened next. Did you escape? Did the Colonel set you free? How did you join Señor Garibaldi again?

Doña Anita: But, Father, do you think you can help me now?

Fra Lorenzo: I can only suggest that. Yes, I believe I can. But much is still up to you. I promise we will come back to that. For now, I should like to know more about your experience.

Doña Anita: As you wish, Father. I didn't speak with the Colonel after that. The next day I prepared some food and washed my clothes. Nothing was in my mind except to be with José. You see, I could believe only that he could be alive, that I looked at every last body on that field. So I watched for my best chance to flee. The guards didn't bother me when I went away from my place to rinse clothes and hang them on the low bushes. Only one soldier worried me. He was from Laguna, Gonçalves Padilha his name, a man who wanted to court me when I was younger, but I refused him back then. I think he would have done me harm if the colonel was not so respectful. But I was able to stay away from him.

On the next day I took a sack to gather my clothes, but I had in it all that I needed. It was almost dusk. When I got to the place where my clothes hung to dry, I folded them into my sack. After I was sure no one was watching, I sneaked through the brush until I reached the fields farthest from our camp. I crawled through the fields to where the woods went down to the river.

The biggest danger was from the sentries who galloped from the camp to their outposts. I waited until one went past and the sky became a little darker. I could not wait long or they would miss me. Across the field I saw the sentry's horse grazing, so I crept closer until I saw the soldier sitting against a tree. His head was hanging and his poncho was pulled up. Asleep, you see. On sentry duty. Not a very good soldier. I couldn't see his musket, but I had to take the chance.

I removed the tongs from the horse's leg and put my hand over his nose. Then I led him step by step to the edge of the ravine, down through the woods and to the river.

Fra Lorenzo: Wonderful! You knew exactly what to do!

Doña Anita: Of course, Father. As I said, I was on horses from before I can remember. Excuse me. I don't mean to speak so boldly.

Fra Lorenzo: No, no, Doña Anita, my dear girl. Never mind. Go on, please.

Doña Anita: Well, at that place the river was still too deep to walk across, so I plunged the horse in and grabbed his saddle horn with one hand. With my other hand I carried my sack high out of the water. On the other bank I led the animal up through the woods to the open fields. I knew we were in the District of Lages. That's all, so I chose a direction at my best guess and rode as fast as I could across the dark fields until I felt the horse grow tired. I spent the night in a small copse shivering and wet, but I didn't dare to make a fire. When morning came, I mounted again.

The open field was like a whole fresh world to me. The sun was already high and warm. I rode as fast as I could with the sun on my left. I knew that soon I could find a trail to the village of Lages. There I would begin again to search for José, a living José. This time to find him alive!

Fra Lorenzo: That thought must have brought you relief, even though you were weary and hungry.

Doña Anita: I didn't feel those the night before but soon I had to stop. The little bit of food I took with me was gone, so I rode to a wooded area where I found a spring for us to drink, the horse and me. It was delicious. Cold and clear. Then I tied the horse near some grazing and slept. We both needed some rest.

The sun wasn't yet up when I awoke. My thoughts were mixed up. I didn't know the time, how long I was running. But the morning air smelled good and I soon cleared my head enough to examine the area. Berry bushes grew along the edge of the copse where we stopped, but you can eat many berries and remain hungry. I also dug up some roots and sipped some water because I knew that it was better for me to reach Lages as fast as I could. There I could get better food. So I saddled my horse and rode without caution. In the next afternoon I reached Lages.

Fra Lorenzo: Amazing, my dear Señora! But you must have felt relieved to be out of danger at last.

Doña Anita: No, Father, not yet. Lages wasn't safe. The Imperialists were back there, and I knew I was in danger of being caught again. So I waited until dusk and circled to the place where José and I had a hut. It was closed up, so I went to the house of two old ladies who were our neighbors. At first they were frightened and wouldn't let me in. I called to them by name and still they wouldn't open the door. Then I loosened my hair and let them see that it was me, Anita. Right away, they welcomed me and put my horse in their shed. I slept through that day in a shelter for the first time in days.

When I was awake the women had food and water for me. What little they had they gave to me, you see? Such sympathetic women who put themselves in danger for me. When we came through there with our Riograndenses the first time, they saw the Black Lancers and they were frightened. All those strange people coming to tell them that they had a new government, a free one. To them strangers only meant different troubles. Freedom from the Emperor meant nothing to them. Better to be left to their meager lives. But still they helped me like family.

Better than the food, they told me that José was in Lages only two days before! He too stopped at the house where we lived. They saw him with their own eyes. After that he left for Santa Vitória. I was beginning to feel my pregnancy, but I couldn't rest.

Fra Lorenzo: With all your other troubles, my dear Doña Anita, that too?

Doña Anita: What choice did I have, Father? The men in Lages were Loyalists, so I couldn't go out freely. The women told me that a man from Saõ Paulo was driving his wagon to Vacaria and said he would take me. But I was afraid. If he was challenged, why would he not give me up? Most important, a wagon was too slow. So I thanked my dear friends and said I would go on my horse. They gave me rice and a blouse, some underclothes of their own, and I galloped out of Lages on the trail to the Rio Pelota and Vacaría to the south.

Fra Lorenzo: My dear girl, to ride so long on a horse in that condition. Was that wise?

Doña Anita: Wisdom, Father? The only wisdom was to get as far from my captors as I could. Never would I give birth to my baby as a prisoner.

Fra Lorenzo: What are you saying, Doña Anita?

Doña Anita: I'm sorry, Father, but I can tell that you know what I mean. Before I let my child be born a prisoner among those who hated us, I would never let that happen. How could I let him begin his life that way? And how could I tell what they would do to us? Better for us to die together.

Fra Lorenzo: But, my dear daughter that is something I cannot bear to hear, as a priest. Do you understand?

Doña Anita: Yes, Father, you are right. Please forgive me. I can see now how wrong that was. But being there at that time, it was different. I am trying to tell you how it was.

Fra Lorenzo: Well, Doña Anita, I am relieved that at least you understand the peril in what you contemplated.

Doña Anita: Yes, Father, yes. But I didn't care to hide or slow down. I stopped from time to time only to rest the horse. I threw all my fears from my mind. I traveled one and one-half days from the time I left Lages. On that second day near dusk, I got off my horse and led her quietly toward some campfires I saw. I sneaked around until I saw José standing among a group of soldiers. In my joy I couldn't hold back. I was impatient, you see. Very foolish! I mounted my horse and galloped toward them. It was a foolish thing I did. The soldiers ran for their carbines. José told me after that they thought the Loyalist guerillas were attacking them. They were ambushed many times by men who lived in the area, so I was lucky that they did not shoot me.

Fra Lorenzo: Praise God!

Doña Anita: Yes, yes, it comforts me to hear you say it. All my comrades were happy to see me. They thought I was dead, you see. They asked many questions, where I was captured, how I escaped, how the Imperialists treated me, who else was captured, killed, ran away. But soon José took me to his place near the edge of the encampment and we slept in each other's arms.

In the few moments before we slept, I told José only that I was treated respectfully. But, Father. I never told him about my search for him on the battlefield--about my sinful thoughts to find him sleeping with Death.

Fra Lorenzo: My dear child, I have no doubt that you are an honest woman. For much of what you have told me, I feel only admiration.

Doña Anita: But, Father, my dark feelings on that field of dead warriors. Even for that short time, I wanted José dead. Wasn't that a sin?

Fra Lorenzo: My poor child, your doubts about your loyalty to Señor Garibaldi, your doubts about his constant love for you? I see what kind of stress you were under at those times, even now from your recollections. But I am not testing you for sainthood. None of the people around you are saints. And you are not now talking with a saint. Only the rarest souls—or fools—are ever free of doubt. I am pleased that you have relieved your anguish by telling me.

Doña Anita: Thank you, Father. Thank you.

Fra Lorenzo: Not yet, my daughter. I have done nothing yet. Save your gratitude for more serious thanksgiving. But for now, let your heart be at rest. I already know that your condition is complicated.

End of third meeting

CHAPTER 35

Fra Lorenzo's Final Instructions

Fourth meeting

Fra Lorenzo: I have conferred with others, and I have reason to give you hope, Doña Anita. But mostly it is up to you and Señor Garibaldi. Now I will let you know what you must do. You must try to learn about your legal husband in Laguna, whether he still lives. Señor Garibaldi has sent word to friends in Laguna to learn what is known there. No matter what comes of that, you and Señor Garibaldi must wait until you are legal residents in Montevideo. After that date. . . . when did you come here?

Doña Anita: In the middle of June last year.

Fra Lorenzo: Good. Just as I hoped, the dates will work out. We will be in time for the Lenten season. If what we learn from Laguna allows us, then we will go ahead with our preparations. I will make all arrangements for your communion. Are you willing?

Doña Anita: I am, Father. But we must not wait too long. You know, don't you, that José has become an officer in the Navy. If something should happen to him.

Fra Lorenzo: I will tell him to take no risks. You do the same.

Doña Anita: But, Father, you do not know how quickly he can act. He has little care about his own safety.

Fra Lorenzo: Then I will explain the most important consideration. He must do everything to protect you and your innocent child. Menotti's soul especially must not be abandoned.

Doña Anita: I hope you can convince him, Father.

Fra Lorenzo: Don't think such things! Of course he will do what is right. His own beliefs, or lack of belief, is not the issue here. Let him carry on his own struggles afterward, but for now the Church must be respected. He has no choice about that.

End of fourth meeting

Fifth meeting

Fra Lorenzo: Doña Anita, I am happy to tell you that we now have all the papers necessary to consider you eligible to marry Señor Garibaldi in formal ceremony. Three friends have signed as witnesses that Señor Garibaldi is qualified, and I have this document witnessed by your mother in Laguna, who has made her mark to affirm that she knows no reason why you cannot marry Señor Garibaldi. With this document she gives you her consent and her blessing, so we may consider her present in spirit, as good as present in body, at the wedding. I have added a statement for you to make your sign, which you should do before a witness. Because you do not yourself read, a friend will read it aloud to you. Keep this now until I send a friend who will bring a witness. Do you suggest such a friend?

Doña Anita: Yes, Father. Doña Feliciana, please.

Fra Lorenzo: Señora Garcia-Belligas?

Doña Anita: Yes, Father.

Fra Lorenzo: Good. That is what I expected. She has become like a Godmother to your child. I trust her to do it and to bring the document to me.

End of fifth meeting

CHAPTER 36

The Marriage Arranged

Editor: Doña Feliciana assured Anita that Father Lorenzo would indeed help, that he was truly sympathetic, full of admiration for her. She soon brought two gentlemen: Don José Garcia, a friend known to Garibaldi, to witness Anita's mark and Don Pablo Semidei, a Notary, to make the signature official. They waited outside for Doña Feliciana to assure them that Anita agreed to the arrangement. When she had, they brought the document that Father Lorenzo had prepared.

Hurrying past Anita's suggestion that she put out some coffee and cakes for them, Doña Feliciana assured her that they would celebrate later. So they got down to the official business immediately with the notary's reading the document aloud, a copy of which appears here:

On this day, 21 March 1842, I, Don Pablo Semidei, A Licensed Notary, due to a verbal order of the Señor Provedor went to Doña Ana Maria de Jesus' house, who tells me she is the legitimate daughter of Don Bento Ribeiro da Silva (deceased) and Doña Maria Antonia de Jesus, and who now of free will wants to marry Don José Garibaldi, who affirms he has no impediment to doing so. And her mother gives Doña Ana Maria de Jesus her permission and maternal blessing to marry Sr. Garibaldi, as she also is aware of no impediment. Doña Ana Maria de Jesus and her mother have not signed the document because they declare themselves unable to write. Therefore, a witness signs for them below their marks.

After Anita placed her mark on the document, Don Pablo wrote her name and signed his own underneath. After the notary affixed his seal, Doña Feliciana thanked them and dismissed them with "Go with God."

An excerpt from Doña Feliciana's follow-up notes is affixed here. Anita protested that she had given no refreshments to the men for their service.

Doña Feliciana: "Please, Anita, my dear," I told her, "did not Father Lorenzo give you the document? It is perfect. As for the

Notary, he has been paid already, believe me. Later we will arrange a celebration for all those who helped. But now I must tell you about some other arrangements.

"First, we have done all that is possible to find out if your first husband, Señor Manoel Doarte, still lives. No one has evidence that he does, you understand? I do not say that we know absolutely that he is dead, just that we have tried but cannot learn that he still is alive. So you must understand that the truth about your first marriage and that accepting our attempts to discover whether he still lives, these are on your own conscience, yours and Don José's. The Church cannot absolve you for what remains unknown.

"Second, Father Lorenzo will make all the arrangements but he will not conduct the wedding ceremony. He will hear your confession, but Dom Zenon Aspiazú will meet you in the Church of San Bernardino on March 26, two days from now, and will authorize your marriage. Father Lorenzo asks me to explain that that date comes during Lent, so by then the bans will be posted only one time, which is sufficient, and, as a consequence, Dom Zenon will not recite the nuptial blessing, so do not expect it. But don't worry about that. To omit it during Lent is proper. Don Pablo and I will be honored to serve as your witnesses."

To Anita's continuing protest that she had no way to thank me and Father Lorenzo, I assured her that, as for thanks, the Good Father wanted me to tell her that after the Church joins her and Don José, then he will pray that God will forgive her, release her from her troubles, and bless her and Don José with more strong and healthy children. After a proper wait, he will baptize Menotti. "So you can see," I was pleased to tell her, "Your troubles are over."

Editor: Doña Feliciana should have added "God Willing," for her final words turned out to be more optimistic than accurate. (See Appendix 3.)

End of Memoirs

Editor's Afterword

I asked a colleague, Professor Ernestine Prine-Halloway, of the Department of English, the favor of reading a preliminary draft of this book. As a result, I learned much about the inherent design of my presentation. For instance, after her initial shock about the way Anita died, Professor Prine-Halloway asked what feelings toward Garibaldi I expected my readers to carry away. I could honestly say that, if my intentions came into it at all, I merely wished to put the three memoirs before my readers and let them form their own opinions of all the persons involved.

When I asked for her own reaction to Garibaldi, she told me that, whereas she found much to admire, she finally felt strongly ambivalent toward him. Well, actually she said she did not like him. On the positive side, she approved of his selflessness, his sympathy for unfortunates, including fallen foes, his untiring attentions to Anita during her most trying times. He could, she felt, have been more sensitive to Anita's jealousy, but that neither diminished nor displaced his abiding concern for her and their children's safety and comfort. Still, she felt something lacking, that his actions were guided more by impetuosity than deliberate judgment, whereby he often did more harm than good, and that his value as a leader was more symbolic than actual.

Respecting Rossetti, Professor Prine-Halloway concluded that Garibaldi's relationship was, in its way, similar. That is, combined with Rossetti's admiration and enthusiastic support was his criticism and his impatience with Garibaldi's impetuosity, his ill-timed outbursts of temper, his ill-guided decisions, and, in a more delicate, personal reference, his neglect of Rossetti's feelings.

Griggs was another matter. The abject opposite to Garibaldi's impetuosity, carelessness, and flamboyance, this seasoned and consummately practical American seaman, she observed, noted flaw after flaw in Garibaldi's drastic lapses in judgment. One such resulted in death by drowning of half his crew. Another was his stubborn resistance to Colonel Canabarro's order for the retreat from Laguna, which possibly resulted in Griggs's fatal entrapment during the Imperial Navy's assault. Over all, she concluded that, at the least, Garibaldi's shortcomings counterbalanced any positive effect he might have had in a revolution that, after all, had failed and which, in any event, he had abandoned.

I asked her to consider his spectacular reputation in the campaign to reunify Italy that followed his activity in Brazil and Uruguay, his effective guerilla tactics, and his inspiration to the Red Shirt Brigades. She shrugged her acknowledgement but asked, "Who today cares about Garibaldi? From what you have told me, several among his evaluators vary in their assessments from negative to ambivalent. " (She is right about that.) "And as for guerilla warriors," she went on, "we have fresher examples to admire, even if we may disapprove of their ideologies." (About that I had to agree, also.)

Back to her observation about the design of my presentation, as she put it, the point of Professor Prine-Halloway's perception was literary. She commended me for having presented three dynamic characters, more complex and sophisticated, she concluded, than Garibaldi himself. Along with their reactions to Garibaldi, they revealed a capacity for introspection, for honest disclosures about themselves. About that, I had to agree with her. Then, those traits, she added unexpectedly to me, makes them truly worth writing about, as any sophisticated novelist would recognize.

I confessed that I would willingly accept credit for fashioning such engaging characters and for recommending them to the reader's enrichment. In truth, however, I had done little more than stumble across—successfully with the help of others—their memoirs and translate what they had already written. My labor, therefore, had been more in the discovery than the design. In short, I had been spared the task I might face if, as my colleague assured me, I ever turned my hand to fiction. Let me say plainly that I have no intention of going that route. The prospect is too daunting.

Finally, I must say that, in the balance, I like Garibaldi, even though my admiration remains mixed. He had unquestioning faith in his own abilities, by which he pushed himself to the fore, to the admirable effect of inspiring others to follow him into danger, often into their own deaths. In short, so firm was his conviction and belief in his own heroic qualities that by sheer magnetism, he attracted others to his image of himself and thereby fixed their destinies to his own.

Now, did his three closest associates approve of all he did? I believe not. In any event, I must let the record I have compiled of their responses guide your own.5`

Chronological Outline of Events

1835, November: Garibaldi arrives in Brazil on board the *Nautonnier*. Meets Rossetti.

1836 Rossetti takes Garibaldi to Young Italians, writes to Mazzini. At the same time Garibaldi does. Garibaldi takes the oath of membership. Garibaldi writes anti-Sardinian article. Draws complaint by Sardinian minister to Brazilian authorities.

March 9: Griggs jumps ship in Port of Rio Grande.

End of March: Griggs guest at Doña Anna's (General Gonçalves' sister's) estancia on the Arroio Grande near Lake Mirim, then on to Piratini to meet Gonçalves

Early April: Griggs back to Doña Ana's estancia.

Garibaldi joins Freemasons in Rio. Saves slave from drowning on Rio waterfront. January: Garibaldi and Rossetti partners in business venture, delivering supplies to restaurants in Cabo Frio. Restless with "macaroni boat," Garibaldi wants to sail as privateer in support of the revolutionaries in the South.

Mid-April: Griggs moves down to a clearing near the mouth of the Camaquã River to work on boats.

September: Griggs shows progress repairing vessels for the revolutionaries' navy.

October: Gonçalves defeated in battle. He, Zambeccari and others imprisoned near Rio de Janeiro. Rossetti visits Zambeccari in prison. Garibaldi established as a privateer.

1837 February: Rossetti takes Garibaldi to visit Zambeccari in prison. Receives letters of marqué signed by General Lima.

May: Arms his "macaroni boat" in secret.

May 7: Garibaldi and Rossetti set sail from Rio. Garibaldi captures *Luisa*, 60 ton Brazilian merchant ship. Renames her *Mazzini* (scuttles his smaller vessel).

May 17: Puts captured crew of *Luisa* ashore at Itapacaroi Point.

May 28: Sails into Maldonado, Rio Platte, to supply ship. Rossetti goes ashore to sell cargo. Uruguayan President Oribe orders arrest and seizure of the , but Garibaldi escapes. Mid-June: Rossetti travels overland to Rio Grande do Sul, rebel headquarters in Piratini. Meets Griggs.

June 14: Uruguayans sympathetic to Argentina send gunboats after Garibaldi.

June 15: In battle. Garibaldi seriously wounded in neck. Sails up the Rio Paraná to Gualeguay.

June 27: Garibaldi, captured, put up in-house of Jacinto Abreu. Put on honor not to go over18 miles from Gualeguay and not to attempt escape. Rest of crew released and returned in ship to Montevideo and then Rio Grande do Sul. Gari learns Spanish and how to ride horseback. Leads quiet life in captivity.

September 10: Gonçalves escapes from prison, returns to Rio Grande do Sul.

December 37 or January 38: Garibaldi attempts escape. Captured. Tortured via strapado. Transported on horse-back to paraná and imprisoned.

1838 April: Garibaldi released abruptly. Takes ship to Montevideo. Rossetti returns from Rio Grande do Sul. Commissioned to start a newspaper for the rebels.

May: Garibaldi and Rossetti leave Montevideo for Piratini. (300 miles overland). After arrival and a few days rest, ride off to meet Gonçalves along the San Gonçalves River. The General leading troops in Battle of Pelotas. After victory, the rebels control the entire province, except Porto Alegre at the head and Rio Grande and San José do Norte at the mouth of the Lagoa dos Patos.

May 15: Garibaldi meets Griggs. Garibaldi put in command of the naval forces of the new republic.

Winter 38: Garibaldi and Griggs raid shipping on the Logoa dos Patos between Rio Grande and Porto Alegre.

September 38: Brazilian fleet bears down on rebel navy. Rossetti produces the first issue of *O 'Povo*.

Summer 1838-39: A quiet time. Social life with Gonçalves families in Camaqua and Arroyo Grande.

1839 Apr17: Rebels' shipyard attacked by guerilla leader *Moringue* (the "Marten").

April 25: General Gonçalves announces intention to move forces north into Santa Catarina. Asks Garibaldi and Griggs about a coordinated approach from the sea.

June 5: With mouth of Lagoa dos Patos blocked by Imperials, Garibaldi and Griggs make plans to transport ships overland at northern end of lagoa and into the Atlantic.

July14: Ships each Tramandai after overland haul and launch the Rio Pardo and Seival into the Atlantic for rendezvous with land troops near Laguna.

July: Griggs makes the journey safely. Garibaldi's ship flounders in surf. Loss of 16 men and all supplies. Garibaldi marches the survivors up the beach to rendezvous. Griggs coordinates the *Seival* with the land attack.

July 22: Colonel Canabarro storms Laguna.

July 26: Proclaims Santa Catarina an ally in the revolution. Navy acquires several additional vessels in Laguna.

July-August: Garibaldi, Griggs, and Lorenzo launch operations against Brazilian shipping in the Atlantic.

Between July and October: Garibaldi begins liaison with Anita, who soon joins his crew.

October: In sea battle, Garibaldi and Lorenzo take cover in Imbituba and fight off the Imperial ships. Griggs separated during the night, returns to Laguna. Garibaldi and Lorenzo follow.

Uprising against Republicans at Imarui, Santa Catarina. Garibaldi and a squad of his sailors sent to sack town. Garibaldi distressed by brutality of his troops.

Mid-November-December: Imperials launch massive attack by land and sea on Laguna. Griggs killed.

Next three months: Rebels retreat southward. Anita stays with Garibaldi throughout. Major battles along the way in Lages, Rio Pelotas, Santa Vitoria, and Curitibanos, where Anita captured and escapes to rejoin Garibaldi in Vacaria. Retreat ends in Villa Settembrina, new rebel capital near Porto Alegre.

1840 May 3: Biggest battle, at Pinheirino, near Taquari. About 6,000 Republicans vs 7,000 Imperials. Anita, 3 1/2 months pregnant, forbidden to participate. Battle ends in Republican victory.

Winter: Garibaldi sent on campaign to take San José do Norte. Anita 6 months pregnant. Battle for San José, August 16, 40. Ends in siege. Finally abandoned. Incident of throat-slitting of Imperial captives. Following campaign, Garibaldi sent up outer banks to San Simon to build battle canoes. Settles in abandoned loyalist estancia and rounds up cattle. Anita settles for winter in house in Mustarda with sympathetic family.

September 16: Menotti born. 12 days old when *Maringue* attacks (September 28). Anita escapes on horseback with infant Menotti in her arms.

Emperor offers rebels amnesty and measure of self-rule, which Gonçalves refuses. Imperial General Caxias enters war, best general on either side. Offers of amnesty repeated, refused.

Early October-late November: Garibaldi and Anita settle in Capivari with rebels. Menotti 2 1/2 months old.

Late November: Rebels in general retreat to western highlands. Rossetti killed in attack by *Moringue* at Villa Settembrina. Cold, freezing rains. Swollen rivers and streams. Climb takes 9 days.

Mid-December: Rebels arrive in Vacaria District. Travel through Lagoa Vermelha, Passo Fundo, Cruz Alta. Finally reach Cima da Serra. Warm, spring weather. Food and grazing for cattle. Reach Cruz Alta. Brief rest.

1841 Mid-March: Arrive at San Gabriel, 130 miles. Retreat stopped (400 miles from Porto Alegre. Garibaldi oversees building of houses for army. Meets Italian family of Francesco Anzani. Menotti 6 months old.

Army thinning out. Many Rio Grandenses yield to Caixias' offer of amnesty. Garibaldi asks for temporary release.

Gonçalves grants Garibaldi permission to collect herd of cattle (900 in 6 weeks).

End of April: Sets out for Montevideo, 400 miles from San Gabriel. Bad luck with cattle. Half drown. Garibaldi slaughters other half for hides, ends up with a few pennies each.

In Montevideo, takes house for seven years. One room for his family, and shared kitchen. Teaches for a while, and works in clothing store. Meets Doña Feliciana.

1842 January: Joins Uruguayan Navy.

Mar 26: Garibaldi and Anita married in Church of San Francisco de Asis.

1848 January: Garibaldi sends Anita and their children to stay with his mother in Nice.

1849 June: Anita leaves their children with Garibaldi's mother and joins Garibaldi in the campaign to free Rome.

Appendix1

Discovering the Memoirs

My search for Griggs, the least familiar of the three, began with correspondence with Mr. Jasper Ridley, whose biography of Garibaldi became one of my most reliable sources. (57) Ridley's research had led him to the Biblioteca Nacional in Buenos Aires, where he and Sr. Jorge Borges (yes, the same!), Head Librarian, found stacked beneath a staircase a complete set of the propaganda gazette—*O Povo*—that Rossetti had written and edited in support of the Rio Grande revolutionaries. Ridley replied that he had found nothing in *O' Povo* to supplement the little that Garibaldi had included about Griggs in his memoirs. (See Appendix 2 for a detailed account of my discovery of Griggs's origins.)

With respect to Rossetti, Ridley did not know that Sr. Borges subsequently found in another location a separate bundle of manuscripts that contained Rossetti's personal memoirs, which included accounts of his and Garibaldi's adventures in Brazil almost from the moment the latter set foot in Rio de Janeiro. Happily, however, Ridley wrote to alert Sr. Borges that I would be in touch with him.

As a final service, Ridley encouraged me to meet with Dr. Wolfgang Rau, of Florianopolis, Santa Catarina, another generous scholar, who had finished the definitive biography of Anita Garibaldi, which came out in 1975, one year later than Ridley's *Garibaldi*. I accepted Dr. Rau's gracious invitation to visit him in Florianopolis, where, following his warm reception, we discussed some particulars of his research into Anita's biography.

In that conversation, he told me about his recent visit to the National Library in Buenos Aires—our paths must have overlapped there—at which Sr. Borges had given him Rossetti's memoirs and noted my interest in them. Sr. Rau suggested that, if they proved useful, he would gladly turn them over to me. Although I offered to help him edit the papers, possibly to bring out a monograph jointly to supplement his biography of Anita, he insisted that, since he had already begun a new project, I should take over Rossetti's memoirs for my purposes.

Even beyond that kindness, he insisted on helping with my search for Griggs's identity, even to the point of accompanying me back to Buenos Aires. We had no hope of finding anything of Anita's writing because, as I have already indicated, she remained illiterate to the end of her remarkable life. Amazingly, however, our assumptions in that regard, were to be reversed.

Back in Buenos Aires, Dr. Borges urged us to re-examine the archives of the Church of San Francisco de Asis, where Dr. Rau had already seen the official records of Anita's and Garibaldi's marriage but not the documents that proved to be the equivalent of Anita's memoirs. They were stored among unclassified church records, nearly one hundred pages of personal notes by a Father Lorenzo, Curate, and a Doña Feliciana. They contained the remarkable record of confidential interviews with Anita prior to her marriage to Garibaldi. Moreover, they solved the apparently insurmountable problem of Anita's illiteracy because both Doña Feliciana and Fra Lorenzo had kept complete and precise records of their conversations with her.

Dr. Borges told us that the contents apparently had been kept separate from the formal records because they contained information that, as the reader will see, might have raised technical questions as to the legitimacy of Anita's and Garibaldi's marriage. Not only were these notes essential to my research but their discovery gave us hope that similar records by John Griggs might exist. So, with copies of Doña Feliciana's and Fra Lorenzo's manuscripts in hand, we returned to our search for Griggs's memoirs.

Dr. Rau and I began by searching—in vain, as it turned out—the waterfront area in Laguna, where the officers in the rebel navy had billeted during their occupation of Santa Catarina. We hoped that, before the rebel forces retreated from that port, Griggs might have hidden something we could use. Local descendants from those far off days in 1839 could offer nothing about John Griggs, but they clearly recollected accounts of Garibaldi and especially of Anita. She, if anyone, they suggested, would have gathered up the personal belongings of her comrades before she left her homeland forever. It was a slim lead, but we continued to inquire at places along the route of the rebels' retreat into the high country of Rio Grande do Sul—itself a fascinating journey—until we reached San Gabriel, the village where Anita, with Garibaldi and their infant son, Menotti, had settled temporarily. They had moved in with an Italian family, the Anzanis until Garibaldi could build a house for his own little family. It was from there that Garibaldi left for Uruguay.

According to reports in San Gabriel, Anita hoped that she and her new family might return after a stay in Montevideo. To that purpose, she had left bundles of belongings with the Anzanis, whose descendants still lived in the village. When we told them about our interest, they let us comb through their well-stored family collectibles. At the bottom of an old trunk we found a slim, green-bound logbook in quarto size wrapped in oilskin. The cover boards were still whole, miraculously preserved because of the weatherproof wrapping and the seamanlike care with which it was tied off in tidy reef knots. Inside on the first page we read the caption "Personal Log of John Griggs, Captain of the War Sloop Seival in Service of The Free and Independent Republic of Piratini. "The text that followed was in clean handwriting in the accepted mode of a ship's log. We could hardly believe our good fortune in this amazing conclusion to our quest.

The Anzanis selflessly relinquished the Griggs's log into my keeping. I have since had copies translated into Portuguese and Italian, which I mailed to the Anzanis with my thanks for their inestimable contribution. Of course, I must give principal credit for the discoveries to Dr. Rau, as I do for the recovery of notes by Fra Lorenzo and Señora Feliciano in Montevideo. When we returned to his home in Florianopolis, we hungrily examined Griggs's log and Doña Feliciana's and Fra Lorenzo's notes. Satisfied with their authenticity and obvious value, I prepared for my return to the States optimistic of success in my newfound project.

Before leaving Florionapolis with copies of the priceless, personal documents in hand, however, I hosted a celebration of Dr. Rau's kindness as the guiding spirit of our discoveries. I could not have designed a more exciting or satisfying conclusion to our labors together.

Appendix 2

The Search for John Griggs

The most direct references to Griggs appeared in five passages in Garibaldi's memoirs. The first tells of his finding Griggs already established among the rebels when he arrived at their headquarters in Piratini, Rio Grande do Sul. In the second, Garibaldi praises his comrade Griggs for his industry, especially his skill, resourcefulness, and perseverance as a shipbuilder, and he coincidentally praises his "young friend" for his selfless devotion to the cause of independence. Garibaldi's third reference contains an account of his own shipwreck in the Atlantic Ocean enroute to his rendezvous with Griggs in Santa Catarina. Unlike Garibaldi, Griggs made the passage without mishap, prompting Garibaldi to offer his explanation that Griggs's ship was better built to withstand the seas, but then allows, "But I must also add that Griggs was an excellent sailor."(.) He mentions Griggs for the fourth time in connection to a battle with Brazilian warships during a raiding foray north of the port of Laguna. In the fifth and final reference to Griggs, Garibaldi recounts the battle in which Griggs died, cut in half by a fusillade from an enemy gunboat. In rushing back out to help evacuate his comrade, Garibaldi found Griggs's legless torso leaning against the bulwarks of his ship. (61)

Several others before me have searched for Griggs. (See Sources for all the biographies and versions of Garibaldi's memoirs.) The most helpful among them, as it turns out, is pure fantasy but which instigated my search among shipping records and related documents in United States Consular Offices in Porto Alegre. More about that later.

Some are works of bona fide scholarship; others are included in semi-fictional accounts of Garibaldi's career. (62), Garibaldi gives effusive praise of Griggs and includes a reference to a letter from Griggs's relatives in North America, asking him to return and receive a large inheritance. According to the timing suggested by Dumas, Griggs was already dead when the letters arrived. In Dwight's translation, Garibaldi mentions Griggs's "rich family" and letters about Griggs's inheritance (63); however, the letters seem to have arrived while Griggs was overseeing the repair of the rebel ships back in Camaquã.) As I suggest earlier, none of the existing assertions I found seems more than speculation, some ingenious constructions but each different from the others. According to one, for example, Griggs was a Quaker divine, to another he was a renegade Irish priest. Still another describes him as a huge, brutal man called "Big John" (João Grande), who did not hesitate to beat his shipyard workers and crew members to keep them at their tasks, unlikely for a Quaker and only remotely so for a renegade priest.

Lisa Sergio, in her semi-fictional biography of Anita Garibaldi, offers a radically different persona—which I refer to above as pure fantasy. Her claims are unauthenticated; nevertheless, they set me on what was to became a successful track of discovery. According to Sergio, Griggs was an adventurer who, reacting to his wealthy parents' political apathy and prompted by "the same passion for freedom that had made his ancestors give their lives in the North American Revolution," joined Colonel Bento Gonçalves' struggle for liberty in Rio Grande do Sul.

Sergio's allusion to Griggs's wealth is based on material in Garibaldi's memoirs, specifically Griggs's refusal to yield to appeals in letters from home for him to return and claim his portion of his family's estate. Garibaldi furnishes no details about Griggs's background other than his references to those letters. According to Sergio's construction, Griggs, as a boy, had visited Brazil with his tourist parents.

Her claim prompted me to examine official records for visas issued for Brazil during the 1820's and 30's, the most likely period for such a tour. That yielded nothing. Still, Sergio's book had served me well, for I expanded my search into other official records. Finally, in U.S. Diplomatic Despatches [sic] and shipping/port reports from Porto Alegre for the same period, John Griggs's name surfaced.

He was mate of the *Toucan*, a small brigantine in the trade between Boston and Latin American ports, including Rio Grande do Sul. His captain was Nathaniel Hamlin, co-owner of the *Toucan*. In an accompanying report I learned that, on the 27th of March 1836, in the channel port of Rio Grande at the mouth of the Lagoa dos Patos, the imperial police boarded the *Toucan* specifically to arrest Griggs, whom they suspected of carrying contraband for the rebel forces. He had slipped ashore just before they arrived.

According to subsequent correspondence among U.S. and Brazilian officials, "Griggs . . . sometime after engaged on board one of the vessels of the [rebels]" (July 1 to September 16, 1836). Other records of the period shed more light on Griggs's involvement in the rebellion, which seems to be a consequence of the swift development of commerce between the U.S. and Brazil. The official dispatches reveal, at the very least, that John Griggs was one among several U.S. citizens who acted in sympathy with the rebellion in Rio Grande do Sul.

So far Griggs's family origins in the United States remain uncertain. My search for those origins leads me to deduce that he belongs somewhere among the families of Griggses with connections in the maritime trade, the sorts of connections helpful to a young mariner's career. As for John Griggs's immediate associates in the merchant service, records in the diplomatic dispatches for Porto Alegre show Nathaniel Hamlin, Griggs's captain, as co-owner of the *Toucan*, whose homeport is Boston.

Subsequent—and exhaustive—searches for Griggs's family origin, which included the services of the late Mr. Philip Thayer, professional genealogist of Hull, Massachusetts, have yielded nothing. However, I did learn that some families of the same surname were involved in trade and shoe manufacturing in Boston. Unfortunately, none of those includes records of children whose dates come anywhere near the approximate birth date for our John Griggs. Their records do include places and circumstances of death that in no way match the end of our John Griggs's career. For now, additional searches are at a standstill.

Coincidentally, at some point during my extensive correspondence with Griggses, I recalled that, far back in 1958, Professor Theodore Hornberger had assigned the name Thomas Griggs as the subject of my bibliographical research for the doctoral seminar at the University of Minnesota. History plays its tricks, large and small.

Appendix 3

The Trouble-filled History
of Anita's Remaining Years

Anita spent six more years in Uruguay, during which period Garibaldi took part in the Uruguayan Civil War as leader of the Italian Legion on the side of the Unitarians. Anita was busy caring for her family, which subsequently grew to four children.

In Montevideo they lived in a one-room apartment with a shared kitchen in a house on Poston Street (later renamed 25 de maio).

Before renewing his military role in Uruguay, Garibaldi worked as clerk in a clothing store (together with Doña Feliciana) and taught in a school for boys. Ironically, Anita was snubbed by the aristocratic women in Montevideo, who ignored her reputation as heroine. The three children the Garibaldi's had during those years were Teresita, Rosita, and Ricciotti. Rosita died in infancy, after which Garibaldi feared for Anita's sanity.

In January 1848, Garibaldi sent them all to live with his mother in Nice, while he stayed on in Uruguay until mid-April, when he sailed with his Italian Legionnaires for Italy. Garibaldi's mother was uncertain about acknowledging Anita, which must have been painful to Anita, especially after all she had been though.

In June, 1849, Anita left her three surviving children in Nice and joined Garibaldi in the campaign to free Rome. This was against his wishes but Anita could not be put off. In July 1849, Garibaldi decided to lead his Legion out of Rome, with Anita at his side. Just before leaving, she rushed off to have her hair cut short and put on a man's uniform. (64) She had four more months to live, but from that moment she resumed her heroic career.

In their retreat from Rome, Anita died miserably in the village of Mandriole, just south of Venice. The dreadful details that close her career follow here.

July 4, 1849, the fugitives reached Monte Rotondo desperately in need of food but were refused by the monks in the local monastery, after which Garibaldi sent Anita and Hoffstetter, a Swiss volunteer, who intimidated the monks into compliance.

Anita also stemmed the increasing flow of desertions. On July 19, on entering Montepulciano, Anita, now well along in her next pregnancy, again confronted Garibaldi for what she thought was his flirting with some young women.

Outside San Marino, where Garibaldi was trying to negotiate safe conduct, Anita rallied the troops. However, she and a few volunteers still loyal to Garibaldi could not hold off their Austrian pursuers. 200 Legionnaires agreed to follow them in their flight from San Marino. With her resistance eroded, Anita developed a fever but insisted on accompanying Garibaldi. At the end of July, they made their escape. Anita, now in very poor condition, rode through rugged mountain passes, then on to the coastal villages of Musano and Cesenatico, south of Ravenna, where they took over some fishermen's boats and sailed north toward Venice.

Their flotilla of thirteen boats sailed past Ravenna with Anita, in the throes of fever, begging for water. They succeeded in reaching the marshes of Lake Comacchio, 50 miles south of Venice, with Austrian vessels in pursuit. A few of Garibaldi's men made it to an island near Magnavacca, where Garibaldi had to carry Anita ashore and hide with her in a field of maze. With help, he sneaked to a peasant's hut, then into a farmhouse, carrying Anita all the way. By now she was very weak and near death. Out of her delirium, she urged Garibaldi to take care of their children. Finally, Garibaldi and his men had to leave her at the Zanetto family farm with promises to return with a doctor. Traveling all the way to Venice with Anita in her extreme condition would slow Garibaldi and his remaining comrades and surely end in their capture, so they decided to make their escape back toward Ravenna. They put Anita in a cart but soon returned her to the Zanetto farm. She fought to keep Garibaldi from abandoning her, as she believed was his intention. So Garibaldi decided once again to take her along.

The boatmen he hired, actually unsympathetic to his purposes, were afraid of being captured by the Austrians, so they dropped the refugees off on an island in Lake Tavbarra di Agosta. One of the boatmen, whatever his motivation, when he learned that the others intended to abandon them, helped get Garibaldi and Anita into the last boat and together with another sympathizer attempted to rescue Garibaldi's party from the island. Once back on the mainland they got a cart and mattress for Anita and escorted the band of rebels safely to the dairy farm of the Giuccioli Family in Mandriole.

A Doctor Nannini showed up there on August 4 and ordered them to carry Anita to a bed up onto the first floor. During that jolting climb, she died. After begging the Giuccioli's to give her a decent burial, Garibaldi and his few remaining followers fled.

From Garibaldi's Memoirs: . . .I have since reproached myself for removing her from her peaceful native retirement to scenes of danger, toil and suffering. I felt most deeply self-reproach on that day when, at the mouth of the Po, having landed, in our retreat from an Austrian squadron, while still hoping to restore her to life, on taking her pulse I found her a corpse, and sang the hymn of despair. I prayed for forgiveness, for I thought of the sin of taking her from her home. (65)

She was buried that same day in a plot of sandy soil, from which her remains became partly uncovered and gnawed at by dogs. Anita was six months pregnant. It was a gruesome ending for so admirable a person.

A decade later, in mid-Oct, 1859, her remains were moved from Mandriole to Nice. Although Garibaldi left a place for her near his grave on Caprera, she was never transferred there. Finally in 1932, admirers moved her remains from Nice and placed them under her statue in Rome at the Janiculum.

Notes

Note numbers appear in the pages of the text above. The substance of the notes derives from the designated sources. Readers may assume that un-attributed information derives from three main sources: Jasper Ridley's *Garibaldi*, Wolfgang Rau's *Anita Garibaldi*, and Theodore Dwight's 1859 translation of Garibaldi's memoirs. Of those, Ridley's biography is my principal source, whereas the other two stand in corroboration. Therefore, for citations readers should refer to Ridley as follows.

For Rossetti's and Garibaldi's experiences in Rio de Janeiro (my Chapters 1, 4, 5), see Ridley, Chapter 4.

For their voyage south to Uruguay, including Garibaldi's troubles there (my Chapters 6 and 9), see Ridley, Chapter 5.

For the inauguration of *O'Povo* (my Chapters 11), see Ridley, Chapter 6.

For the comrades' adventures in Rio Grande do Sul (my Chapters 11, 12, and 13), see Ridley, Chapter 6.

For the occupation of Santa Catarina, Garibaldi's disaster at sea, Anita's entry into his life, Griggs's death (my Chapters 14-25), see Ridley, Chapters 7 and 8.

For the rebels' retreat from Laguna, the failed campaign in The South, Rossetti's death, the birth of Anita's first child (my Chapter 8), see Ridley, Chapter 8.

1. That interest piqued with the discovery of a mysterious footnote, "a United States Citizen, John Griggs" as one of Garibaldi's comrades in the revolution." See Amfitheatrof, p. 78.

2. Garibaldi-Dwight, p. 9.

3, Garibaldi-Dwight, p. 23.

4. In his heading, Griggs refers to his memoirs as a personal log. . . : For a discussion of ships' logs, see Gibson, pp. 177-78.

5. The people in that inland stretch. . . . For details about the gauchos, see Agassiz, Denis, and Freyre

6. Some of my own kin. . . . The Boston City Directory for 1847-48 lists, among other Griggses, John B. as partner with William Forbes as boot and shoe makers, which could connect them via the import of hides, one of the principal exchange cargoes from Rio Grande do Sul. The connection rests on my own speculation in my unpublished paper "Identifying John Griggs."

7. But they show their best energy . . . : For details about horses and tackle, see Nash and Graham.

8. The General asked after Captain Hamlin . . . : American ships and contraband. Even though the U.S. maritime trade with Brazil was well established at the time, several events preceding Griggs's flight, and the subsequent wreck of the *Toucan* show why the Imperial Brazilians suspected that U.S. citizens dealt clandestinely with the rebels. As the following accounts indicate, the Brazilian authorities' edginess was understandable. As early as 1834, consular notices for January-February, show that the *Brown*, a brig registered under American ownership, was found to be carrying false coins. Captain Samuel Pierson of New York was arrested and imprisoned but escaped. The subsequent entry for January 1-June 30, 1834 reads: "Brought copper coin manufactured in the United States, and shipped thence most probably in Brazilian accounts, the Capt imprisoned—and American Flag disgraced—the owner for . . . Register of this vessel is Paulo J. Figuera, a Portuguese (naturalized) resident in New York." According to the dispatches for the period January-June, 1835, two other American ships were detained and searched for copper coins at Rio Grande: the *Trafalgar* and the *Arabian*, but both were cleared of any charges.

9. To begin with, he told them about. . . . :For information about earlier Griggses, see Thomas Griggs in Hakluyt, XI, 34-39; Fairburn, II, 851 ff; Albion, 167.

10. Of course, now that I have become a marked man. . . . : See U.S. Diplomatic Dispatches: July 2, '36, formal report of Griggs's flight; July 17, '36, *Toucan* now 5 mos in port, still in Porto Alegre after 20 days detainment in Rio Grande.

11. I've got to admit that sort are the exception on most American vessels these days: See Gibson, 52ff.

12. Each of these vessels displaced approximately 25 tons . . . The *Toucan*, built in 1834 in Duxbury, Massachusetts, was 92' 4" long, 22' 3" wide, with a depth of hold of 11' 2 1/2", and registered at 207 36/95 tons gross. The Sampson family built, owned, and were the original operators, with Levi the registered owner, Simeon the master, and Augustus the master carpenter and builder (Boston Ship Register, 1834), by courtesy of Mr. Paul J. O'Pecko, Reference Librarian at Mystic Seaport Museum.

13. Griggs's ship-fitting compound. . . . Dimensions of the Lagoa dos Patos: The lagoa is twice the length of Long Island Sound, twice as wide at most points, but much shallower throughout. It is almost completely landlocked, accessible only via a gap between two fortified towns at its mouth, Rio Grande and San José do Norte. The entrance is actually one mile wide, but during the period relating to this study, it was obstructed by sandbars impassable except for a narrow channel. Here even the small U.S. traders had to wait for a favorable tide before they could clear the bar and enter the lagoa proper. Once inside and cleared by the authorities, they proceeded cautiously northward in a relatively narrow channel to Porto Alegre at the head of the Lagoa. In a letter to U.S. Ambassador John Forsyth in Rio de Janeiro (July 17, 1836), Vice Consul Ralph W. Peacock writes that vessels drawing "15 palms of/11 feet/ water very frequently cross the Bar. . . ," although most preferred 14 palms to avoid delay.

14. The Brazilians have all range of designations according to skin color—mulattos, mestisos, moranhos, mamelucos, caboclos,

cafuzos, cambos, cabujos and others reflecting unions of whites, Africans, Indians. See Desmond, 89.

15. Garibaldi-Dwight, p. 23.

16. Garibaldi-Dwight, p. 24.

17. Garibaldi-Dwight, p. 24.

18. Garibaldi-Dwight, p. 25.

19. Garibaldi-Dwight, p. 25

20. Garibaldi-Dwight, p. 25

21. Garibaldi-Dwight, p. 26.

22. Garibaldi, it seems, had been caught in a political crossfire: For a dependable account of the political and geographical details relating to the general unrest in this area, see Calogeras.

23. Garibaldi-Dwight, p. 34.

24. After all, I am simply following the good example set by the first U.S. Navy: See Tuchman's *First Salute*, Ch. IV, p. 43, about the transformation of merchant vessels for military use by American revolutionaries.

25. Garibaldi-Dwight, p. 37.

26. Garibaldi-Dwight, p.39.

27. Garibaldi-Dwight, p. 26.

28. Garibaldi-Dwight, p. 26.

29. Garibaldi-Dwight, p. 45.

30. Garibaldi-Dwight, p.44.

31. For Garibaldi's complete version of the attack on the galpoa, see Garibaldi-Dwight, pp. 46-9.)

32. The transportation was glorious! For photos and paintings of the rebels' ships, including the transport to the sea, see Rau, pp. 94, 99, 100, and 161. For Garibaldi's complete version of this operation and the disaster that followed, see Garibaldi-Dwight, Chapter VIII.)

33. Garibaldi- Dwight, p. 52.

34. Garibaldi- Dwight, p. 58.

35. Garibaldi- Dwight,. p. 61

36. Garibaldi- Dwight, p. 59-60, I include the last words of this entry—more appropriately, I believe—in Appendix 3, p. 249 above, in the account of Anita's final days (" I have since reproached myself . . .").

37. Garibaldi-Dwight, pp. 65-6. For Garibaldi's full account of this punitive task, see Chapter X.

38. Garibaldi-Dwight, p. 106.

39. Garibaldi-Dwight, p. 63.

40. Garibaldi- Dwight, p. 64.

41. Garibaldi- Dwight, p. 67.

42. Still, we have showed them our front sides. . . . Ridley makes a relevant point about the scale of the battles in the revolution (pp. 97-98). The engagement at Vacaria, Santa Vitoria, is recorded as larger than most, yet the rebels claimed 50 Imperials killed and 15 captured, whereas, by their figures, only 25 rebels died.

43. Garibaldi-Dwight, p. 68.

44. Garibaldi-Dwight, pp. 68-69.

45. Garibaldi-Dwight, p. 69.

46. Garibaldi-Dwight, p. 70.

47. Garibaldi-Dwight, pp. 92-93.

48. Rossetti failed to note one nasty incident to the discredit of the rebels. . . . See Ridley, p. 101 for the incident of the rebel's brutal execution of captured Imperialists.

49. I wanted to put that observation down. . . . Readers may be interested in comparing Rossetti's conclusions to Griggs's. See p. 37 ff. For Garibaldi's complete account of that venture, see Garibaldi- Dwight, p. 26ff.

50. Garibaldi-Dwight, p. 93.

51. Garibaldi-Dwight, pp. 93-94.

52. Garibaldi-Dwight, p. 94.

53. Garibaldi-Dwight, p. 96.

54. Garibaldi-Dwight, p. 98.

55. It was a long time before he returned to the village. See Ridley, 87. Well, the men in Laguna teased me a different way after I rode back on his horse with his whip in my hand. See Calogeras, 12. I am like the Empress Leopoldina, who was herself a great rider: I can ride the most fiery horses without fear. See Calogeras, 72.

56. An Indian Goddess from the earth in Santa Catarina: See Nash, 10. And there was the other, the heroine in the Bahiana revolt. See Walsh, 127.

57. That was life to me before José came to Laguna, after Manoel was taken into the Imperial Militia. See Ridley, 88.

58. My best friend. One quick embrace. I left her my little scissors to remember me. See Rau, 67.

59. But, Father, my feelings were twisted around. See Ridley, pp. 194-5 for Garibaldi on mortality.

60. See Footnote 43.

61. Appendix 2: My search for Griggs. . . . In his letter to me, July 25, 1980, Jasper Ridley wrote that he had found "an almost complete collection of *O Povo* for the years 1838-40 in the News-paper Section of the Biblioteca Nacional in Buenos Aires" but that he saw no references to "Griggs in the extracts from *O 'Povo* which I took." In that same letter, Ridley suggests that I write to or visit Dr. Rau in Florianopolis.

At this point, I must offer a special note of gratitude to all li-brarians. Of course, I have Sr. Borges in mind, but to his name I add Dr. Ralph Stenstrom, at the time Head Librarian of Hamilton College, who ordered for me the official U.S. documents in which I finally located John Griggs.

62. Garibaldi-Dumas, p. 85.

63. Anita may have been influenced here by the Brazilian woman who put on her brother's uniform and fought in his place (see her conversation with Doña Feliciana above, p. 204)

64. Garibaldi-Dwight, p. 60.

Sources

Agassiz, Louis and Elizabeth C. *A Journey in Brazil*. Boston: Tickner and Fields, 1868.

Albion, Robert G. *The Rise of New York Port [1815-1860]*. New York: Scribner's, 1939.

Amfitheatrof, Eric. *The Children of Columbus* (Chapters 4-5, pp. 65-104). Boston: Little, Brown, 1973.

Bandi, G. *Anita Garibaldi*. Florence: Doria-Bandi, 1932.

Bernstein, Harry. *Origins of Inter-American Interest (1700-1812)*. Philadelphia: U of Pennsylvania Press, 1945.

Bowditch, Nathaniel. *American Practical Navigtor*. Washington, DC: US Government Printing Office, 1943.

Burns, E. Bradford. *A History of Brazil*. New York: Columbia U, 1980.

Calogeras, João P. *A History of Brazil*. Chapel Hill: U of North Carolina, 1939.

Camacho, S.A. *Brazil, An Interim Assessment*. London: Royal Institute of International Affairs. Oxford U, 1952.

Candido, Salvatore. *Giuseppe Garibaldi nel Rio della Plata*. Firenze (no publisher), 1972.

Collor, Lindolfo. *Garibaldi e a Guerra des Farrapos*. Rio de Janeiro (no publisher), 1938.

Denis, Pierre. *Brazil*. New York: Scribner's, 1911.

De Polnay, Peter. *Garibaldi*. New York: Thomas Nelson, 1961.

Desmond, Adrian and James Moore. *Darwin's Sacred Cause*, Boston: Houghton Mifflin Harcourt, 2009.

Despatches from United States Consuls in Rio de Janeiro, Brazil, 1811-1906. Washington, DC: National Archives Trust Fund Board.

Despatches from United States Ministers to Brazil, 1809-1906. Washington, DC: National Archives Trust Fund Board.

Despatches from United States Consuls in Rio Grande do Sul, Brazil, 1829-97. Washington, DC: National Archives Trust Fund Board.

Ewbank, Thomas. *Life in Brazil*. New York: Harper, 1856.

Fairburn, William A. *Merchant Sail*. Center Lovell, Maine: Fairburn Marine Education Foundation, 1945-55.

Freitas, N. *Garibaldi in America*. Buenos Aires (no publisher), 1946.

Freyre, Gilberto (Samuel Putnam, Trans.). *The Masters and the Slaves*. New York: Knopf, 1946.

Fuentes, Carlos. *The Campaign*. New York: Farrar-Straus-Giroux, 1991.

Garibaldi, Anita. *Garibaldi in America*. Rome (no publisher), 1932.

Garibaldi, Giuseppe (Alexandre Dumas, Ed.; R.S. Garnett, Trans.) *The Memoirs of Garibaldi*. New York: Appleton, 1931.

_____. *Autobiography of Giuseppe Garibaldi* (A. Werner, Transl.). New York: H. Fertig, 1971.

_____. (Dwight, Theodore, Ed.-Trans.). *The Life of General Garibaldi*, Written by Himself. New York: Barnes, 1859.

_____. "From General Garibaldi to His English Friends." *Cassell's Magazine* (New Series), Vol. I. London: 1870.

Gerson, Brazil. *Garibaldi and Anita*. Rio de Janeiro: Editoria Souza, 1953.

_____. *Garibaldi and Anita*. São Paulo (no publisher), 1971.

Gibson, Gregory. *Demon of the Waters*. Boston: Little, Brown, 2002.

Grademigo, Gaio. *Garibaldi in America*. Montevideo: "Don Orione," 1969.

Griggs, Thomas. "Certain notes of the voyage to Brasil [sic]. . . ." in Richard Hakluyt. *The Principal Navigations, Voyages, Traffiques & Discoveries of the English Nation*. New York: Macmillan, 1904.

Griggs, Walter S. *Genealogy of the Griggs Family*. Pompton Lakes, NJ: The Biblio Co., 1926.

Hendrickson, Robert. *Yankee Talk*. New York: Facts on File, 1996.

Hibbert, Christopher. *Garibaldi and His Enemies*. New York: New American Library, 1996.

Hill, Lawrence F., *Diplomatic Relations between the United States and Brazil,* Durham: Duke U, 1932.

Hutchins, John G.B *The American Maritime Industries and Public Policy, 1789-1914*. Cambridge: Havard U, 1941.

Kirkland, Edward C.*A History of American Economic Life*. New York: Appleton-Century-Crofts, 1951.

Klemp, Egon (Ed.), Margaret and Jeffrey Stone (Trans.). *America in Maps*. New York: Holmes & Meier, 1976.

Levine, Robert M. *Historical Dictionary of Brazil*. Metuchen, NJ: Scarecrow Press, 1979.

Libra de Casamentas (Church of Danto Antonia de Los Anjos, Manuscripts). *Laguna, Sta Catarina*, Brazil, 1832-44.

Mack Smith, D. Garibaldi: A Great Life in Brief. New York: Knopf, 1970.

Pam Manning, William R. (Ed.). *Diplomatic Correspondence of the United States, Inter-American Affairs, 1831-1860. Vol. II, Bolivia and Brazil, Documents 388-722.* Washington, D.C.: Carnegie Endowment for International Peace, 1932.

Ministério da Marinha. *Capitania dos Portos do Estado de Santa Catarina: Directoria de Portos e Costas 1516-1944*. Florianópolis.

Morison, Samuel E. *The Oxford History of the American People*. New York: Oxford U, 1965.

Murphy, Caroline P. *Murder of a Medici Princess*. New York: Oxford University Press, 2008, p. 57.

Nash, Roy. *The Conquest of Brazil*. New York: AMS Press, 1969.

Naylor, Bernard. *Accounts of Nineteenth Century South America*. London: U of London, 1969.

Notes from the Brazilian Legation in the United States to the Department of State, 1824-1906. Washington, D.C.: National Archive Trust Fund Board.

Notes to Foreign Legations in the United States from the Departmemt of State, 1834-1906. Washington, D.C.: National Archives Trust Fund Board.

O' Povo. Rossetti, Luigi (Ed.). On file in Biblioteca Nacional. Buenos Aires.

Rau, Wolfgang L. *Anita Garibaldi*. Florianópolis, SC, Brazil: Editora Lunardelli, 1975.

Reichardt, H. Canabarro. *Ideas de Liberdade no Rio Grande do Sul a Guerra dos Farrapos*. Rio de Janeiro (no publisher),1928.

_____. *Bento Gonçalves*. Porto Alegre, RGdS, Brazil: Barcellos, Bertaso, 1932.

Ridley, Jasper G. *Garibaldi*. New York: Viking, 1976.

Rippy, J. Frederick. *Rivalry of the U.S. and Great Britain over Latin America (1808-1830)*. Baltimore: Johns Hopkins U, 1929.

Ruschenberger, William S. W. *Three Years in the Pacific.* Philadelphia: Carey, Lea & Blanchard, 1834.

de Saint-Simon, Henri Comtell. *Selected Writings*, ed. and transl. by F. M. H. Markham (Oxford: Basil Blackwell, 1952).

Sergio, Lisa. *I Am My Beloved.* New York: Weybright and Talley, 1969.

Shaw, Paul V. "José Bonifacio and Brazilian History." *The Hispanic American Historical Review,* November, 1928: 527-50.

Shorto, Russell. *Manhattan, Island in the Center of the World.* New York: Vintage, 2005.

*State Department Registers of Correspondence, 1870-1906.*Brazil, May 29, 1833-November 11, 1862.Washington, D.C.: National Archives Trust Fund Board.

Trevelyan, G.M. "Garibaldi in South America." *Cornhill Magazine* (New Series, XXX) 1911.

_____. *Garibaldi's Defense of the Roman Republic.* London: Phoenix, 2001.

Tuchman, Barbara W. *The First Salute.* New York: Random House, 1988.

Varzea, V. (C. Petti, Transl). *Garibaldi in America.* Rio de Janeiro (no publisher), 1902.

Walsh, Robert. *Notices of Brazil in 1828-29.* Boston: Richardson, Lord & Holbrook, 1831.

Whitaker, Arthur P. *The United States and the Independence of Latin America, 1800-1830.* Baltimore: Johns Hopkins U, 1941.

Acknowledgments

Mr. Jasper Ridley's biography of Garibaldi and Dr. Wolfgang Rau's of Anita are consistently the most thorough and reliable of the sources I used. Also, both authors have been prompt correspondents, especially with respect to my search for John Griggs. Other especially helpful members of the Garibaldi community are Lisa Sergio, biographer of Anita, Dr. Anthony P. Campanella, biographer and custodian, and Dr. Lino S. Lipinski de Orlov, Associate of he Meucci Museum.

I thank Hamilton College for granting me a leave of absence and for other financial support toward this project. My thanks go also to individual members of the Hamilton College community. First is my good friend Dr. Ralph Stenstrom, Director of the Hamilton College Library (now retired), who acquired photocopies of the Despatches [sic] from the U.S. Consuls in Rio de Janeiro and Porto Alegre, Rio Grande do Sul. Next are members of the library staff: Ms. April Caprac, Assistant to the Director and Ms. Lynn Mayo, Reference Librarian, for their generous assistance in all phases of my research. Professor Robert Paquette, History, also deserves special thanks for his prompt and perceptive reading of my paper on John Griggs. My thanks go also to Father John Croghan, Newman Chaplain, for authenticating Fra. Lorenzo's doctrinal procedures in preparing the way for Anita's marriage to Garibaldi.

Ms. Katherine Collett, Assistant Archivist, deserves special mention here. She identified a long deceased member of the Hamilton faculty, Dr. Christian H.F. Peters, who had an interesting connection to Garibaldi not long after the Brazilian years. Dr. Peters was conducting studies in astronomy near Naples during the time of Garibaldi's Sicilian campaign. He dropped his studies and donned the "Red Shirt" as a member of the Garibaldi Brigade. Dr. Peters subsequently joined the Hamilton College Department of Mathematics and Astronomy, at the time undifferentiated disciplines. He was, as Ms. Collett understands, the first Ph.D. on the Hamilton faculty.

As to the examination of the counselor dispatches, Dr. Scott Gwara, currently Professor of English at The University of South Carolina, Columbia, who served as my undergraduate assistant, discovered John Griggs, U.S. merchant mariner, among them. My gratitude also goes to my former Hamilton College student, Helena Nejman, for translating my correspondence with Sr. Rau, as well as passages from the highly stylized, 19th Century Portuguese publications.

In my search for John Griggs's family origins, I enjoyed correspondence with individual Griggses from Maine to California, all generous in their desire to be helpful. Also cooperative were staff members of numerous institutions, including genealogical societies, state historical and academic libraries all along the East Coast from Maine to South Carolina. Among them, I single out two persons: first, Ms. Shay Allen, Research Director of the City of Boston Archives, who guided me patiently and thoroughly through all the possibly pertinent records at hand; and the late Philip S. Thayer, Genealogist, whom I mention in Appendix 2.

With respect to the preparation and presentation of this book, I shall remain indebted to the Editor of Branden Books, Adolfo Caso and his wife, Margaret, for their unsurpassed patience, perception, and precision.

Finally, beyond any ordinary expression of gratitude, I single out my dear wife, Irma, for her inspiration and her persistent urging to "get on with Garibaldi."

Made in the USA
Charleston, SC
26 May 2015